The Wildon boy an
and hop a few beds
incriminating, very ~~~~~~ ~~p~~, and a mystery
drug that turns common lovers into consummate love
machines. And what do they find?

The perfect pet who can shape her piquant body to
one's most stratospheric desires.

The nasty punk rocker reduced to a whimpering
body by a sensuous flick of the wrist.

The high-gloss model who can turn herself on with
a kinky surprise between her exquisite legs.

For Dirk and Honey, half the fun's in getting there.
The other half's in the hottest family reunion that
ever happened behind cool, closed doors.

Also by Roland De Forrest
and published by Futura

THE EROTIC QUEST OF DIRK AND HONEY
DIRK AND HONEY: SIN-DICATED

THE
WILDON
AFFAIR

ROLAND DE
FORREST

Futura

A Futura Book

ISBN 0 7088 4330 1

Typeset, printed and bound in Great Britain by
BPCC Hazell Books Ltd
Member of BPCC Ltd
Aylesbury, Bucks, England

Futura Publications
A Division of
Macdonald & Co (Publishers) Ltd
66–73 Shoe Lane
London EC4P 4AB
A member of Maxwell Pergamon Publishing Corporation plc

ACKNOWLEDGMENTS

With nefarious assistance by:

Sonny Lemontina, Carlos Valdez
Jacques Le Frère, Mama Gordita

To SHAYLA

Always Sweet Inspiration

THE
WILDON
AFFAIR

1
DIRK

By the flickering light of a torchlight, he could make out four ladies sharing a jay in the hot tub. Dirk stopped at the end of the large steaming pool of water built into the side of the hill and, smiling down at the buxom beauties, dropped his towel. 'May I join you?'

The brunette directly below arched her head, looking up his long legs, her fleshy white breasts floating on top of the water like pink-nosed dolphins. 'My, aren't you a tall sight.'

'No one need ask to join a hot tub,' the platinum blonde directly across purred, nailing him with a come-hither stare.

'Get in,' the third, a curly black-haired girl, invited, her eyes not rising above his balls. 'The heat's good for what ails you.'

'What ails me will require more than heat,' Dirk said with a wink. 'But it's a damn good start.' He stepped down into the hot water between the black-haired girl and

11

the brunette. Slowly he lowered into the over-hundred-degree water, sighing as his balls dipped.

'Don't burn anything useful,' the blonde cracked, her small breasts pertly pointing up at the star-filled sky.

Sitting on the tiled seat, he eyed the fourth young lady, who had been moaning softly, eyes closed, head tilted back onto the coping. He recognized her from her hit TV series – a sitcom that had changed her overnight into a national sex goddess. Strawberry blonde, soft and cuddly-looking, girl-next-door type, with large, firm breasts that jiggled in the dark water like bowls of some heavenly dessert. She let out another groan of pleasure.

Probably diddling herself, he mused and drew the girls on either side closer to him with friendly arms. They nestled into him, the black-haired girl snuggling one soft breast into his trunk, the brunette beginning to trace his thigh with exploring fingers. Dirk stretched his legs out, freeing his works. The tub was large, over eight feet square, and floated on the brim of the hill overlooking the sparkling lights of the entire Los Angeles basin. The gentle hand on his leg grew bolder, rushing to cup his balls with a squeeze of intimate greeting.

'Ahhhhh,' sighed the TV starlet across from him, her eyes popping open, blank with ecstasy. Immediately in front of her, bursting out of the water like Jaws himself, a bald head shot up, gasping for air, spewing water and crying joyfully, 'Hot shit!'

Dirk recoiled in surprise. 'What the – ?' he roared, then burst out to join the laughter of the women as he recognized his host. 'Damn, Sol, you got a submarine down there?'

Sol grinned proudly and wiped the unmistakable drops of silvery cum from his mouth. 'What was it?' he threw at the platinum blonde with the pert tits.

She glanced at the wristwatch on the ledge. 'Three minutes, forty-seven seconds.'

12

'Not bad, huh, girls?' Sol boasted, his thin chest panting.

'Hell, Sol,' the brunette with Dirk's balls in hand cooed, 'you can muff dive me anytime.'

'In or *out* of the water,' the platinum blonde rejoiced and kissed him loudly, throwing her arms about his neck.

Dirk shook his head in amazement, his cock hardening under the brunette's expert fondling. 'Damn, Sol, how can you munch pussy underwater without choking?'

'Lung power,' the film producer boasted. 'Every morning before I leave for the studio, I swim underwater laps in the pool. Hell, on good mornings I can get four and a half minutes on one lungful.'

'But not with your mouth full,' Dirk quipped.

Sol guffawed and stuck out a hand. 'Welcome to Xanadu, Dirk.'

They shook and Sol introduced the ladies – all but the TV starlet whose eyes were still closed, riding the downside of her underwater treat. The brunette, Heather, began stroking on Dirk's ever-hardening cock with a steady, determined beat. Sol sank his wiry frame onto the submerged seat and pulled the platinum blonde onto his lap, speaking to Dirk over her shoulder. 'When'd you get into town, buddy? Last I heard you were off in Bali doing some spread for *Esquire*.'

'Couple of hours ago. Just dropped my bag off at the Bel Air and headed up here.'

'Got plenty of room if you want to stay here – that is, once the party mob clears out.'

'Thanks, anyway,' Dirk said, appreciating Sol's gesture, but preferring the ones underwater. The rock music from the pool area up the hill behind them filtered down, and for a while all just sat in the steaming water, its darkness covering the below-the-line sexual activity. The vast carpet of twinkling lights spread out before them: Beverly Hills high life at its best, Dirk thought as he delicately rubbed between the silken thighs of Heather. She parted them invitingly and tugged on his cock.

He slipped his middle finger inside and explored the ruffled ridges of her outer twat lips. She was moist and swollen already. Probably banged at least three times this evening, he thought and probed deeper, pushing through to her distended clit. She sighed broadly and threw a leg over his knee. Meanwhile he was using his free hand to caress the soft pliable boobs of Susie, the black-haired lovely on his left.

Across the tub, the TV starlet stirred out of her blissful stupour and stretched languidly, purring like a contented kitten, her large tits swelling out of the water like emerging volcanic islands. 'Oh, Solly, that was delicious. Your tongue's quicker than a serpent's.'

'Fast but not forked,' Dirk said, smiling at her. The snatch on his hand was thrusting wildly now, raising waves that lapped the sides of the tiled tub. He pressed his palm to her bush, middle finger buried completely, and just hung on to her thrusting pelvis. Everyone was watching the contortions of her face. 'Go for it, go for it,' the platinum blonde chanted softly.

Abruptly Heather's hips shifted into a slower gear, her eyes fluttered and closed. With his fingertip, he sought her clit once more. As soon as he grazed it, she began to squeal: 'Yes, yes, yes . . .'

'Let's see it,' Susie, on his left, urged. 'I wanna see.'

Sol bent forward eagerly. 'Yeah, let's see it pop.'

Dirk twisted to Heather, withdrew his finger and clasped her around the waist with both hands. With a strong heave, he lifted her up out of the water, sitting her on the tiled edge. He spread her legs, offering a clear view for all. Her cunt lips were wide open like a split cabbage. Squealing, she fell back flat, planting her heels flat on the edge, lifting her hips, moaning with paroxysms of pleasure. The sticky moisture began oozing out like liquid

14

pearls, dripping off the trembling lips and falling slowly to the deep blue tile.

Dirk winked at the gaping faces. 'Preview of coming attractions.'

'Helluva shame to let all that go to waste,' Sol muttered and lunged the platinum blonde off his lap. He dove head-first between the raised legs of Heather, who squealed with more delight.

'You must have fantastic fingers,' Susie praised.

'I think she started without me,' Dirk said, grinning.

'You're Dirk Wildon, the photographer, aren't you?' the TV starlet asked suddenly.

He smiled. 'Yes, but it's pronounced "will-done" – short vowel sound. Not "wild-on." '

A flush of hurt colour tinged her cheeks. 'I've only seen it in print.'

He shrugged it off, trying to make her feel at ease. 'You're Lia Lorne . . . I've seen your series. Very good.'

'Tits and ass show,' she muttered, glancing into the sparkling distance. 'And I'm stuck for another five fuckin' years.'

'Come on, Solly,' the platinum blonde pouted, tweak-ing her host's pink ass. 'Come up for air, dammit.' But Sol was occupied, his head bobbing between Heather's firm thighs like a pile-driver.

Silently Susie sank below the water and vanished. Instantly he felt her face on his groin, her lips seeking the knobby head of his bird of paradise. She sucked it in, grazing it with her teeth, painfully. He grabbed her hair underwater with both hands and shoved his bird deep into her throat. She managed to get in two good hard pulls of suction before she coughed. It was audible even above water. She broke to the surface, choking and red-faced like an angry seal.

The platinum blonde teased, 'Didn't look big enough to choke a horse.'

'Wasn't the size,' Suzie sputtered. 'It's the fucking water.'

'If the water could fuck,' Lia replied disdainfully, 'we wouldn't need these bastards.'

'You'll have to take lessons from Solly,' the platinum blonde said to Susie. 'Increase your lungs.'

'Looks like her lungs are very healthy as is,' Dirk said and flicked Susie's extended nipples. He pulled her onto his lap, her love cushions flattened against his chest, and she straddled his hips.

Susie lowered her wet pussy onto his perpendicular dick-head and he shoved into it forcefully. He wrapped his arms around her trim waist, resting them on her full hips as she worked feverishly up and down. He could feel his cock swelling inside her. She was tight and juicy.

She smacked her lips, staring deeply into his eyes. 'Fuck me . . .'

Silently he pumped, not holding her any longer, but grasping the tiled seat near his flanks for better leverage. Beside him on the tub's lip, a series of explosive moans erupted from Sol's munchmate. 'Oh, Lord, here I go again.' Heather yelped and threw her head back, arching for the heavens.

Susie, bouncing on Dirk's bird, began whispering heatedly, 'Oh, baby, you're so good . . . so-o-o-o good . . .' Her slippery hot cum began bathing the tip of his buried prick.

Dirk glanced at Sol just as Heather jackknifed and went down on Sol's thick, hard peter. Almost instantly, Sol too began to climax and yanked her head away with a gasp, shooting silvery geysers from the slit of his purple-hued cock. The cum hit Heather's lips and cheeks and she licked it with fervour from her skin. 'Geez, Sol, you come faster than a dog.'

The platinum blonde rose out of the water petulantly. 'Come Fido, time to play host.' She tugged Sol up and wiped his still-hard dick on a towel.

16

He winked. 'Ladies, time for a little snow. Dirk, see you up at the house.'

Susie, on Dirk's lap, whispered, 'You're a good fuck, Dirk,' and pulled off to climb weakly out of the tub.

'Hell, I was just the doorknob,' he said lightly, admiring her rounded ass. He waved to Sol and his entourage of lovelies as they headed back up the grassy sweep of lawn to the Mediterranean-styled mansion on the hill.

Lia, alone on the other side, batted her eyelashes. 'You didn't come, did you?'

He laughed and stood, his cock thrusting out like an angry lance. 'Plenty of time. I just got here.'

'You going?'

He nodded and bent for his towel. She paddled to just below him, peering up provocatively. 'You want to do a camera study of me?'

'Maybe . . . sometime,' he said casually and wrapped the damp towel around his waist. His bird was falling slowly but still tented the front of the towel.

She raked his toes with the back of a long fingernail. 'There isn't a photographer in the world who can capture a woman the way you can . . .'

'I'm easy . . . flattery always works.'

'So don't run away.'

'I'm hungry. Didn't eat on the flight.'

'You can eat me.'

'But is it nourishing?' He winked and turned toward the house on the hill. She was beautiful, but not magical. So far he had not found the one face of the evening.

In the den, the action was even hotter. Under a bright ceiling-spot, a former NFL quarterback, his naked body pale, beefy, hairy, knelt and thrust his wet, hard cock into a small mountain of snow on the coffee table. His lady friend, wearing only a Dodgers baseball cap, patted the coke tenderly over the top of his tool, coated it and pulled it out, jiggling the excess off. Promptly, and with a wicked

17

leer, the ex-jock thrust his powdered prick into her willing, open mouth. Greedily she began sucking and licking.

Someone pressed a crystal jet-atomizer inhaler under Dirk's nose. An explosion of pure flake ejected into his nostril. He grinned at the sudden rush and sought out the supplier – a small, young lady in a see-through kaftan, her body lean, gymnastic-looking, her taut breasts resting like hard muscles on her slim torso. 'You looking for company, Dirk?' she asked and offered more coke.

He took a good strong blast. 'Have we met?'

'No, but I know who you are. Bet every lady here knew within five minutes after you arrived. They're all dying to meet you,' she said quietly.

'You in the business?' he asked, but was studying the back-lighting effect on a couple in the corner humping like crazy.

The trim little lady nodded.

'Actress, right?' he asked, returning his focus to her.

Again she nodded, leaning her hips into his towel, rubbing her hard snatch.

'Want a snow job?'

She took his hand, leading him to the mirrored coffee table with the coke piled generously in the centre. She yanked off his towel and surveyed his equipment with a jaundiced, good-natured eye. 'I've seen bigger.'

He chortled and took hold of the diaphanous material of her robe, tugging it over her head. He grinned at her taut breasts. 'I've seen bigger too.' She laughed huskily and dropped to her knees. She took his limp peter lovingly in both hands, kissing it softly, and began to lick its length. He watched dispassionately until he could feel the blood rushing into it, thickening it, lengthening it. He closed his eyes and let it happen. Soon he was hard enough for the coke. He kneeled and jammed his ready-to-fly bird, wet with her saliva, into the centre of the pile. She dusted it motherly before extracting it. Hungrily she fell onto it and began sucking off the snow.

His eyelids fell closed. The lady was good. Damn good. Someone taught her well. A bona fide graduate of the fine art of plating; she could play the flute and swallow the music, he mused as he felt the rising tide tingling at the base of his balls. His eyes drifted open and he stared across the book-lined den. Then he saw the one face of the evening. Pure magic.

Directly opposite on the green velvet couch, she sat haloed in a diffused spot from above. Her face was classically beautiful, erotic, alluring with exquisitely proportioned features; her lustrous black eyes held a thousand secrets and they were staring directly at him.

He felt the fire in his loins suddenly increase. Another few seconds and he would come. Gently he pushed away the head clasped firmly onto his twitching organ. In puzzlement she looked up, but he was already moving magnetically toward the mysterious presence. Mesmerized, he did not hear the plaintive wail from the gymnastic cock-sucker on the floor.

He stopped before the magic. She was even better in close-up. A gentle smile tugged at her sensitive lips, the deep black pools of her eyes grew limpid as she waited for him to speak. He could not find his tongue. His mind was a welter of precise camera information on how he would shoot her – what lens, what film, what f-stop, what angle, what lighting. He also had an irresistible urge to stick his trembling hard bird into her luscious mouth.

Gracefully, she reached out a tentative hand as if to touch the demanding red bulb on the end of his swollen dick. A tap on his shoulder roughly shattered the moment. Like a startled doe she drew back into the shadows.

'Got a minute, Dirk?' It was Sol, in a blue terry-cloth bathrobe, his tanned, gaunt face strained with seriousness.

'Better be important,' Dirk growled good-humouredly.

19

'I don't know,' Sol replied, latching onto an arm and tugging him away. 'You have to tell me.'

With one last look at the delectable being on the couch, Dirk reluctantly allowed himself to be led away. Up a carpeted staircase, down a long hallway leading to the master bedroom suite, and into a comfortably furnished, masculinely appointed screening room which held a giant Advent TV screen. Sol closed the door quietly behind Dirk and moved to a cluttered desk. 'This just came by special messenger.'

Dirk glanced at the brown-paper-wrapped package in Sol's hands. On the top was written boldly in ink printing: FOR DIRK WILDON'S EYES ONLY. There was no other writing, label or return address.

Perplexed, Dirk took it and started unwrapping. 'Who the hell knew I was coming here?'

'Someone must have.'

'*I* didn't even know until I got here.' He tore away the paper, revealing a black plastic video-cassette. 'Oh hell it's just some model's audition tape. I get these all the time.'

Sol tightened the belt of his robe. 'Who knows till you take a look at it?' He walked to the door. 'Put it on the machine. I'll keep the room off limits.'

Dirk tossed it back onto the desk. 'I'll catch it later. I found the one I was looking for in the den.'

Sol looked oddly agitated. 'Dirk, listen, it wasn't delivered by any messenger service I know. This guy looked like he was auditioning for *The Godfather*. Look at the damn thing, for Chrissakes. And then tell me everything's okay, okay? That jerk gave me the fuckin' shakes.' Sol split and shut the door quickly.

Somewhat pissed at the interruption, Dirk slammed the tape onto the video player, switched on the power for both machines and hit the play button. While the cassette was dropping into place, he spotted a rosewood liquor cabinet and poured himself a straight Glenlivet Scotch on

20

the rocks. On the six-by-six foot screen, the bright image began fading in. He stared, casually curious.

Three nude figures writhed on a bed of red satin – two strong muscular black bodies and a white chick. The black male had a huge hard-on that looked a good foot long, and half that thick; the black female – easily over six foot – was built like an Amazon, the muscles and tendons rippling under the ebony skin like a jungle cat's. The blackness of their skin contrasted vividly with the creamy white of the chick buried between them. Her body was softly luscious, full, voluptuous.

Dirk was lost for a moment in the pure beauty of the shot – the camera angle was low, the lighting natural not harsh, the magnificent bodies erotically presented without being trashy. So it's a fuck film, he thought. Even if it was as good as these opening shots, why the hell would someone send him a fuck film? Perhaps it was someone's idea of a joke that –

Suddenly he choked on his Scotch, coughing it up in an explosion of shock. It was the fiery red pussy of the white chick that clued him in first. 'Oh my God,' he breathed aloud, sinking like a stone onto a leather couch.

The chick in the middle was his own goddamned sister! Her beautiful red-furred pussy was being eaten by the big black beauty while Honey's pink lips enveloped the huge head of the giant black cock.

His mind went blank with confusion. Dazed and intent on the raunchy activities unfolding in vivid colour before him, he did not hear the hall door open, nor the soft padding of bare feet across the thick carpet; nor did he see the slender, naked figure gliding to his side and bending to kneel. Only when her mouth sought his cock did he jerk with a start and look down at the magical face he had left below in the den. The dark luminous eyes peered up at him from the end of his stiff prick, which he had also been unaware of, as she slowly slipped it into her mouth.

But he could not keep his eyes off his sister; her full

body being projected larger than life. He was both drawn to and repulsed by the sight. Like a nymphomaniac in heat, she was sucking the biggest cock Dirk had ever seen. The camera zoomed in on an extreme close-up of her exquisite profile. Her mouth, stretched as wide as it could open, was swallowing only the fist-sized head of the hard, black log. Dirk's own cock was getting the same attention, but the sensitive warm mouth of the magical face had all his full-blown bird inside her milking throat.

At that particular moment, he felt that his cock was as large as the black's. In fact, in his stoned and highly aroused state, there was no differentiation between the sweet mouth sucking on the screen and the one on his own throbbing cock. He was one with the video image, both observer and participant. His balls tightened into him, his legs went askew, his breath erupted in hot gasps, his eyes locked on Honey, his brain reeling. He could not hold it any longer. It rushed over him with the force of an avalanche, burying him under the mounting tension, until he erupted.

The black stud came at the same instant and Honey pulled back, her mouth grotesquely full of dripping, thick, ivory cum, and still the black cannon shot loads onto her pale, delectable, beautiful face. Dirk's load was considerably smaller. The magical woman kneeling before him raised her head, freeing his last feeble squirts to arc onto his stomach. She lowered to lick them off.

Drained, Dirk fought to regain his equilibrium and felt the righteous anger building inside his chest like a ball of fire. He flopped an arm behind him and hit the rewind button of the video player. As the tape stopped and the screen blanked, he forgot the lady in his lap and his earlier desire to photograph and fuck her. All he could think of was *what the hell was Honey doing*? Allowing herself to be taped like that, opening herself up to untold damage both to her highly respected journalistic career, as well as her own personal life. 'Honey Wildon,' he groaned to

22

himself, 'you have gotten your sweet ass into one helluva mess of trouble.'

Angrily he stood, bent and kissed the soft, sensitive lips still moist from his own cum. 'Another time, another place, I promise . . .' He pushed the eject button, downed the last of the Scotch, and when the cassette emerged, snatched it off and headed for the door. He had to find Honey . . . and find her fast. But knowing her, she could be anywhere, doing anything – or anyone. This Honey never stuck anywhere for too long.

2
HONEY

She crossed her shapely, silk-encased thighs and asked 'Who were your boyhood heroes, Generalismo?"

At the sound of the soft hissing, the general added several more drops of sweat to his already clammy brow '*Por favor,*' he rasped, leaning forward over the desk 'I would like you call me, Miguel. My name, Miguel. More friendly, sí?'

'Sí,' Honey said, all business, and uncrossed her legs with a slight whoosh. She placed her sensible sandals flat on the tiled floor. The dreary office, a temporary one assigned to the general during his week-long stay in Brasilia for the conference of Latin American military leaders had no air conditioning and she could feel the dampness collecting on the back of her knees, trapped there by the rarely worn silk stockings. Her low-cut peasant-style blouse was sticking to the back of the leatherette chair. She was dying for a drink of anything cool, but

25

more so, she was damned determined to get an interview out of this squirmer.

She raised her pad, unconsciously parting her pale thighs and glanced at her copious notes. 'So tell me, Miguel, who *were* your boyhood heroes?'

Click, whirr, click, whirr went the automatic forwarding camera from the corner of the room. Carla Kopit, Honey's girlishly attractive photo assistant, checked the light meter and moved to the Venetian blinds. She snapped them open, flooding the dusty space with sharp cross shafts of bright light.

'My heroes?' the general repeated, looking puzzled and frowning at his interpreter, a tired, thin man with a tired thin goatee. The interpreter whispered the translation and the general beamed, a picture of a cooperative military man in his tan, crisp uniform. 'Juan Perón,' he answered directly.

Honey made a brief note in her pad, checked the amount of tape left on her recorder and accidentally hiked up her dark green cotton skirt, exposing a bit more of a creamy thigh, lightly clad in a dusky silk. 'Why was he your hero? What did he do to inspire you?'

'Got to top,' said the general, one of the most powerful men in all of Latin America, and raised his black brows in a distinct leer. His flashing eyes dropped again to the narrow opening beneath her skirt and for a brief moment, they narrowed to slits as though he were trying to X ray her underclothing.

Innocently she raised a flank of thigh to cross her legs at the knee, flashing a bit of the black garters that dug into her flesh. His eyes bulged noticeably, his already-red face flushed deeper and he knuckled his crisp, black mustache repeatedly.

Honey, aware of the effect of her propitious choice of undergarments, pressed forward. 'Is getting to the top more important than raising the standards of living for your fellow countrymen?''

26

Her question caught him off guard. He raised his eyes guiltily from her silk-covered legs and gulped, 'But of course. I am not stupid.'

Immediately the tired interpreter bent to whisper heatedly in the general's ear and Honey smiled to herself, turning her head casually to watch her assistant bend her graceful, lithe form to obtain a better angle on the general. Carla's tight little ass, packed neatly into a pair of Pierre Cardin jeans, beckoned alluringly. Damn, what a lovely protégée, Honey thought, and remembered Carla's energized lingual activity in the ladies' room of the airport. The very memory ignited a glowing ember between her legs. She could not wait to get her little pet alone.

Honey's revery was interrupted by the general, wrathfully shouting to the interpreter in Spanish, 'Shut your fucking mouth, you stupid shit! I'm going to fuck this hot cunt if I have to tell her my real hero was Hitler!"

Honey, who spoke fluent Spanish, among several other international tongues, understood clearly and congratulated herself on her thorough research. The tidbit of gossip she had discovered deep in the files of *World News*, the giant, international newspaper and magazine chain for which she worked, had proved accurate. The general *was* a nylons-and-garter-belt freak. And she was pleased that she had gone to all the trouble of wearing the appropriate if constraining apparel. She had not wanted to use them, however, to get what she wanted. She usually preferred to let her professional skills as an interviewer break open a subject. But General Ratton was proving to be a difficult subject. It would take some extraordinary skills outside of her professional ones to get his core.

'Carla,' she said sweetly, 'be a luv and take a powder. I'm sure you have what we need.'

Carla nodded her pixie bangs with a curt 'I read you' toss, grabbed her Nikon camera bag, and headed for the door with a friendly wave, 'Ciao, all.' Her tight-bunned ass twitched provocatively out the door.

The general did not seem to be disappointed to see Carla go. In fact, he promptly dismissed his goateed interpreter, who left in a huff of bureaucratic dust, tossing a sour grimace at Honey.

She ignored it and rose, gliding to the window to peer out at the limited segment of the futuristic city. It was not her first visit to Brasilia, nor would it be her last, but next time she hoped she would be able to enjoy more of the sights and specialties. This present jaunt was definitely a rush job, a last-minute assignment insisted upon by her boss, Humboldt Hamilton.

The general eyed her covertly in stunned silence. This gringo interviewer was a most strikingly beautiful young woman. Tall – even in her sandals – long-legged like a thoroughbred colt, with heavy, swaying breasts which strained to be free from the thin fabric of her scoop necked blouse. Her most striking feature was her hair – a deep, burnished red, which framed the delicate oval of her creamy white face like a fiery halo of soft waves. Sensuality poured out of her unchecked, raising his hopes and fevering his bowels. He had never encountered a woman, from any country, who had so affected him. She smouldered like a red-hot tamale ready to be devoured.

Observing her silhouette against the light, her breasts sticking out ripely like melons in the marketplace, the general began to rub the hardness in his lap – a persistent boner he had possessed ever since she had strode into his office. He had been in agony ever since. Now he gulped audibly.

She turned and caught his hand squeezing the thick lump in his lap. A faint smile tweaked her lips and she walked to him slowly, full hips, full breasts swaying gently, her soft thighs whispering silkenly. She sat one haunch on the corner of the grey metal desk. Tearing his eyes from the pushy mound in her tight, wraparound skirt, the general looked up into hers. Their bright blue had deepened in colour, like the sultry sky before a summer storm.

She leaned forward intimately and asked in Spanish her voice more husky than honey, 'Is it true you are planning a military coup to overthrow the populist government in your country?'

His gaze rested on the soft whiteness of her breasts which spilled the colour of fresh cream over the top of her drawstring blouse. It was with some surprise that he found himself nodding in agreement to her question.

'And you have the full support of all three branches of the military?' she asked, again in perfect Spanish, the tone more suggestive of the boudoir than the boardroom.

Again he nodded minutely, transfixed by her nipples.

'When?'

'Soon,' he rasped. 'Before the year is out.'

'Is there no compromise?'

'None.' Suddenly he thrust a clammy hand under her skirt. For a second she did not move. His trembling fingers grazed the tops of her stockings and touched one of the garter snaps.

His already florid face intensified in hue and the mound in his pants twitched noticeably. She stood and, with the same movement, swept his hand away as she moved casually to the other side of the desk.

'*Conjo!*' he growled in frustration. 'What do you want me to tell you?'

'Nothing more, thank you,' she uttered with a disarming smile and switched off the recorder. 'You have been most candid. I know my faithful readers of Honey Wildon Interviews will not be disappointed.'

He blinked in confusion. 'What did I say?'

'I'll send you a copy. Once it's in print,' she replied breezily and stuffed the recorder into her large, leather carryall.

The general seemed genuinely pained at the abrupt termination of the torturously pleasurable experience. '*Gordita*,' he oiled, 'surely there is more you want to know about me?'

'Yes,' she admitted quietly. 'But "off the record".'

'Private?'

'Yes.'

He beamed, his full, dark cheeks bunching his eyes to near oblivion. 'Anything, *gordita*. What is it you want to know?"

She returned slowly to his corner of the desk and sat, placing one toe of a sandal on the arm of his chair. Her wraparound skirt fell open on one side, revealing a generous amount of gartered thigh. The general needed no further invitation. His thick fingers began kneading her flesh around the garter straps as if it were pastry dough. His breath wheezed out of him.

She allowed him to reach under her skirt to feel the garter belt crisscrossing her soft belly, and watched with a detached air. 'Generalismo Miguel Ratton,' she whispered, 'what is it you want most?'

'Your pussy.'

'And next? After me?'

'Power. Total. Irrevocable.'

'I thought as much,' she said aloud to herself and helped him with the tie of her waistband. Her simple skirt fell down to her feet. She kicked it free and leaned back onto the desk, allowing him full view of her well-chosen underthings. In addition to her sand-coloured silk hose, she wore a thin black lace garter belt and the briefest of French bikini panties of pale, pink silk. The deep red of her bush was plainly discernible through the thinness of the material.

The general fairly squealed with delight and jumped to his feet, sending the roller chair crashing back into the metal filing cabinet. 'Don't move,' he panted. 'Stay as you are . . . exactly . . . as . . . you . . . are . . .'

He hiked up the bottom of his military tunic and fum-

30

bled with his pants zipper. In a flash, it was down, and his thick brown stubby cock sprang out at full attention, a drop of moisture already on its slit.

'Ahhh,' she observed with growing interest. 'The one eyed monster at last.'

He thrust its mahogany-coloured head onto the pale soft flesh of one thigh and rubbed its under-ridges over the three textures – the silk of her stockings, the smoothness of her skin, and the roughness of the elastic garter. An expression of exquisite bliss passed over his face and his eyes fluttered closed.

He was not bad-looking, she was thinking, handsome in sort of a cloddish, bovine way, like a labourer from the fields, which is exactly from whence he had emerged. But it was not his rustic looks that had turned her on. It had been and continued to be the absolute electric energy he transmitted – an overwhelming self-confidence, an unshakeable belief in himself and his ultimate victory. He generated an almost tangible smell – like the air after lightning, an odour with which she was vastly familiar. It was the acrid smell of power. And it was the one aphrodisiac over which Honey had little control.

The general was thrusting his stubby cock between her thighs, crashing its thick brown bulb into the silk of her panties. She opened her legs farther, raising her hips slightly until his hard weapon rubbed the lubricating lips of her vagina. She could feel them parting, the crotch of her silk panties becoming more slippery, the trench of her cunt more pronounced through the filmy material, until she was so wet that the pink silk clung to her love-lips like a second skin.

Only then did he move to free her love canal from the silky wet barrier. He roughly yanked the material aside, enough to expose the glistening, rose-coloured petals of her pussy, offset by the deep, fiery red of her bush.

Taking a deep gulp of air, the general paused to study the succulence spread open before him. Her pussy

31

yawned like a sliced fresh mango, juicy and mouth-watering. He bent to inhale her aroma – sweet, natural, like a rose garden under the summer sun. He nuzzled the top of her slit with his prominent nose, deeply inhaling her intoxicating essence. The hair of her bush was soft and tickled the sides of his nose. He nudged deeper, his nose an explorer on a journey of undeniable adventure, and touched the hard island of her clit. Nodding into her, he teased that love button with his probing proboscis. Again and again he nuzzled it, like a pig unrooting a truffle with his snout.

Honey gasped at the general's nasal adroitness; waves of intensely delicious sensations coursed through her groin, rushing out and upward like shock waves, filling her every pore with delectable explosions of white-hot heat. So quickly had he raised the flames, her cunt seemed an unquenchable conflagration. He clawed at her garters, snapping them sharply into her tender flesh, adding volatile fuel to the intensifying flames. She began to moan harshly, coiling like a tight spring within the cage of herself. And still his persistent nose thrust at her until she felt she would be consumed by the flames, burnt to a cinder by her own insatiable heat.

She exploded with the suddenness of a string of Chinese firecrackers, flooding his nose with hot vanilla cream and instantly overloading her pleasure circuits. She collapsed back onto the hard desk like a rag doll. 'Where did you ever learn that?' she managed to gasp, overcome with admiration for his talents. The general lifted his proud, dripping face. 'A girl from your country,' he boasted. 'In the Peace Corps. From a school called Well-es-lee.'

She pushed to her elbows with a throaty laugh. 'I should have known. *I* went to Wellesley.'

He slowly licked the white cream from his thin moustache. 'Is that a sex school?'

'It's a highly respected institution.'

32

'So is sex,' he said and pushed her back roughly. 'Now it is my turn.'

Without further warning, he rammed his still-stiff staff into her cunt. She yelped in surprise, then melted with joy. His thrusts were quick, sure, short but sweet. Standing, humping like a piston, he rested his weight on his hands on the desk, his arms rigid, not touching her anywhere except with his cock and balls. The latter slapped into her like a sack of walnuts. She raised her legs, hooking her heels over his shoulders and bringing his face in touch with the silk of one stocking. He twisted his neck and began to tongue the silk near the hollow of an ankle. That small point of wet warmth localized a new arena of conflagration and she had the incredible sensation she had two pussies – for each area was rich with incandescent sparks.

He came without a sound or without altering his expression. Her only clue was the tiny vat of thick warm pudding that quickly lubricated her love-channel walls. He started to pull out, but she jerked him forward by a quick tug of her heels on his shoulders. 'My turn again,' she insisted.

She ground her ready-to-detonate clit into the bone of his pelvis and surged again into the fleecy white clouds of sensual free-flight. The general struggled to remove himself but her heels held him until she climaxed with another string of six or seven quick explosions, banging her softly rounded ass into his thighs with each one. With the last higher-than-ever peak, she threw her legs off his shoulders and waved them in the air with a spontaneous kick of lustful enjoyment, adding a zesty, saucy laugh that seemed to come from her cunt itself.

Stuffing his fast dwindling peter back into his pants, he stared down, watching her cameo face wildly transmogrified. Gringo ladies, he thought – all crazy. But this one craziest. Never had he met any woman who so openly enjoyed fucking. One hot little *conchita*.

Still purring with contentment, Honey swung her long legs gracefully to one side, scooted off the desk and, with a swoop of her swaying breasts, bent to retrieve her skirt. She snapped the crotch of her panties back over her cunt and wrapped the skirt around her waist, tying it as she said, '*Mucho gracias*, Miguel.'

With military precision, he straightened his tunic. 'It is usual the man thanks the woman.'

She winked, reaching for her bag. 'Not at Wellesley, bèbè. Thanks again.' And she was out the door.

They sat on a full couch in the centre section of the roaring jet and Honey hugged her pet closer. 'But it's true,' she laughed. 'His cock was nothing. His nose everything.'

'The nose knows,' Carla giggled.

'And I gave him a helluva nose full.'

They rocked with gentle laughter and Honey held out the thin joint of strong Colombian grass she had prepared for the short flight back to Rio. The general had been so overcome with the extraordinary episode atop his temporary desk, he had insisted that she and Carla fly back on his private military jet, Boeing 707.

The two were the only passengers; the steward had long ago disappeared into the cockpit, leaving them alone in the specially designed interior that more nearly resembled a luxurious living room than a military transport plane. Entwined on the couch, Honey ran her fingertips through Carla's short locks. 'It was a fair exchange. *He* gave me an earful. I have a hunch my article will create quite a stir.' She began caressing the sweet breasts beneath the halter top.

'Par for the course,' Carla voiced admiringly. 'You're the best interviewer in journalism today. Bar none.'

'My sweet pussy,' Honey whispered, and kissed her sweet lips.

34

'I'm more to you than just a pussy, aren't I?' Carla asked, overserious.

'Of course you are,' Honey answered, rushing to assuage. 'Pussy is just a word of endearment. Like Stein's nickname for Toklas.'

Carla's large, expressive brown eyes peered up questioningly, 'Who?'

Honey sighed. 'I should have never snatched you out of college.'

'You didn't snatch me,' Carla protested, raising her breasts to be explored more fully. 'I snatched you, remember? Right after your last lecture. Boy, did you rock the New School. Can't believe I was the lucky one who caught your eye.'

'How could I miss you? You camped on my doorstep for two weeks straight,' Honey laughed and traced the teasing nipples poking through the stretch fabric. 'But sometimes I do wish you'd stayed on in school instead of becoming my photo assistant.'

'Why?'

'Either that or read more.'

'Again why?'

'So you wouldn't ask such ill-informed questions as "Stein and Toklas", who?' She stroked her dear protégée's delightful tight cheeks so compactly packed in blue denim.

Carla was silent for a moment, her tongue busily wetting the cotton material over a hardening nipple, then said in a rush, 'I can't go back to college. I could never leave you.'

'Pussy,' Honey said softly, bending over the girl's innocent face, 'catch the joy as it flies and live in eternity's sunrise.'

'I've heard you quote that before, right? It's sort of your motto, didn't you say? By Bill Blake, right?'

'William, pussy. William Blake.'

Carla reflected pensively. 'So you think this joy we share will fly on by, is that it?'

'This too shall pass, Pussy.'

Carla pulled up into a seated position, pouting ingenuously. 'I think that's cruel.'

'I prefer to call it honesty,' Honey offered slowly. 'Look, pet, it's glorious while we have each other. I think you are irresistibly adorable and I am crazy about you.'

'But it won't last?'

Honey put her arm over the slight shoulders, drawing her close. 'My pet, it lasts as long as it lasts. Each of us is constantly growing, changing, exploring. Such is life, no?' Impulsively she kissed her, lingering for a tender time.

When they parted, Carla smiled. 'I love you, Honey. For however long it lasts.'

'Our love will not diminish,' Honey assured. 'It's only how we choose to express it that may change.'

Carla leaned close, breathing seductively. 'And how do you choose to express it right now? This moment?'

Honey grinned conspiratorily and with one quick movement brought Carla's stretch halter up over her ears. Carla's breasts were fully tanned with dark aurorae, looking like two healthy helpings of raisin-centered coffee ice cream. Honey fell upon them, kissing them feverishly. Her blood simmered with desire and she could feel the jump in Carla's heartbeat.

Honey shed her blouse and pressed into her pet; their nipples rubbed together like warring thimbles, their tongues dueled in a heated, passionate exchange. Carla with difficulty slithered out of her tight jeans, exploring the bristly hairs of her twat, which looked like a triangle of sagebrush growing over her hill of love.

'Suck me there,' Carla pleaded urgently.

Honey scooted around to place a knee on either side of Carla's ears and leaned down to the offered oasis of love. Hidden delicately under the kinky outcropping, Carla's tender twat glowed a healthy pink, its crinkled edges deepening in tone to a blushing red. Honey sucked on her pet's pussy, forcing her tongue deep into the slash until it located the turgid, tumid tumor of her clit. Lashing it savagely with a flicking tongue, Honey lowered her own increasingly moist gash over the eager profile of her assistant.

'Suck me, you little bitch,' Honey ordered, her words muffled by the muff on her mouth.

'Likewise, you cunt,' Carla shot back, underscoring her words with sharp, goring jabs of her conelike tongue into the innermost reaches of Honey's inflamed twat.

Honey clutched at Carla's tight, runner's ass and licked her trench open wider with an ardent, urgent action. Deeper and deeper she probed, and with each thrust she returned to the hard protuberance of the clit. In similar manner, Carla attacked with raging lust Honey's own extended button of desire. Soon each was groaning in exquisite anguish. Carla's legs clamped tightly around Honey's ears and a deep spasm rocked her trim hips. She thrust her cunt hard against Honey's face and erupted with a rumbling release that rolled on and on, her thick creamy liquid gushing from her gash in astonishing quantities. Its salty-sweet-sour taste set Honey off and she jammed her hips down on Carla's head, spewing forth a less violent but equally satisfying series of sensual bursts, a delicious fun-house ride of lengthy proportions.

Exhausted, dripping with perspiration, the two naked figures – one full, ripe, voluptuous, the other slender, tight and girlish – wrapped around each other in blissful repose, their bodies reeling with sweet waves of left-over tremors.

Carla tweaked a protruding nipple of Honey's heavy, full snow white breasts. 'Bet you graduated summa *cum* laude.'

'Only magna,' Honey laughed. 'Senior year I skipped half my classes to have an affair with my journalism prof.'

'Just like I'm doing.'

'Touché.'

'Is summa more *cum* than magna?' Carla asked teasingly.

'Bucketsful, Pussy, bucketsful . . . just like you.'

3

DIRK

He landed at Rio's Aeroport Santos Dumont only hours after Honey, and hurried off the first-class section of the giant jet, eager to locate his roaming and errant sister. Though it had taken him longer than he had hoped to track her down through her New York offices at *World News*, he was still angry as hell at her, his judgment of her scandalous behaviour undiminished. In his camera bag was the damning, inflammatory evidence against her – the video cassette of her cavorting so lustily with the giant black couple. He could not wait to confront her with the overwhelming evidence of her indiscretions. All through the long, direct flight from L.A., Dirk had cursed her under his breath. The more he dwelled on the subject the angrier he became. Usually it was Honey who had the fiery temper, but now he felt ready to match any outburst he had borne from her.

The customs area was sticky with humid heat and the official in a military-styled uniform handled each piece of top-of-the-line equipment in Dirk's camera bag with an irritating slowness. 'If you don't mind, I'm in a hurry,' Dirk said, annoyed.

'What's this?' the official asked.

'A video cassette of some of my TV commercials,' Dirk hastily said. 'Just standard prime-time stuff.'

The customs officer set the cassette aside. 'I will give you a receipt.'

'What for?'

'For it,' the official answered in a bored tone. 'All visual material has to be viewed before entering our country.'

Dirk blanched. 'Viewed? This is absurd – you don't understand,' he said urgently. 'It just contains my TV commercials. I direct them. Pepsi . . . MacDonalds . . . that trivia.'

The customs man shrugged and scribbled on a printed pad. 'It will be viewed within the hour.' He tore off the slip and handed it to an incredulous Dirk. 'You can wait if you wish.'

Dirk slapped down the receipt. 'I refuse to grant you permission to view my personal property,' he said with mounting despair. 'It is an invasion of my privacy.'

'The law requires it. We do not allow smut into our –'

'Smut!' Dirk railed. 'How dare you call my work smut! I demand to speak to your superior. Who's in charge here?'

Dirk's angry protestations fell on deaf ears even with the airport's top customs official, who smiled apologetically. 'But, señor, it will only take a moment. We have all the machines.'

'Look, see my cameras? All my equipment? I am a professional U.S. cameraman. What happened to the friendly neighbour policy?'

'Please, señor,' the headman asked coldly. 'You are creating a disturbance.'

'That's nothing to what I'm going to do when I get out of here,' Dirk yelled, out of control. 'Give me back my cassette! I'm leaving your damned country!'

'Impossible, señor,' the official responded. 'You have already officially entered. Your passport has been stamped.'

Dirk's knees trembled. Forcing himself up to his full six-foot-two height, towering over the little man, Dirk roared full voice, 'I'm calling the U.S. consulate! The ambassador is an old, *old* family friend!'

'Please feel free,' the official sighed. 'In the meantime we will view your tapes.' He whirled and smartly marched away.

In aggrieved astonishment and profound resignation, Dirk stared after him. 'Goddammit to hell,' he muttered and grabbed his camera tote bag. He stormed through the swinging doors into the crowded waiting room. Unseeingly he pushed through the milling mob and headed directly for the pay phones. He stopped before them, his shoulders drooped. He could not drag the ambassador into this. What a horror show that would be.

Slowly, Dirk turned in defeat and moved through a nearby glass door. Barely conscious of his surroundings, he gradually discovered that he was on a small exterior balcony between two giant cement pillars, overlooking the rear end of a large parking lot. The afternoon air was thick, even more humid as he slumped dejectedly on the railing to light a cigarette.

Of all the damned rotten luck, he was thinking and promptly cursed himself for being so pigheaded that he had failed to consider all the possibilities and ramifications of his sudden excursion. He sucked in the smoke, wishing it were a good jay instead. Thankfully, he had not brought any of that into the country for it too might have been discovered, adding considerably to his already horrendous problems.

His eyes fell on a vision of loveliness dressed in black, moving grandly below on the sidewalk. Instantly he forgot everything but her enticing beauty. Carrying a vanilla ice cream cone, her carriage erect but naturally graceful,

41

she was eloquently proportioned, her slim, elegant frame clad in an expensively tailored, almost severe suit. She looked like an aristocratic society matron, her undeniable beauty on the verge of fading. Her black hair was streaked attractively with silver grey and swept back into a tight French roll at the base of her neck; at her throat, earlobes and wrist, diamonds sparkled brilliantly in the white, hot sun. But it was her face that had attracted and held his entire attention. Its delicacy was at once sensual and aristicratic, proud and vulnerable, like Goya's 'Naked Maja.' In spite of her advancing age – perhaps over fifty – she was bewitching.

He leaned over the balcony's railing, watching her slip with a crisp, clean movement into the rear seat of a sleek, grey Lincoln Continental limousine with smoked-glass windows. The only occupant was a small white toy poodle with an English shawl-cut, which frantically yelped a greeting. She shut the rear door and settled back onto the leather seat, holding her white pom-pom dog on her basic-black lap. She bent to lick the fast melting ice cream. Her side window was fully open and yet when she sat back again, Dirk could only see her from the waist down. She placed the toy dog on the generous, carpeted floor-space and her legs suddenly parted.

In total suspension, he watched the mysterious presence below yank up the hem of her skirt, baring her trim thighs. She was not wearing any panties. Her black bush looked like a triangle of cat fur on her dark skin, a veritable black pussy between her legs. He could see her long fingers reach down with the dripping cone, her rings flashing. She patted a bit of ice cream on her vagina's lips. Instantly the white poodle was between her legs, licking frantically, obviously engaged in a favourite treat.

In utter blissful astonishment, Dirk observed the erotic proceedings below, aware that she was unconscious of his presence above. His pecker bloomed bone-hard. The toy dog lapped at the cool delicacy of her cunt, a blur of white against the black of her bush. When the dessert was finished, the little dog raised its head, its sharp nose twitching for more. Again her fingers dabbed more ice cream on her twat and again the little dog performed his oral duties. Dirk could not stand it a moment longer. He had to see this up close.

Running, he bounded inside and down the nearest stairs, emerging on the sidewalk leading to the side of the grey limo. There was not a single person at this end of the parking lot. As the rear window was darkly tinted, he could not see her. Carrying his camera case in front of his raging hard-on, he walked swiftly to her open window and stopped, not bothering to bend down.

The poodle raised its head, yelping fiercely. With a flurry of flying hands, the woman covered herself and hastily rolled up the window. Dirk faced it squarely and removed the camera case from in front of his bulging slacks. He just stood there letting his ready-to-fly bird of paradise speak for him. She must have liked what she saw, for she leaned forward to glare up at him with a look of annoyance barely masking her obvious interest. Her eyes darted over his face and landed down on his long, lean bird straining to be free of his pants. She opened the door.

He ducked into the cool, air-conditioned interior and before he could slam the door, she was all over him, her lips pressing against his, her hand clasping his hard cock with desperate, urgent fingers. Deftly she unzipped him and brought out his engorged member. He had never seen it look so magnificently primed for action.

The poodle had not stopped barking since his arrival, as though crazed with territorial rights. In annoyance, she dropped Dirk's fluttering bird and scooped up the toy pooch, threw it into the front seat, and promptly pushed the button that electronically raised the glass partition. The unhappy little mutt was shut off before it could hop back over. His white fluffy head bounced against the glass as he barked furiously at them, the volume distinctly lower because of the barrier.

That attended to, the elegant, bejeweled lady fell on Dirk's prick like a starving refugee leaping upon a substantial morsel of nourishing food. Unexpectedly she jammed the remains of her ice cream onto the head of his hard cock. He shrank from the sudden cold and then surged to his glory again as she began licking and sucking off the cool cream, replacing the cold with the heat of her wet mouth and tongue. She finished off the last drop, then patted her mouth with the curved back of a hand before resuming tasting his cock sans sweet-treats.

As she worked her wonders on him, he managed to get a hand up under her skirt and a finger into her cunt. Its lips were still cool from the ice cream, but inside she was a liquid furnace. Abruptly she sat up and partially stood in front of him. She crouched, her black-tailored skirt bunched around her slim hips, and taking his stiff prick upright with one hand behind her, she gradually lowered herself onto his straining shaft. He slid into her like a hot poker through a snowbank. The lady had been stretched many times before, but what she lacked in tightness, she more than made up for in adroit, heated moves.

Her erect back to him, she faced her toy poodle beyond the partition – barking even more frantically now – and began to rise up and down on his ever-hardening prick, like a ballerina doing leg squats. He did not have to move a muscle, only lean back and enjoy the ride. Wishing he could see her magical face, he reached around and cupped her small breasts – each a handful – beneath her white silk blouse. Her precise but determined strokes jarred loose the tight roll on the back of her neck and several thick strands of black grey hair fell unheeded.

Along the length of his cock, he could feel the internal walls of her tunnel of love contract and undulate, milking him toward completion. He pressed back into the luxurious leather seat and eyed her slim ass – flatter than he

44

normally preferred – gyrating furiously. Her diamond clustered hands flew out to catch the back of the front seat.

With each bounce of her flat buttocks, the little dog's barking became more frenzied and he pawed at the glass as if mad as hell for not being allowed to bring her off. The damned mutt was grating on Dirk's nerves but not enough to decrease the enormous pleasure of dipping into the tantalizing, creamy twat. His balls tightened into him and the unmistakable sensation of impending fireworks increased to the brink of agony.

She started coming with a quiet efficiency, merely a tiny whimper from the back of her throat. He could feel her hot juices washing over the head of his pushing cock. He closed his eyes, ready for his own explosion. The next thing he knew, she had lowered the partition and allowed the poodle to join them. A cold, hard nose grovelled between her legs just as Dirk started to come. A rough tongue lapped over his balls at the commingled drippings.

Before Dirk was even finished shooting his wad, the dignified lady jerked upward off him and pushed his still squirting bird down between her legs. With a disgusting slurping sound, the pooch licked the sticky residue from Dirk's exploding prick. He pushed upright, pulling away from the pesky poodle, disappointed he had not been able to come totally inside the magical, mature beauty.

Not looking at him, the aristocratic woman yanked down her skirt, smoothed her white blouse into the waistband and sat as far away from him as possible, lowering her hemline decorously over her knees. She picked up the now-quiet poodle and placed him in her lap. Dirk grinned and crammed his licked-clean-as-a-whistle cock back into his pants, zipping up with a satisfied flourish.

Instantly he remembered the overwhelming and potentially disastrous circumstances that were the cause of his detention at the terminal. His stomach hollowed. 'Do you speak English?' he asked quietly.

Shaking her head, staring at the dog, she patted into place the stray strands of hair. He noticed her slender fingers, and well-manicured nails with a clear gloss lacquer. 'Español?' he asked hopefully, although his proficiency was minimal in that tongue. Again her handsome head said no as she coolly petted the tense dog in her lap.

Dirk gazed out the window toward the modern terminal. 'If Honey were here, she could talk to you,' he said more to himself. 'I'm the dumb one in the family. And I'm in a mess of trouble.'

The magical face did not respond or look in his general direction. She had cut him out totally. He opened the door and stepped out onto the sidewalk, the hot rays of the sun searing him quickly. Bending down, he smiled into the far reaches of the limo's backseat. 'Mucho thanks, anyway. I'll never see an ice cream cone without thinking of your cunt.'

Only the toy poodle looked at him and barked triumphantly. The beautiful matron, whose face now was drawn into an unflattering tightness, stared ahead as if waiting stoically for someone else.

Dirk winked glumly at the damned dog and slammed the door. Walking toward the front of the terminal, he happened to glance up at the balcony from where he had first seen the cone-lady. A pair of native maintenance workers in overalls grinned foolishly down at him, whistling and catcalling, congratulating him. He laughed in spite of his pending troubles and waved.

A few moments later his spirits plummeted to the depths of despair. The head customs official stood in front of the terminal along with three beefy, uniformed security guards. All of them scanned, as if their lives depended upon it, the emerging and arriving crowd.

Dirk ducked behind a cement pillar before they caught sight of him and clutched his camera bag to his chest as though it might offer protection. He had to get out of here fast, he decided, and ran crouched alongside the parked cars until he found an available taxi. Slipping into the backseat, he shut the door quietly and spoke hurriedly to the portly driver: 'Hotel Copacabana Palace, and hurry. Please hurry!'

The cab shot out of its stall with a screech of tires, squealing past the main entrance with a deafening roar that bounced off the cement overhang. Dirk had folded out of sight below the windows, hoping like crazy he had not been seen.

4

HONEY

On the rumpled bed before the open doors to the balcony and the grey blue Atlantic beyond, Honey lay nude, her legs spread, and huskily spoke into the phone's receiver. 'Hum, why don't you join us? It's glorious down here.'

Carla, also naked, raised her head from Honey's snatch and grinned lustily, whispering, 'It's glorious down here too!'

Honey cheerfully waved her pet back to business and returned her attention to the phone conversation. She was speaking with her powerful employer and lover, Humboldt Harrison Hamilton, founder and chairman of *World News*, the largest international chain of newspapers and magazines with over one hundred and sixty publications in eighty-nine different countries. 'Hum,' as she endearingly called him, had phoned to ask about the general's interview.

'It went marvellously,' Honey sang out and patted her

pet's head. 'I just finished wiring it to headquarters. You'll be proud of me.'

'I'm always proud of you, Honey,' came his tender reply. 'You are a real professional.'

That praise, along with Carla's wicked tongue, raised gooseflesh along her arms. 'Thank you, darling. I owe it all to you.'

A loud, demanding series of knocks began on the outer door. 'Someone's at the door, Hum. Have to run. Bye, my love.' She let the receiver fall and promptly forgot about everything but the intense flames mounting in her loins.

The banging on the hall door resumed, more urgent, more insistent. 'Oh, cripes,' Honey groaned and pushed off the bed, kissing Carla on the nose. Her knees rubbery from the clitoris interruptus, she tugged on her emerald green, silk travelling-robe and moved unsteadily into the sitting room. 'Who is it?'

'Dirk,' came the curt reply.

'Dirk?' With a burst of joy, she unlocked the door and threw it open. He stood glaring down at her, his sandy blond hair uncombed, his tall frame rigid and and unmoving.

'Dirk!' she squealed again and dragged him into the room, giving him a welcoming hug. He was strangely unresponsive and she pulled back. 'What on earth are you doing here?'

His boyishly good-looking face was set in a hard frown and the splash of freckles across his nose erupted with colour. 'You should be ashamed of yourself,' he sputtered.

'Now what?' she sighed, long used to his brotherly admonishments and overly protective nature. 'No, don't tell me,' she quickly added. 'I've done nothing to be ashamed of, so it's your problem, baby brother. All urine, as we used to say.'

'That's where you're wrong, Honey,' he said sourly and

gave her curvacious frame a quick once-over. 'You look like you just got up from a roll in the hay.'

'What's the matter, Dirk? Didn't you get laid last night?'

He jerked his unruly hair toward the partially closed, bedroom door. 'Who's stashed in there?'

'Carla,' she replied. 'My photo assistant.'

'Can you trust her or should we talk out on the balcony?'

She burst out in a flare of hot temper. 'That, Dirkson Horace Wildon, borders on a direct insult!'

'Tough titty. You're in *big* trouble. And because of you, so am I. So I don't give a shit who knows. No sweat off my balls, lady.'

She had never seen him so deeply angry with her before. Towering a good four inches over her, his lanky, long-legged frame fairly trembled with rage. It pained her to see him so distraught, whatever the reason, be it real or imagined, accurate or exaggerated. She took his hand and led him out onto the balcony off the sitting room. Before the spectacular view of the luxuriant green mountains pushing down into the narrow strip of golden sand far below, she reclined on a yellow-padded chaise longue and lit a thin jay of Columbian grass. She inhaled deeply and passed the peace offering. He took it wordlessly and savoured a lungful.

With a rush of expelling air, he began with a renewed burst of temper. 'How could you allow yourself to be video-taped like that? Fucking and sucking is one thing. But recording it for posterity, for the whole fucking world to see, is an entirely different matter. I always credited you with more brains. Honey the smart one. Honey the college grad. Honey the big-shot journalist. Jesus, Honey, it was a goddamned stupid move!' He paused to inhale on the weed again and continued speaking through held breath and gritted teeth. 'Surely you must have considered the serious repercussions – if not to your personal

51

reputation, at least to your professional career. To mine even! And what if Humboldt Hamilton sees it? You think your goddamned boss and lover is going to put up with a low-class act like –'

'I haven't the foggiest what you're raving about, Dirk,' she interrupted coldly.

'How many sexual episodes have you video-taped, dummy?'

'None.'

'I saw it with my own eyes,' he railed. 'Screwing and cavorting around with that black couple like you single-cuntedly invented the term *ménage à trois*!'

She thought briefly. 'A couple of black what?'

'People – what else? Or is there an animal sequel?'

'A video tape of me screwing around with a black couple?'

'And giants too – that dude must have a foot-long cock.'

'Oh my, I'm sure I'd remember that,' she said with mounting concern. 'Where did you see this tape?'

Hurriedly he described how he had come to view the raunchy cassette. As she listened, a cold lump of fear hardened in her breasts. When he had finished, she sat up taking his hands and pulling him down beside her. 'I swear to you, Dirk. I have never allowed even a nude photograph of me – surely *you* must know that. Let alone allow myself to be video-taped . . . never, never.' Her voice cracked and she shivered under her silk robe. 'You have to believe me, Dirk. Because if you don't, no one else will. I swear on the graves of Mom and Dad, I know nothing of this. I must have been drugged or something.'

'Honey, you were wide-awake and enjoying the hell out of every dirty second of it. Hell, you even winked at the camera once.'

She held his deeply serious gaze and felt tears welling in her own. 'Wasn't it Voltaire who said, "It is one of the superstitions of the human mind to have imagined that virginity could be a virtue"? Hell, I haven't been a virgin

52

since I was twelve. You know that. But I have my standards – and high ones at that. You used to know that too. I can't believe you would think I would lower myself, put myself into such a compromising position . . . it's a . . . a horrible nightmare.' She broke down completely. She had been trying not to cry but the mere thought that her dear, younger brother, of all people, did not trust or believe her stabbed deeply into her heart.

He tugged her hands from her face and kissed her wet cheeks. 'Don't cry, Honey, please. Save it for later. I've only told you half the mess we're in.'

'Oh God,' she cried. 'There's more?'

Unwillingly, Dirk explained the problem with the customs officials. She pulled back in alarm, her tears drying up rapidly. Her eyes deepened in blue, and with firm resolve she leaped off the lounge and plunged back into the sitting room.

'Carla,' she called out with loud conviction, 'get dressed. *Toute suite!*'

Dirk loped into the room. 'What're you going to do?'

She whirled, her body vibrantly alive, sparks of determination flashing like crystals in her now deep blue eyes. 'I'm going to get my hands on that fucking tape before it blows my goddamned career out of the goddamned water!'

Within the hour, Honey – demurely but expensively attired in a forest green suit by Chanel, her burnished red hair in a modified Gibson girl roll – sat in a hard-metal folding-chair facing a trio of stern-faced customs officials. It was obvious from their stuffy, military-tribunal bearing that they had seen the tape. The atmosphere in the long, narrow, harshly lit conference room was thick with hostility, judgment and contempt.

She began with a dazzling, disarming smile, her trademark on the interview circuit. 'Gentlemen, as my passport states, I am Honey Wildon, citizen of the U.S. and I sincerely hope –'

The taller official in the centre broke in sharply: 'Where is your husband?'

'My husband?' she asked before it dawned on her. 'Oh, you mean my brother, Dirk, Dirkson Wildon, the third.'

Behind the long table, the trio exchanged confused glances before the middle one turned to her. 'Señorita, he has broken our laws and he must be dealt with severely.'

'Dirk had no idea such a law existed here,' she explained patiently. 'I realize ignorance is no –'

This time the shorter, more rounded official, cut her off. 'It is *you* on this tape, is it not?'

She felt her face flame in spite of her cool control. 'To be frank, I don't know. I've never seen the tape. That's –'

The third man, harder-faced with a lean, cruel mouth, waved her to silence and again there was a hurried huddle, their heads bent together like a trio of magpies on a wire fence. Nodding, they reached a decision. The cruel-mouthed one smiled with oily charm. 'As you are not positive it is you on the tape, *we* are not positive it is you. If you remove your clothes, we will determine for ourselves.'

'Wha – ? You can't be serious,' she struggled to say.

'Sí – serious.' They all agreed, heads bobbing.

'This is too much,' she said firmly and stood. 'I am calling my embassy.' She stalked to the door, the epitome of outraged probity.

'In that case,' sliced the knife-edged voice, 'you are under arrest.'

Incredulous, she spun around. 'For what?'

'Performing in and being part of a conspiracy to smuggle in pornographic materials. A warrant will be put out for your brother also.'

With a measured pace, she returned to her chair. 'And if I do as you say?'

The thin one supplied the expected: 'You will be permitted to take your filthy, disgusting tape out of our country.'

'It's that good, is it?' she quipped and stepped out of her low-heeled leather pumps. Methodically she slipped out of her suit jacket and skirt, folding them carefully over the back of the chair. In only her high-necked blouse of pale green satin, which barely covered her matching silk panties, she paused to look at the men behind the table.

Plainly visible from her angle, each was rubbing hotly, and squeezing a hard lump in his lap. With a burst of good spirits, she decided to give them their money's worth. Unbuttoning her blouse with a steady rhythm, she reached the last and coyly turned her back. She lowered it slowly over her shoulders, gradually revealing their graceful, creamy white curves. She threw them a glance over one shoulder and dropped the blouse. she began inching down her panties, taking her time, knowing for certain that her softly rounded ass was definitely one of her major assets. Ostensibly to yank free the panties from her bare feet, she bent and projected her delicious derriere at them. She made certain that they had just a glimpse of her rose petaled pussy-lips hanging between her legs before she stood upright. Letting the panties flutter to the chair, she discreetly covered her breasts with an arm and placed one hand over her flaming bush. She turned to face them, hanging her head as if in shame.

All three had their cocks in their hands now, pumping like crazy. 'Drop your arms,' one ordered in a raspy wheeze.

She did so and stood proudly erect, her bounteous breasts thrust forward, her red bush, like a blaze of hot fire between her legs, setting off to perfection her alabaster skin. Her bright blue eyes twinkled with humour as she surveyed the panting trio.

They were so taken by the voluptuous sight before them that their tongues, as well as their stiff cocks, were

55

hanging out. She rose from the floor like a classical statue sculptured out of the rarest white marble. Her softly rounded figure was earthly in its sensuality and striking in its pristine purity of form.

With a lusty cry, the three were out of their chairs as one, bounding around the table, their stiff cocks bouncing before them like hardened scouts preceding the attack troops. They leaped upon her, clasping her with rough, sweaty hands, and dragged her to the table, pushing her down upon it, holding her there.

Their sudden actions had startled her; she certainly had not foreseen or desired this reaction to her disrobing. Now she bordered on fright. Their fingers dug painfully into her soft flesh as they spread-eagled her legs. She opened her mouth to scream but a fat cock was stuck in it, gagging her with its thickness Another had flung his heavy, hard prick onto her mountainous breasts and was beating her there as if he were wielding a riding crop. Still another rammed his heated pole into her cowering cunt without so much as a nudge of greeting. It was the first time in ages that a cock – or anything for that matter – had been inside her twat without the benefit of her own lubrication. The angry, dry thrusting of the good-sized cock was rubbing painfully raw the walls of her love canal.

She struggled to be free of her tormentors, bucking and twisting, trying to wriggle away. But they were too strong and only increased their fervid activity – the pumping in her mouth, the flailing on her breasts, the rutting in her sensitive, raw gash. Intense discomfort and pain permeated her every pore. It became so extreme, she verged on hysteria and even blacking out.

But then an odd thing occurred. She first noted it with great surprise and no little relief in her tender twat – she was no longer dry. In fact, the attacker's pushing prick was fairly swimming in her libido liquids. Next, her nipples took up the alarm by thickening, lengthening, extending into full hardness under the other's thrashing hard thwacker. And her tongue, as if with a mind of its own, began caressing the apple-hard head of the invading prick.

By the moment she was actively conscious of the changes in her body, it was too late to do anything about them. Like a flash fire, the lust spread over her, inflaming her, scorching the very soles of her feet with an extreme incandescence. All cerebral activity fled and total animalistic behaviour took charge. She became like a tigress in heat – writhing, twisting, moaning. She clutched out at them, squeezing their balls, rubbing their black leather belts, tearing at the polished buttons of their uniforms, scratching at their faces – wanting only that they fill her up even more completely.

Unceremoniously she was dumped onto her side and the one with the cruel mouth, his cruel cock still pumping deliciously inside her stretched out to lay facing her. Another's stubby fingers pried at her asshole, priming it with abundant juices now flowing out of her courageous cunt. With a grunt, the anal attacker pushed his lethal weapon into her asshole, stretching her wide with a great deal of hard flesh. And still the cock in her mouth pushed at the back of her throat. She was filled to bursting in every orifice. Sweat gathered and trickled off her, pooling on the hard table beneath her. Her limbs tensed, quivering expectantly.

Suddenly, a cataclysmic eruption from the very depths of her soul blasted her overly stimulated senses to near oblivion. She began to come, shaking, her quakes trembling the table as she climaxed again and again, ejecting thick, creamy cum in great quantities.

Before she knew it she was lying on her back again, the trio of hot, horny men kneeling over her, jacking off. One by one they came, covering her face, breasts and belly, bush and thighs with white gobs of sticky cream. She rubbed it into her skin, smearing her lips, licking it, tasting its salty sweetness.

57

They stood on the table glaring down at her. Her eyes widened as they began to piss – heavy, hot acid streams of urine blasted her like from firehoses, drenching her hair, running yellow rivers down her snowy breasts, flooding the plain of her belly and into the red forest of her thick bush and the hidden valley of her still-coming love channel. She could not control herself. She raised her legs and let forth her own steady stream of piss, geysering it up by sheer muscle control and splattering their shiny black boots.

With a cry of outrage, they leaped down from the table. One spat on her, another called her a 'whore pig.' They packed their worn-out meat back into their wrinkled uniforms and marched out single file, slamming the door behind them.

With a great effort, Honey gathered herself off the table and forced her stiff legs to move her to the outer door. She shook her head, like a wet dog, to rid herself of some of the excess fluids and threw open the door. She spoke to the startled, horrified receptionist in the sweetest tone she could muster: 'Dear, you got a towel?'

They gave her barely ten minutes to clean up in the ladies' room and to dress again before hustling her, under armed guard, out into the main corridor.

As Honey emerged, still dazed, Carla, who had been waiting nervously and whose sweet face now was a mask of concern, rushed forward to speak. But Honey signalled her with a small shake of the head to 'move on.' Carla, the quick-thinking sweetheart that she was, caught on swiftly and veered past them, rushing to greet effusively a total stranger. As she passed by, Honey made certain that Carla glimpsed the black-boxed video-cassette clutched tightly in her trembling hands.

Within minutes, Honey was placed on the first available flight out of Rio and found herself bound for Cuba.

58

5

DIRK

Two days later, he found her where he knew she would most likely be – their deceased parent's favourite vacation home on the northeast coast of Kauai, not far from where *South Pacific* was filmed. The isolated beach house was so buried in the dense vegetation of the shoreline, nestled in tall palms, surrounded by lush, brilliantly hued tropical flowers that its grey slate roof and wide veranda were barely visible. It was the one place to which both he and Honey retreated in times of great stress or for just getting away from the often frantic and hectic schedule of their full, rich lives. Since it had no phone, Dirk had to rely on his gut feelings that she would be there – but then, he knew her better than anyone.

Arriving by taxi from the Lihue Airport, he climbed the wide stairs to the cool veranda and ambled into the dim, breezy interior. The white wicker furniture, which had belonged to their mother, still graced the spacious white, yellow and green living room. Honey was curled up on the floral print couch wearing only a faded pink T-shirt and brief, ragged, cut-off jeans. She looked up in surprise and he noted that her exquisite face was strained, solemn; her eyes dulled, lifeless; and her gorgeous Titian-coloured hair lacking sheen, as if unbrushed since he'd seen her. It pained him deeply knowing she was in such a state.

Wordlessly she greeted him with a vague kiss and he joined her on the couch. For a long while, they sat silently, side by side, holding hands, sipping frosty glasses of piña colada and absorbing the spectacular view out the open-shuttered French doors across a wide expanse of golden sand and into an ocean shimmering like a piece of iridescent blue foil.

She began talking, hesitantly, without her usual verve, telling him of her unexpected but short-lived jaunt to Cuba, of the long, tedious flights to reach this sanctuary. When he asked if she had viewed the tape yet, she waved a weary hand at the colour TV set and video-playback system – one of the few modern conveniences they had installed over the years.

'I've seen that damned tape so many times,' she groaned, 'I could duplicate every grunt. Providing, of course, I had that gorgeous black couple again.'

'They were something else all right. Especially the Amazon lady. I'd sure as hell like to waste a dozen rolls of Panatonic X on her.'

'I pray I run into them again soon,' she said with some of her usual sass, and then grew pensive again. 'You were right, Dirk. Getting as mad as you did in Rio. But for the wrong reasons. This hot little exhibition was done *without* my conscious, verbally expressed permission. I feel I have been violated in the most obscene manner.'

'But how could it have been made without your knowing?'

60

She nodded. 'And why? That's the hardest one. And why was it sent to your eyes only? With no follow-up or threat of blackmail or extortion? Someone is out to get at me through you. But who? Why? For God's sake *why*?'

'I was hoping you'd know.'

She crawled to the end of the couch, a soft portion of her white flanks poking out from the jean fringe, and brought back a yellow legal pad with her neatly penned writing. 'I made some notes on things that will be useful to us.'

He studied her, recognizing the 'determined professional' side of her multifaceted personality. 'You're not planning on *us* tracking this down? Let's hire the best private eyes and let –'

'Not on your life,' she interrupted sharply. 'No one is to know of this, except us. *No* one, understand?'

'How about the black couple? Not to mention the Rio customs officials. By the way, how *did* you get the tape back?'

'Never you mind,' she said dryly. 'Now listen . . .' She scooted closer, her heavy, full breasts swaying against the flimsy T-shirt, her nipples pushing hard to be free. 'In the tape, I'm wearing a gold waist-chain. Remember it? Hum had it made for our third anniversary together – it has a little ebony clasp.'

'So?'

'So I lost that beautiful belt in Morocco. Perhaps it was stolen. But when I got to Gstaad, it wasn't with my things.'

'When was this?'

'I arrived at Hum's on the fourth of last month,' she said quickly and yanked a *Le Book* appointments log into her lap. 'Which narrows down the period this tape could have been made. Now look . . .' She opened the black, leather-bound calendar to a marked page and pointed to the third of the previous month. In contrast to the heavily scheduled appointments of most of the surrounding days, the third was a totally blank page.

His eyes narrowed. 'What happened on the third?'

'That's just it,' she said strongly. 'I don't know. The week before, I was in Libya at Tarabulus covering the OPEC conference. I wrapped up on Friday and was going to fly to Gstaad to Hum's, but he got called to London. Subsequently I found out my darling Disa Dichter was in Tangiers. So I winged there to surprise her. Disa had the use of a baron's villa and we spent a glorious evening and Saturday together, frolicking in the surf. On Sunday morning, I took her to the airport to fly to Rome and returned to the villa for a rare day all by myself.'

'And?'

'Not long after I arrived back, I began to feel sick to my stomach – woozy, you know? So I went to lie down. I awoke on Monday morning, tired, muscles aching, but well enough to fly, so I left for Gstaad and joined Hum. That's it.'

'How long would you say you were passed out?'

'Twelve . . . fifteen hours. At the most.'

He stood. 'Then that's *got* to be when.'

'But what *have* we got? Not much, Dirk.'

Pacing, Dirk began thinking aloud: 'A missing gold waist-chain . . . and a missing twelve hours.' He stopped and looked at her. She looked so forlorn, he had the urge to draw her into his arms and comfort her. 'Let's watch the tape,' he suggested. 'See if we can spot anything else that might trigger your memory.'

He closed the full-length shutters, darkening the TV alcove, and switched on the playback machine. He settled next to her and stretched his long legs out. The episode began with a long shot of the three bodies rolling heatedly together on the bedspread. The walls of the bare room were white stucco and in the rear above the large bed was an unusual star-shaped window

62

opening. Dirk hit the freeze frame on the remote control. 'That window . . . can't be too many of those in Tangiers. Have you seen it?'

'No. It's not from the baron's villa. Which means I was abducted from my bed and returned.'

'Jesus,' he sighed. 'Somebody went to a helluva lot of trouble.' He played the tape forward again and they watched the passionate heated display in silence. With growing unease and discomfort, Dirk began to fidget. The explicitness and tangible heat emanating from the trio on the tube had started a chain reaction in his groin that he had no control over and was embarrassed to admit even to himself.

Honey happened to glance down at his lap and a slow smile graced her lips. 'I see my performance gets one hundred per cent on the Peter Meter.'

He scowled and scooted upright. Sitting tensely, he concentrated all the more, keenly conscious of the warmth of her full body next to him. The screening took only twenty-eight minutes, but it was the longest, most excruciatingly embarrassing and tension-filled period he could remember. With relief, he finally shut the machines off at the tape's conclusion. Without a word, he stood, throwing back the shutters with an angry noise.

'I've harvested some of our home-grown,' she said evenly. 'Let's go to the grandpa tree.'

Sharing the jay of rich, potent grass, they walked barefoot in the sand along the isolated cove, discussing over and over what they had discovered and what could be behind it. The beauty of their surroundings did not go unnoticed – the soft fragrant breeze, the gently lapping waves, the familiar landmarks. As children they had spent every Christmas here with their parents. But after the tragic airplane crash in Alaska, which had claimed their parents, the beach cottage had been closed up by the trustees of Wildon Enterprises – an empire of fish, timber and mineral holdings – and had not reopened again until Honey had reached twenty-one. Since then, Dirk recalled, he and his sister had rarely been there together at the same time. Memories of their carefree weeks there as kids flooded over him and he recalled vividly chasing Honey down this very beach and her joyous screaming laughter when he had caught her.

Now Honey took his hand and drew him into the dense forest of roots and trunks of the centuries-old banyan tree which they had dubbed 'the grandpa tree'. Inside its recesses, protected from the sun and rain, they had played endless hours among the maze of twisted intertwining trunks.

'Remember what we used to play in here?' she asked.

'Yeah. Doctor. And I was always the patient.'

She laughed. 'What naughty children we were.'

'Correction. *Still* are.'

She hesitated. 'Do you regret we messed around like that?'

'Are you kidding? I only regret we stopped.'

She averted his gaze. 'With Mom and Dad gone, it just didn't seem right. I was aware that as the older, it was up to me to put an end to it. I think I was afraid the trustees would find out and separate us permanently.'

'Which they damn near did. Packing you off to school in Switzerland. Me to that goddamned military academy. I never forgave them for that.'

'They were only trying to do what they thought best,' she said and reflected for a moment. 'Do you think of Mom and Dad?'

'Rarely now. Used to, but not much now. You remember them better. Had two years more with them than I did.'

She nodded, delicate tears forming in the corners of

64

her expressive blue eyes. 'The two sweetest people on earth.'

Dirk broke the mood deliberately. 'Hum is worried about you. I phoned him to try to track you down after Rio. He said when I found you to tell you he sends his love and please call.'

She nodded noncommittally. 'It will be difficult facing him with this damned conundrum hanging over my head. He can be so . . . so damned inquisitive.' She clutched his hand. 'Dirk, you promise you'll help me get to the bottom of this?'

Playfully, he held up a thumb and pinky finger and she quickly matched the gesture with the same. They pressed their extended digits together as he chanted their childhood oath of allegiance, 'Here's to Dirk and here's to Honey/With all their luck and all their money/Both for one/Both for fun . . .'

She joined in on the last line: 'Side by side life is so sunny.' Her eyes quickly teared again and she clung to him.

He swept her up in his arms, lifted her off the trunk and held her tightly. The closeness of her beautiful cameo face, the fresh scent of her windswept hair, her soft full breasts pressing into his chest, the distinctly noticeable pressure of her mons veneris on his thigh – all took their toll on his anatomy. His cock bloomed fast and furious.

Kissing him, she broke free and slid down his trunk to stand. 'What'll we do about ol' bird of paradise?' she teased, referring to his pet name for his peter.

'All he wants is a warm nest,' he joked self-consciously.

'We *are* rather isolated out here,' she teased. 'Guess we'll have to –'

'Make the best of it,' he interrupted and laughed too loudly. Hand in hand, they started for the beach cottage.

On the veranda, Carla Kopit, Honey's photo assistant, was waiting in a rattan peacock chair, her suitcase by her feet. Honey squealed with delight and ran to her as Dirk hung back, both pleased and disappointed. 'Dirk, you darling,' Honey cooed when she learned that he had arranged the surprise visit. 'And what if I hadn't been here? You would have had her all by yourself,' she laughed.

He could not help but make comparisons between the two – though Carla was lovely in a fresh, prep-school kind of way, her body lithe, almost boyish, her breasts small and teasing in her simple cotton sundress – it was Honey who held his eyes. Her full, womanly figure, her classically perfect features, the stunning mass of deep red hair . . . of all the beautiful women he had photographed in his illustrious career, there was no doubt in his mind. Honey was the most extraordinary. With a half-hearted attempt at easing away, he walked into the house to unpack, cursing his generosity.

Much later that night, Dirk found himself on the veranda outside of Honey's bedroom, surreptitiously watching through the shutters her and Carla on the candle-lit bed. He had not meant to end up there but sleep had been impossible.

All throughout dinner he had felt strangely tense, irritable. With each burst of convivial laughter from Honey, who had miraculously regenerated her usual zest and spunky spirit, Dirk had sunk deeper into a moroseful self-exclusion from the festive reunion. He had retired early hoping to escape into a deep sleep. But even the soporific effects of all the extraordinarily good wine, food and smoke had not been able to ease him into a blissful, escapist slumber. He had tossed and turned, all too aware of the subdued noises and intermittent giggling that had started from Honey's room.

Finally in frustrated despair, he had risen and in his birthday suit had wandered out onto the moonlit veranda to smoke still another jay. The heavy breathing and ecstatic moans, distinctly more audible from out here, had drawn him to Honey's window like a moth to a flame. Now, with baited breath, he peered through the partially opened slats of the shutter and watched them in a mesmerized state of suspended time and place.

In the soft, vacillating glow of the single candle on the end table, the two forms were melted together in the classic sixty-nine position. Honey, her feet to the shutter, was on her back, knees raised; Carla's short-cropped head bent into Honey's unseen pussy from above, her own legs straddling Honey's head. Their passionate activity was febrile but silent now, a meshing and melding of mouths and cunts into a humanistic machine created for one express purpose – getting off.

At the far top of the bed, the small cheeks of Carla's tight little ass humped into the concealed face below, like a dog humping a leg. With a helpless little groan, her head snapped up, her eyes staring at the very shuttered window through which Dirk observed.

Through Carla's soft, brown eyes were unfocused, glazed over with a recognizable passion, Dirk took a step backward, withdrawing further into the deep shadows. His hand found his fluttering bird of paradise and he began to pump determinedly. With the raising of Carla's head, he had been suddenly blessed with an unobstructed view of the most beautiful, succulent, lust-inducing pussy he had ever laid eyes on.

The glistening, deep rose petals of Honey's snatch riveted his attention. Only in the X-rated video tape of her *partie à trois* had Dirk ever been witness to that particular view of his sister's adult anatomy. Now, in the flesh, it was even more exciting, more stupendous, more sensational than he could have hoped – the absolute, perfect, fantasy cunt. Boarded by the burning bush of her silky pubic hair, its delicate deep-toned ridges were wet, glittering with the dew of passion. The petals rippled and undulated before him like a separate living organism sensually mouthing its desire to be fed.

But it was Carla's feeding time and she groaned again, biting her lips to refrain from a louder outburst. Her neck arched, throwing her head into the air, her features frozen in a state of exquisite delight. With a tiny yelp, she collapsed first on her side, then on her back, pulling her partner around with her until it was Honey on top. The pale, pear-shaped globes of Honey's soft ass now faced him, its light purple anus staring back sightlessly, her knees far apart over Carla's prone head below. Honey bent into the brown nest of her pet protégée; her snow white breasts hung heavily over the nearly flattened mounds of Carla and jiggled and swayed, their distended nipples pointing down like two divining rods.

He concentrated on the deep rose-hued trench hanging open beneath her white, full ass. Carla's finger concentrated on the clit area. As she poked, Dirk stroked. And stroked on his hard bird, pumping it with long, firm movements, relishing every second, not wanting it ever to stop. His eyes felt welded to that awesome treasure so openly displayed.

The overwhelming sensation centred in the ballooning head of his cock teetered dangerously on the brink of ultimate satisfaction. He slowed the beat on his painfully throbbing prick and held off, waiting for his sister to take the lead. He did not have long to wait. Emitting a soft cry, she began to be wracked by bucking orgasms. Thick, silvery fluids rolled out of her petaled pussy like white-hot molten lava from an erupting volcano. Hips still high, she slammed her torso onto Carla's belly and hung on to the the pillows with clawing fingers, her ass waving in the air like a flag on a windy day. Carla's head leaped to lick her rewards, blocking Dirk's view of the hypnotizing magnificence of Honey's incandescent cunt.

By then he was coming anyway, shooting great cannon-balls of sticky gism onto the windowsill. It was a spectacular climax, and he quickly concluded it was the next best thing to being there.

6

HONEY

It was not without some trepidation that Honey showed up on the doorstep of Hum's ancestral home, Hillsprings, in the foothills of the Allegheny Mountains in old Virginia. In a personally chartered flight, she had flown into his private airstrip without notifying him – something she had never done before. But she had something she desperately wanted from him, a pressing favour to ask. And because she had disappeared out of his life for four days – both personally and professionally, the latter resulting in one missed deadline and the first failure of her international column to run on time – Honey believed she could not in all good conscience make such a presumptuous request over the impersonal instrument of Alexander Graham Bell.

The elderly, dignified butler who answered the ring expressed a reserved surprise at her unannounced arrival but told her 'the master' was down in the springs. She thanked him and hurried down the long wood-panelled

71

hall strewn with rare Persian and Chinese silk rugs. Hillsprings was a beautiful and elegant home filled with priceless antiques and family heirlooms handed down for hundreds of years. Coming there was always a special treat for her, but today she nearly ran to the rear of the house, through the glass-walled solarium filled with blooming orchids, and down the interior stairs. Past the bowling lanes, the gymnasium and the large indoor swimming pool she breezed and through a heavy door into the steamy, sulphuric-tinged atmosphere of the natural hot springs. The strains of Vivaldi's *Four Seasons* softly played on the stereo speakers beyond in the cavelike room.

Swiftly, in a small, carpeted anteroom, she removed every stitch of clothing and stepped with eagerness through the brick archway. Natural daylight filtered in through the giant windows that overlooked the immaculately groomed flowering shrubs of a very formal English knot garden. Around and above the large sunken, stone basin of the bubbling pool, hanging ferns and large potted plants thrived in the warm, humid air. But it was her nude bathing lover who held her eye.

All six-foot-four, two hundred and forty pounds of Humboldt Harrison Hamilton floated, barrel chest up, beefy arms straight out, his eyes closed, like a relaxing bear in a mountain pool. With a growing excitement flourishing in her loins, she tiptoed down the stone stairs and into the hot, steaming water, which gurgled up in large bubbles. When the water was over her hips, she kicked out in a modified breaststroke and swam to his outstretched legs. Her watery movements were covered by the bubbling springs and the Vivaldi. She paddled directly between his legs and unceremoniously clasped her mouth over his floating cock. Like a sleeping thick snake suddenly awakened, it jerked powerfully away.

He rose with a sputtering explosion of surprise and gaped at the silent cocksucker. 'Honey!' he greeted gruffly. With a burst of softening laughter, he gathered her into his strong arms and hugged her to his broad-chested frame. Their feet drifted down to touch the smooth, warm stones on the bottom. He kissed her fiercely on the lips, draining out of her the last drop of excited breath. Lovingly she encircled his neck, driving her tongue into his mouth, slicking the insides of its roof while grinding her hips into his. She pressed her mons veneris into a heavy thigh, tickling him with her silken bush, feeling her libido juices already flowing freely. Of all the men she had ever been with, Hum could make her hotter, faster than anyone.

When they broke for air, his prick had swollen between them, poking insistently at her like a demanding child wanting attention. He eyed her sternly from beneath his greying, bushy brows. 'And where have you been?' he growled in an authoritarian tone that was too posed to be genuinely threatening.

'I just had to get totally away from it all,' she breathed into his heavy neck. 'Forgive me?'

'Did that "all" include me?'

She pulled back, admitting, 'You know I can't think straight sometimes when I'm around you. You're the only one I know who makes me feel like an awkward inexperienced schoolgirl.'

'Perhaps that's only because you *want* to feel that around me,' he said with a pleased grin and cupped a handful of her ass.

She trembled. 'You didn't say you forgive me yet.'

'I didn't hear an apology.'

'Oh, Hum, I *am* sorry,' she blurted and wrapped her long legs around his substantial waist. 'Really, I am. But I just had to escape to my own sanctuary. To gather my bearings again.'

His gun-metal grey eyes pierced her with an inquisitive gaze. 'Pressures?' He watched her nod and she felt the heated bulb of his upright prick nudging at her ready,

73

willing and able lips. 'Anything you want to share with me?' he asked softly.

'Yes . . . my pussy with your cock.'

A smile formed on his craggy, maturely handsome visage and with one quick thrust of his hips, the tomato-sized head of his urgent cock parted her cunt lips and sank into her waiting box, like a welcome fire-log. She gasped with pleasure and pushed down on it, wanting it totally inside her. He complied readily, plunging the entire length of his hard member as far as it would go. For a brief span, he stood – her legs wrapped around him, the steamy water bubbling up like hot champagne – before he began a slow, unhurried, confident stroke.

'Oh, that feels marvellous,' she murmured huskily. 'Fuck me, Hum . . . fuck me, fuck me, Hummmmmmmmm.' Her full breasts pushed so tightly against his rib cage that she could feel the hammering of his strong heart, its animated, energetic rhythm energizing her own.

The frothy water effervesced her skin like a million butterflies kissing her. She tingled inside and out and could feel his swelling farther inside her vanquished vagina. His strokes increased in speed, accelerating steadily like a powerful auto gaining momentum. She reached under her suspended ass and found his fuzzy balls, floating free like heavy stones suspended in a fish net. She propelled him on faster, using her hips, maximizing her rapture.

All too soon – way before she knew he was ready – she shrieked shrilly, her strident cries echoing off the stone walls of the grottolike room, overlaying a pleasingly discordant instrument to the violin section of the Vivaldi score. With hip-wracking spasms, she began to come, adding her own lubrication to the water.

'I'm coming too,' he croaked unexpectedly. 'Here it comes . . . right . . . now?' Hot geysers of his thick semen shot into her fartherest recesses and he bucked her

74

wildly with each detonation. Once he had finished, she floated free on her back, still in the delicious throes of sensuous waves cascading over her like a gentle waterfall. Enveloped in warm liquids, she felt totally immersed in their own cum.

They made it twice more before they finally dressed – once in the nearby, cedar-lined steam room on the hot wooden slat benches, and again, just outside, in the warm spring sun on the down-soft carpet of grass of the putting green of his private eighteen-hole course. Both times she finished before he did.

Later that afternoon, Hum took her for an invigorating horseback ride on the many trails crisscrossing the wooded thousand-acre estate. The gentle, friendly landscape near the Shenandoah Valley was unmistakably feminine – softly rounded tree green hills, like gently sloping shoulders, swept smoothly down into alluring valleys unspoiled and untouched by man.

The estate had been in Hum's family since before the Revolutionary War; George Washington himself had discovered the hot springs around and over which the huge main house had been built. Balneology, the science of bathing in therapeutic, natural mineral waters, had been a part of Hum's ancestor's daily life and he carried on the tradition. Rarely a week went by that he did not travel, from wherever he was in the world, back to Hillsprings to partake of the soothing beneficence. But it was also the land he came back for and he surveyed it now from the back of his coal black thoroughbred as if he were seeing it for the first time.

Honey rode expertly beside him on her usual mount, a frisky Arabian mare, and out of the corner of her eye she studied the man she loved the most in the world, excluding her brother. In direct contrast to the land, Humboldt was distinctly masculine. Ruggedly handsome with iron grey hair, he had a deeply tanned face composed of rough-hewn planes, as though his features had been cast in bronze. Though over twice her age, he exuded a youthful, zestful energy, vigorous and determined. To her thinking, he was the only true genius she knew. Singlehandedly, Hum had built, by dint of painstaking work and awesome dedication, an enormous, influential empire worth over a billion dollars. A demanding but fair employer, he inspired complete devotion and matching hard work. But above all this, it was his magnetic power that attracted and held her.

In her journalistic career, she had interviewed heads of states, military forces, conglomerates, social and political leaders, men and women who wielded tremendous power. But no one came close to Hum's personal magnetism. It flowed out of him in tangible waves of energy and strength, purpose and conviction. Being with him again, she felt under his spell, marvellously alive and whole. If it had not been for the pressing favour she felt compelled to ask, she would have felt totally at ease.

They reined to a halt on a hill looking back over the valley to the large brick house in the distance, gracing the green expanse of the golf course like a stately centrepiece on a natural wedding cake. Hum cleared his throat, looking at her. 'Your piece on General Ratton. Hard hitting. Thorough job. It's creating quite a stir. Even the White House called about it.'

'Terrific! That's what I love to hear. He *was* a difficult subject. Quite reticent to open up.'

'Such a gift you have, Honey. No one has gotten such a revealing portrait of him on paper. Someday tell me your secret.'

'*You* taught me everything I know,' she laughed. 'The very first thing you told me, that afternoon you plucked me off the society page of the *New York Journal* after you had added it to your chain – you said, "young lady, your first rule is 'be prepared.' " Like the Boy Scouts. I've done my homework ever since.'

'Very impressive, the hours you spend on research. I admire your tenacity too. Not giving up until you've gotten fully what you want. Most young people, as fortunate as you, endowed as you are with nearly unlimited trust funds, end up throwing their lives away. Worthless. Meaningless existence. But not you. I'll never forget the surprise when I learned you were one of the wealthiest heiresses in the country.'

'Thanks to my dear dad and his hard work with Wildon Enterprises,' she voiced sadly. 'You would have adored him, Hum. Brilliant, gregarious, fun-loving . . . just like you.'

His thick brows bunched. 'I do not wish to be a father figure to you, Honey.'

She reached out and touched the sleeve of his cashmere riding coat tenderly. 'Hum, I didn't mean it that way. You're everything to me – my hero, my teacher, my boss, my lover – everything *but* my father. You treat me like an equal. From the very first you saw my potential, nurtured it, challenged it. I owe my very adult life to you.'

'My darling Honey,' he said hoarsely and pulled her into his arms across their saddles. 'You have brought me so much joy.' He kissed her heatedly and she felt the fires leap to life within.

She pulled back, gasping, 'Last one to the stables has to eat the winner for a whole hour!' Digging her boot heels into the mare's flanks, she tore off at a blistering gallop, laughing at the pure exhilaration of the race.

Though it was a heated, neck-to-neck run until the final moment, Honey won and received her just desserts sprawled in the straw of one of the stable's stalls. Knowing Hum had let her win did not diminish her pleasure. He was always a gentleman. He even ate her longer than the required time.

Dinner that evening was served intimately in the sitting room of his bedroom suite before a crackling fire. They had just finished the exquisite lemon soufflé of the last course when she finally voiced her request. 'Hum, darling . . . I would like to take this next month off completely. I may not even see you for a while. And I don't want you to ask why.'

As for all his dinners, they were formally dressed – he looked dashingly debonair in his black tie and tuxedo, and she coolly elegant in an ice blue chiffon evening gown by Yves St. Laurent. Strapless, backless, barely covering her ample bosoms, it clung to her every curve with a delicate assurance. Her Titian hair glowed in the firelight; diamonds and sapphires – a Christmas set from Hum – glistening at her throat and earlobes like cold fire as she waited nervously for his response.

Hum took a slow sip of their wine, a Château Latour, 1959, and set the Baccarat goblet carefully on the white linen tablecloth. 'You leave me no choice but to say yes.'

'I promise to tell you everything once this month is up,' she said gratefully and added quickly, 'Regardless.'

'Regardless of what, my dear?'

She flashed a radiant smile, dazzling as her diamonds. 'Just "regardless." Are you terribly upset with me?'

'No,' he said easily. 'Only disappointed that I cannot share this – whatever it is – with you. May I offer any assistance, help you in any way?'

'You've done too much for me as it is,' she said and finished her wine. She felt slightly tipsy and vastly relieved.

He grinned jovially. 'Knowing you as well as I do, I realize how pointless it is for me to probe further.'

'On the contrary,' she said, her voice deep with seductivity. 'Your reward for your generosity is that you get to probe as deep as you want. Providing it's not with words.' She stood and glided to the white bearskin rug in front of the roaring fireplace. With one simple tug on the sides of her long gown, she brought it down over her superstructure. The blue chiffon fluttered gracefully to the fur rug, and she stood nude except for her exquisite jewels and her slender high heels.

A golden aura cast by the fire brushed the soft curves of her luscious body. The fiery triangle nestling in the thrust of her thighs made her skin seem pale in comparison. The full, heavy curve of her breasts swelled across her torso like snow-clad peaks.

At the intimate, elegant table, Hum appraised her expertly, like the experienced connoisseur of fine art which he was, and enthusiastically passed approval by an appreciative burst of applause. 'May I have my cigar first?' he laughed.

'Why not both at the same time?' she breathed huskily.

'Capital idea,' he said, bounding to his feet and tearing off his tux. 'I do love the way that brain of yours works.'

Sinking to her knees, she gracefully inclined on one full hip, facing him. 'And I do love the way that cock of yours works.'

Once he was naked, he grabbed one of his favourite Havana cigars from the humidor and lit it on his way to her, his rugged large form accented sharply in the middle by the thick angle of his rising cock.

She fucked him hard and furiously on the white fur rug, attacking his burly body with the fervour of an insatiable nymphomaniac. But then, Hum always brought that out in her. The whole while, he lay on his back, puffing his sweet-aroma cigar, not lifting a finger to interfere with her administrations to his bodily needs. Squatting over him, she rode his bludgeoning prick like a jockey on a sweepstakes' winner. Using the whip of her flat hand on his hip with sharp, stinging little blows, she urged herself on faster, faster, faster until they both crossed the finish line at the same time.

Rasping, panting, jubilant with mutual victory, they bathed each other in lusty fluids, and shortly he flopped over to tap the long ash of his forgotten cigar into the hearth. He noted the remaining length and smiled. 'Good. I still have some left.'

That night, as Hum slept soundly wrapped in her arms in the giant, four-poster bed of his great-great-great-grandfather, Honey stewed about the video tape and what Hum's reaction would be if he ever found out about it. Heaven forbid. Worrying about the upcoming month off and whether it would produce the desired results – getting to the bottom of the horrid horror show – she had difficulty falling asleep.

7

HONEY

Immediately upon checking into her favourite suite in the Ritz Hotel in Paris, Honey dialled her dear old school chum, Disa Dichter. To her extreme disappointment she learned that Disa was not presently in town. Disheartened Honey left word and hung up, falling back against the plump pillows of the Regency bed with a sigh.

Darling Disa, daring Disa, delectable Disa, she mused forlornly, and conjured up the delicious dimples on the derrière of Disa (which rhymed with Lisa). If anyone could help track down the why and wherefores of the sex tape, dimpled Disa was the one. Not only did Disa know everyone who was anyone around the world, plus the raunchiest gossip of the varied, exotic locales frequented by the leisurely wealthy, she also had at her roving finger-tips every source of major and minor kink to be had on the continental party circuit. Surely Disa would have an idea, an inkling as to who was behind this appalling invasion of privacy. After all, Disa had been there that very morning in Tangiers, winging off to Rome just before Honey had 'passed out'.

Honey cursed herself soundly for not wiring Disa of her impending arrival. Knowing Disa's penchant for travel, the lovely lass could be anywhere in the world. And here *she* was, all alone in one of her very favourite cities, without her usual favourite tour guide and sexy, zany playmate. Feeling antsy, but having no immediate outlet, Honey slipped out of her travelling ensemble, a smart suit by Anne Klein, and drifted into the bathroom for a hot soak.

She had been in the large, claw-footed tub, luxuriating in the soothing bubble bath only a few minutes when the white and gold, stand-up phone next to the tub rang. It was Disa returning her call!

'Damn, why aren't you here?' Honey asked breathlessly. 'And where *are* you anyway?'

'Monte Carlo, darling,' Disa reported in her low, sultry voice. 'Where *you* should be, *ma chère*. Everything's hopping down here. *Toujours gai.*'

'When are you coming back here?' At the very sound of her first lover's voice, Honey's fingertips automatically began exploring the furled edges of her pussy portal. 'I have something terribly serious to speak with you about.'

'How mysterious,' Disa purred. 'But I just got here. Darling, why don't you fly down? We're all heading out on Tremont's yacht this afternoon. For Portofino.'

Beneath the soapy water, Honey inserted a single, long finger and began flicking at her lust trigger with a well-manicured nail. 'Damn, I wish I could, but I promised Hum I'd do just one more interview before I take my month holiday.'

'You? A holiday?' Disa echoed disbelievingly. 'Oh, *merde*, this is rotten timing. I don't remember your ever being free from that dreadful column since you went to work for Hum.'

'It is my first break, at that,' Honey said. Her internal

temperature, due to her fast flicking finger, was now far above that of the steamy water surrounding her. She slowed the pace of her prodding digit. 'Of course,' she laughed lustily, 'there are those who will insist my life is nothing but one long vacation anyway.'

'*Pas moi, chère amie.* I, for one, know how hard you work.'

As they chatted on gaily for several minutes about mutual friends and about Honey's continued relationship with Hum, Honey raised her feet to press against the porcelain tub and imagined it was Disa's firm tongue inside her. It was a lovely, pleasant sensation and with Disa's warm tones in her ear, she could have come easily at any moment. Unexpectedly, Disa broke out in a series of sharp, staccato, unmistakably 'coming' groans.

'Why Disa Dichter,' Honey panted in her own throes. 'Whatever are you doing?'

'The same thing you are, darling,' Disa moaned. 'Making love to you over the line. I can almost taste your sweet cunt.'

'And I yours . . .'

Shortly they both came together again, sharing their lusty vocalizations over the line with wild surrender. Finally, with fervoured cries professing their undying love and a promise from Disa to call within the week, they rang off. Replacing the receiver, Honey felt a renewed wave of melancholia. Even her own hand in her cunt seemed tired now, dispirited, even disenchanted. She withdrew it and pledged firmly to find at once a more able partner for the evening. If she could not make progress on her pressing quest, at least she could have some fun.

It took no time at all to arrange the latter.

That evening, promptly at eight, exquisitely gowned in a red satin evening dress by Givenchy, her lustrous hair swept into a dignified French roll, Honey arrived by taxi in the exclusive residential area near the Seine. She was met at the door by the wickedly handsome host, Pierre LaComber, who embraced her warmly, his roving eyes twinkling with barely hidden amusement: 'Honey! *Très chic, très jolie,*' he praised and added in perfect English, 'Good enough to eat.'

'Am I the main course?' she joshed and squeezed his tuxedoed arm. Pierre was a notorious playboy, the only heir to a vast banking fortune, and one of the perennial jet-setters who crisscrossed the world like a butterfly in heat, landing momentarily before flitting on. She had met him the year before at the Berlin Film Festival, introduced by his then paramour, Disa. Though Honey found him much too handsome and suave for his own good – frivolous too – she also knew that he had a sterling reputation for presenting amusing, decadent evenings. And that was exactly what she was in the mood for. A little kink to spice up a dreary day.

In the high-ceilinged drawing room, Pierre made a grand show of presenting her to the other guests – three divinely attractive couples also formally attired – and seemed to indicate in his manner that with Honey, tall and magnificent on his arm, he had captured the prize of that or any other season. Over cocktails, the conversation was witty and titillating, the guests eyeing one another with obvious approval. When dinner was announced, Pierre latched onto Honey's arm, whispering confidentially that it was Disa who had phoned urging him to find some amusement for her dear friend, Honey. He said now he hoped she would not be disappointed. She replied that she was ready for anything.

The moment she walked into the luxurious dining room with its dark brocade walls, Honey knew something most extraordinary was in store for them all. The unique table was her clue. Glowing under a candlelit crystal chandelier, a large scalloped circle contained eight individual recesses, the entire table covered to the plush carpet with a flowing, white damask cloth. Within each half-circled indentation, a tapestried, cushioned chair awaited. Pierre seated each of the women in alternating chairs around the table, placing Honey next to him. He himself sat only after everyone was in his proper place.

'Before we begin our repast,' he began cordially, 'may I request that the ladies remove their undergarments and place them on the tray in the centre. And gentlemen, please slip out of your trousers and shorts. Jean-Louis will collect them.'

A burst of boisterously excited laughter followed, but everyone swiftly moved to comply with the host's request. For a brief spell, the soft rustling of garments being hastily removed beneath the table was the only sound in the room. The glamorously attractive guests swayed in their chairs around the large, white shell table as though each were treading water. One by one, the lovely young women threw their silk panties into the silver tray before them all. Then it came to Honey's turn, she smiled bewitchingly, and explained, 'I didn't want to be over-dressed.' The men appreciated her remark a great deal and laughed heartily as they handed their trousers and shorts to the passing uniformed butler.

Pierre grinned wickedly, his dark gaze turning to each as he spoke. 'Tonight, we are reintroducing a favourite pastime of the court of Louis XIV. It was – and is – called La Grande Bouffe. Underneath this table, a young woman is secreted. A lovely young woman, I may add. Totally nude. She has been instructed to find the most appetizing genitalia exposed below and to service it – be it cunt or cock.' Like a proud peacock, he paused to let the delicious news filter into their evening's sexual menu and began again theatrically: 'The object of the amusement – *mon petit divertissement* – is exactly this: if you are so fortunate to be chose by our lady of the lap, you must not let anyone else at the table know that it is you. It is a supreme test of your willpower and endurance to enjoy your pleasures in complete secrecy and total privacy. The

85

rest of us will proceed with our dinner and our conversations, trying to determine just who is being eaten.'

'Impossible,' a flashing-eyed contessa protested. 'Who can keep *that* from showing?'

'I can,' boasted an English lord of barely twenty-six.

'What's the penalty if we let on?' Honey asked, already into the challenge and the spirit of the contest.

He winked at her. 'The loser has to do what I bid later this evening.'

'I say, old fellow,' the young English lord humphed, 'you mean if I lose, I have to do you?'

Pierre's roguish eyes narrowed provocatively. 'Or anyone – or anything – I command. After all, I am the host. Do we agree to these rules?'

No one dared say anything, each was so excited at the teasing prospect. Pierre nodded like a ringmaster. '*Bon*, ladies and gentlemen, spread your legs. Dinner is being served. *Bon appétit*.' He lifted the tablecloth and leaned down. 'And to you, *mon petit chou*.' To much laughter, he rang a silver dinner bell. On silver platters carried by six young servants all in black, the salmon course began arriving.

The cold salmon was delicate and delicious and Honey adored both it and the fantasy of the guests' nude lower halves beneath the table. From the waist up, it could have been a thousand other dinners she had attended, but oh la la, underneath – *that* was the big difference. She smiled to herself, secretly wishing it were she under there. She had had her eye on the delicate but tomboyish young contessa directly opposite, and would have loved to have been able to glimpse her lower anatomy up close. Everyone was most merry, the first wine exceptional – a premier champagne Louis Roederer Cristal, '71 – and the conversation covered many topics, but Honey knew each was thinking as she. Who the hell was the lucky one?

The first course concluded, the second commenced – a truffle dish – and still Honey had no idea. Then with a slight start, she felt a pair of soft, warm hands on her thighs, parting her wider. As gentle as a doe nuzzling for tender grass shoots, a curly head nudged between her legs and an expert tongue found the lips of her clam shell. The tongue slit her open like a skilful surgeon and was so sure of itself, Honey soon began to pump savory sauces of her own.

Casually she sipped the second wine, Château Margaux, '75, and, commenting on its velvety balance, felt the invading tongue working wonders on her love truffle. She was determined, however, to win this amusing event and therefore made a concerted and deliberate effort to keep up her end of the free-ranging conversation.

'Pierre,' she said during a small lull, 'you failed to mention what the winner gets if he – or she – comes without signalling.'

He smiled devilishly, a naughty little boy. '*If* there is a winner, he or she gets to have anyone here. Or *all* of us for that matter.'

'Hear, hear,' the lord grumphed appreciatively.

By the third course – a *coquilles St. Jacques*, which was excellently complemented by the superb choice of a '71 Corton Charlemagne – Honey was having difficulty breathing normally. Tongues of searing flames lashed out at her and she was positive her facial colouring had deepened considerably. She was thankful that the candlelight was dim, very romantic. Hopefully it was too dark for anyone to see her clearly. The subterranean sucker was one of the very, very best that Honey had had the pleasure of experiencing. Not a furled ridge of her liquefying lips was being missed, not a centimetre of her kindled cunt was being slighted. Though the teasing of her love button was exquisite agony, she delicately sipped her dry white burgundy, savouring its lingering rich spiciness.

The culinary and cunnilingual banquet moved steadily into the main course, an irresistible pheasant stew. Honey felt on the verge of either fainting or screaming, it was so difficult to hold back even the tiniest sigh or to shift her position in her chair unduly. It took enormous will-power on her part to steel her resolve. She clamped her thighs tightly around the loose curls of the head wedged below and hung on for dear life. The tormenting tongue did not cease its worthy efforts, and even seemed to redouble the tender affliction. Honey's hands trembled as she tried to bring the heavy, solid-silver fork to her mouth. She was positive Pierre detected the minute flutter, for he eyed her deeply.

'Everything OK, *ma chère*?'

'Perfect. Everything is just perfect,' she said, cooling her facade. 'I'm afraid, though, I've positively reached my satiation point. I couldn't handle another morsel.'

'We've only one more,' he said winking.

By the dessert, a *tarte aux pommes*, served with rare Roederer Cristal champagne, she had fallen silent, her apple pastry untouched, her knuckles white from clasping the stem of her fine crystal glass. Fortunately, by then everyone else was filled to the bursting point with so much fine wine and excellent cuisine that they were not paying close attention to anything except their own overindulgence. She bit the insides of her cheek to prevent even so much as a swelling of her cleavage. But she was fast losing ground, sinking rapidly into blissful oblivion. She pushed lower into the feminine profile still devouring hungrily as if her cunt were the most delectable feast imaginable. Honey's bare cheeks and the tapestried cushion beneath were awash with her succulent sauces.

Finally, her love kettle was boiling so heatedly, she could not contain it one moment longer or she feared she would burst open all over the lovely assemblage. Much to her consternation and self-admonishment, she allowed a minute moan to escape, a little release of the unbearable pressure that had been building for what seemed hours.

'*Mon Dieux*,' she whimpered.

Instantly Pierre pointed an accusing finger, declaring drunkenly, 'Aha! You lose, my pussy.'

'*Au contraire,*' she gushed and sank lower into the face, coming like a burst dam, overflowing a tidal wave down the valley of her love delta. The other guests were surprised and delighted, applauding like happy children who had just seen a clown act, offering their astonished congratulations for maintaining her beautiful, charming, captivating façade.

When the lady of the lap had withdrawn her lingual licker and Honey had been completely drained, Pierre bent to call out the cunning cunnilinguist. And who should arise from beneath the white shell, looking like Botticelli's Venus, but the dazzling, very blonde and very nude, Disa Dichter.

'Disa!' Honey squealed, rushing to throw her arms around the lusciously curved figure filmed with a glowing sweat. She pulled back to appraise the ravishing blonde, whose hair was a mass of newly styled soft, golden ringlets. 'I thought you were on your way to Portofino!'

'How could I resist Pierre's little subterfuge?' Disa confessed girlishly. 'I was in bed with him when you and I spoke this morning.'

Honey hugged her tightly, relishing the firm breasts pressing against her own. 'I should have known it was you under there. No one but no one has a more talented tongue.'

'And no one but no one has such a red and ripe pussy. Just like a juicy tomato,' Disa laughed.

Much to Honey's joy, Pierre announced grandly that the loser had to serve not him – but Disa. 'How divine,' Honey exclaimed. 'May I take her back to the hotel with me?'

'As long as you fulfil your end of the bargain,' he replied graciously.

'To be sure, I will,' Honey said emphatically. 'It will be *my* pleasure.'

*

Within a half hour, she and Disa were sprawled naked on the big bed of Honey's elegant hotel suit, whiffing some excellent coke from a tortoiseshell compact mirror and later melting together like two ice cream bars in the summer sun. They were evenly matched – both tall, leggy, full breasted, and hot boxed. Their differences, however, were striking. Disa's hair was as radiantly blonde as Honey's was lustrously deep red; and Disa's soft, flawless skin was tanned the colour of golden honey, whereas Honey's matchless satin was as pale as fresh milk. Milk and honey flowed together, responding to and re-exploring each other's bodies and libido with the deft assurance of old lovers.

She and Disa had been practising these very same routines and techniques every chance they got since they had been budding, ripening pubescent girls. At the exclusive Swiss finishing school near Lucerne, when they first met they were only twelve, but they had been instinctively drawn to each other. Their natural affinity and mutual regard had quickly blossomed into a tender and exploratory love affair. Later, as each had matured, the affair bloomed until at one period it had been an all-consuming passion for both of them. As they had gone their separate ways after graduation – Honey to college and Disa into the social whirl – their reunions were far between, but the love that bound them together had remained. And now, together again, it was like coming home. Tender and secure, torrid and deep-felt, simultaneously fresh and familiar. An expression of a lasting, genuine love and mutual commitment.

At one point, Disa reached to the floor and from her beaded handbag brought out *chef de gare*, producing it with a great flourish. Honey giggled with delight at the sight of the familiar tool. It was an antique ivory dildo of unique design. The thick, long scimitar-shaped shaft was double-headed, allowing each to insert an end. Soon they were riding once more in tandem 'the station master' as they had nicknamed it so long ago. The ancient instrument of pleasure was Chinese by design and had been presented to Disa on her thirteenth birthday by her mother with the expressed wish that it would bring the child as much pleasure as it had brought her. As her mother had died of an overdose of sleeping pills not long thereafter, Disa had always carried it with her, following the sage advice as often as she could. Like now, once more with Honey.

Disa pulled off from her end of the mutual thruster and, without missing a stroke, wrapped her mouth around the now free end, the other still in the suction cup of Honey, and began to move it slowly in and out of the steamy dampness with maddeningly slow thrusts. Twisting around the curved ivory two-headed monster connecting them mouth to cunt, Disa placed her unattended cutlet over Honey's gaping mouth. 'Eat me, you fiery cunt you,' Disa ordered sternly.

Honey wordlessly, enthusiastically obeyed, repaying in kind some of the acute attention Disa had so lavished upon her earlier that evening. Diving into Disa's box was like opening a jar of thick honey – the muff was as golden and the juices as sweet and thick. Lapping in the lap of luxury, Honey teetered on the edge of popping. The hard bulb drove deep into her flap, perforating her puffy pasty. With each thrust she received from the teeth-pushing Disa, Honey in return broached the lids of the honey-jar and dirked deeply inside the damp, sweet den. With distinctly guttural growls of glee, Disa began coming; thick, viscous fluids oozed slowly like nectar of the gods. The thrill of bringing Disa off first pushed Honey into a groundswell of rolling tremors. She twittered and twisted on the ivory dick wedged to its half-way mark within her welling well. She bucked and boned and let loose with a lasciviously lustful howl, her cunt smelling faintly of roses.

Later, foot to foot, cheek to jowl, in the high-sided tub

with pale pink bubbles up to their chins, Honey and Disa unwound at a wickedly slow rate. Honey was longing to tell Disa everything about the horrid, incriminating tape, and knew that her dear friend would give unconditional support and all assistance she could, unasked for. But Honey also remembered her vow with Dirk – no one would know about this outside of the two of them. And any bond, tacit or verbalized, with her brother Dirk was stronger than even for love for Disa. Therefore, not wanting to raise suspicions, she began a most delicate inquiry into that fated Sunday in Tangiers.

After answering many questions, Disa was naturally curious; what was so damned important about that one day so long, long ago? Honey professed that it was such a vividly perfect memory of a stunning, sensual weekend, she wanted to relive each precious moment of it again. Disa appeared touched by the admission and step by step, moment by moment, they recalled that Sunday morning together: the breakfast on the terrace overlooking the crowded, tiled roofs sloping down to the beach; what each of them ate – dates and cool goat's milk for Honey, a croissant and black coffee for Disa; even details of who prepared the food – the plump old wife of the elderly caretaker; the exact time Honey dropped Disa off at the airport for her flight to Rome; whether they had a snack or drink in the bar. Disa's answers were straightforward and coincided exactly with Honey's recollections.

'And the baron?' Honey asked casually. 'Where did you say he was – that entire weekend we had the run of his villa?'

'Visiting his ex-wife and children in Johannesburg,' Disa replied and yawned from the other end of the tub. 'Such a pity about him, wasn't it?'

'About what?'

'Surely you heard?' Disa said lifting her head. Her full tanned breasts rose from the bubbles like curious seals.

'He was killed last week. In Tanzania. Trampled by a wild elephant.'

'Oh, no,' Honey exclaimed sympathetically, even though she had never met the baron.

'Flatter than matzah brei.'

In the big bed, filtered light flowing in from one sheer, draped window, bathing their warm full bodies in soft luminescence, they lay wrapped peacefully in each other's arms and Honey asked even more questions of the rapidly fading Disa. Honey wanted to know about the elderly couple who ran the villa for the now-deceased baron. Disa, her long, golden lashes resting on her tan cheeks, barely whispered that the 'dear old things' were working now for an exotic male dancer in Cairo. Honey's memory of them was exactly that – a kindly, generous, helpful old pair who wouldn't harm a mouse in the flour barrel.

All the more bewildered and befuddled, Honey assessed the beginning of her month off as not very propitious. She fell silent, allowing Disa to drift to sleep with a soft kiss on her brow. It took a long while for Honey to shut off her fast-turning mind; she went over and over everything they had discussed and still nothing clicked into place, nor were there any jagged edges or glaring omissions to mar the purity of her memory of that morning. It was a completely baffling mystery.

8

HONEY

'Joe Scurvy adds no new dimensions to the term *punk*,' she hastily jotted in her notebook and scribbled beside it a list of adjectives to use in her column: *arrogant, egomaniacal, surly, paranoid, hostile, offensive, stoned, horny*. In the near darkness of the large, empty auditorium of the Olympia, she adjusted the improvised cotton earpads she'd concocted out of tampons to block out the horrible amplified shrieking coming from the brightly lit stage of the famed showhouse.

Joe Scurvy held centre stage as if it were his God-given right. Short – barely five-four in his knee-high Buccaneer boots – emaciated-looking, his face gaunt, hollow-eyed, his sallow skin ravaged by acne, he gave the appearance under his spiky, brown hair, of a pale skull infested by maggots. With a fed-up gesture, he waved to a ragged silence the shrill, simplistic, out of tune sounds of his band, The Epidemics.

As he fiddled his phallic-shaped microphone, the four

members of the band behind him – dressed in a hodge-podge of ill-fitting smelly rags, straight out of the days of the plague – picked their noses, dug at their assholes, spit on the stage, carved dirty words into their instruments and pissed on the wing curtains: in general, they behaved as if they were bored silly and couldn't wait to run outside, overturn a car and set it on fire.

Honey had never seen such a collection of motley, scraggly, ugly, no-talent, gutter-rollers in her life. That morning was turning out to be a real bummer. She had hated leaving Disa curled so soundly and sensually in the big bed – especially knowing that Disa had to fly off to Munich later that afternoon to meet with her generously doting father because of something about an overdraft of a half a million marks. And to make the already tedious day more of a drag, Honey – by direct orders of Hum – had to obtain a decent interview from this skinny jerk before the end of the day. Or miss her deadline for the second time that month. She took her responsibilities seriously. As Hum did his. Besides, she owed him one.

The seedy band launched unevenly into their number-one best-seller and Honey jammed her fingers into her cotton-stuffed ears. Joe slouched to the microphone stand like a mean, mangy rat, snatched it with clawlike hands and snarled the lyrics in a gravelly monotone. 'Suck me! Suck me! Suck me sublime! So suck me! Suck me! Suck me sublime!'

Silently Honey gathered her things and went out to smoke a jay.

After the sound-check rehearsal had ground to a halt, she ventured backstage and knocked at their dressing-room door. 'Go away, ya bleedin' ass'ole!' a near-male voice shrieked inside. But the door was thrown open anyway.

A female equivalent of Joe Scurvy sneered. Her scrawny body was covered by an army camouflage suit her

96

dirty feet visible through open-toed, fifties-styled wedgie sandals; her hair was two-toned, the crew-cut side was chartreuse, the scraggly longer side was day-glo orange. The unappealing apparition popped a wad of bubble gum and blocked the open doorway with an arm wound with a grey, bathtub chain. 'So? What the fuck do you want?'

Honey coolly held her ground, not bothering to flash her trademark 'entry' smile. 'I'm Honey Wildon, here to interview –'

'Show the bitch in,' came the interrupting growl from inside. 'Let's 'ave a look at this piece, mates.'

The tub-chained arm hesitated, the gum snapped, the heavily made-up eyes slitted in hostile suspicion before Honey was allowed to enter.

Howls of dirty approval greeted her, along with cries of: 'Dig them titties! They fer real? Blimey, she's a big box, ain't she? Can I pee on them tits, scuz?'

She stood patiently, waiting for Joe to look at her. He sat before the light-rimmed dressing mirror – shirt off, ribs protruding – having one arm tattooed. His pig-faced drummer was just finishing the *me* after *ea*t in a childish block print, jamming the black India ink under the skin with a tarnished hat pin.

Joe jerked his arm away with a howl. 'Shit, man! Ya douche bag! Watch wha'cha fuckin' doin' or you'll be singin' soprano!'

The lead guitarist, who looked like an ugly Keith Richard, sprawled in a chair beside Honey, his flaccid cock in his hands as he stared in fixation at her ass. Wishing she had worn something other than her tight designer jeans, she pulled the yellow, western-styled vest over her russet T-shirt and said pointedly to Joe, 'Anytime you're ready, maestro.'

He leered up at her tits. 'I wanna suck on them boobies.'

The drummer guffawed. ''N jam me sticks up her pee 'ole.'

She surveyed them all and returned to Joe. 'Some other time, perhaps.' She spun on her heel and strode out of the room. Squawks and cries of disappointment followed her. So did Joe.

He caught up to her halfway down the hall, his heavy boots clomping like grown-up shoes on a small kid. 'Hey now, where're ya goin'?' he panted.

'I have better ways to spend my time,' she said easily and kept moving.

'Oh now don't go actin' 'igh 'n queeny with me, bitch,' he snarled. 'I know fer a fact meself ya *got* to interview me. My agent done tol' me the whole scam. So make it easy, cunt, or I'll shit on your shoes.'

She threw at him, 'Piss off,' and breezed through the side doorway, out into the alley.

'Hey, bitch!' he screamed, running after her. Just outside the door, he froze and blinked in the harsh light and shrank against the wall. 'Jesus, it's fuckin' bright. Where're me shades?'

She turned, watching him as he patted the pockets of his baggy tweed sports coat frantically. He looked so momentarily off guard, so vulnerable cowering in the sun as if Dracula were a direct ancestor, she began to soften. He was just an angry little boy who needed some motherly love and attention. She held out her large sunglasses, smiling her concern. 'Here, use mine.'

He crabwalked to her with scurrying, furtive steps and grabbed the glasses out of her hand. Clamping them on, he grinned, his uneven, yellowed teeth missing a bicuspid. 'Say, you're a piece o' all right, a' that.'

'Apology accepted,' she said warmly and took his arm. He flinched like a maltreated dog but did not pull away. He smelled far less than she had feared and she leaned down maternally, a heavy wave of her red hair brushing his cheek. 'Have you eaten today?'

He grinned boyishly. 'Yeah – three pussies and two cocks.'

She laughed lightly. 'Well, not bad for breakfast.'

Honey treated him to a light lunch al fresco in a side-walk café on Champs-Elysées. The healthy meal appeared to have little effect on Joe's antisocial behaviour. He belched, bitched, farted, and grumbled through the entire repast, pissed that the other customers and the strollers-by were paying more attention to her than to him.

Intermittently, she thought of a question and poised it but rarely obtained more than a monosyllabic sentence. He refused any direct questions about his background, even about where he was from in England. Or was it New Jersey?

Undaunted, she shifted gears, deciding to focus on Joe as a personality of 'today's scene'. 'Tell me, Joe, who were your heroes?'

He sunk lower in his chair. 'Ain't got none no how.'

'Even as a kid?'

He pondered that weightily for several moments. 'Naw, not really. I kinda dug Morrison, a heavy fox. The first real punk.'

'Jim Morrison of the Doors?'

'Naw, Big Mama Morrison of Bologna,' he chortled.

She smiled. 'Did you know he was buried here in Paris?'

'Dead, is he?' Joe looked up surprised. 'Thought they put the bloke away for flashin' his pecker.'

'Would you like to see his grave? Père La Chaise is a lovely, old cemetery. With some extraordinary names out of history. Balzac, Chopin, Piaf – even Oscar Wilde.'

He shot his cuffs as if 'dolling up'. 'Say, 'ow'd ya know I dug boneyards? Fer a chick with big knockers you ain't 'alf dumb.'

Inside the stately gates of Père La Chaise, they started up the gently inclined path through the gardened walk-ways, past large marble crypts and raised tombs. The gnarled old maple and alder trees formed a lacy canopy over their heads, breaking the sunlight into a mottled carpet of light and shade. As they walked, she lit a jay of her own Kauai homegrown. Inhaling, she swelled her breasts and he watched her grand expansion out of the corner of his eye, nervously darting a tongue over his lips. With a rush she expelled the smoke and passed the joint. 'What do you like? TV? Movies? Comic books?'

'Naw . . . jus' sittin' 'round's the best, now ain't it?'

Her lips parted, glistening like ripe strawberries, and she recalled something from Kafka – a favourite quote of Hum's and she murmured it now. 'There are two cardinal sins from which all others spring, impatience and laziness.'

'Sins, eh? Ya don't look no religious type.'

'Only about life,' she said and led him off the main walk, down a well-trod, dirt path between and behind two large stone crypts over twenty feet high. There, in the centre, hemmed in by the rear of two more tombs, lay the simple, flat slab marked James Morrison. A cheap bouquet of plastic flowers rested on top. Graffiti – hymns to the Lizard King – were scrawled in lipstick or chalk, and scratched and painted onto the backs of the surrounding dark mausoleums. The small space smelled of cheap wine, urine and semen. Discarded bottles and cans lay scattered about.

'Ayeee,' he growled in appreciation. 'Ain't this lovely now? Littl' bit o' 'eaven, eh what?' He plopped down flat on the marble marker, assuming a corpselike pose, hands folded across his thin chest. 'This is how I wants me shot on the cover of *Rollin' Stone*,' he said seriously. 'A fuckin' classic, eh?'

Suddenly he started giggling insanely, wiggling his butt around like he had fire ants in his pants. 'Oh, James, me boy, now ya just cut tha' ou', ya 'ear?' He laughed and sat up. 'Oh, James here, minute I sat down, up pops a big ol' Hampton Wick, pokin' me in the bum.'

She lowered herself slowly to sit on the edge of the slab. 'What are you afraid of, Joe? What are your fears? Death?'

'Naw,' he grumbled. 'I ain't scared o' nuthin'.' He made a grab for a breast. 'An' I still want to suck on these.'

'Is that why you insisted only I interview you?'

'Natch.' He grinned lewdly. 'Wanna see my pecker? I'll show ya mine if'n ya show me yours.'

She eyed him steadily. 'Okay, you first.'

He pretended he did not hear and sat back on his haunches. 'Hey, what's worse than a dead cat on your piano?'

She shrugged. 'You're stalling.'

'Naw,' he said impishly. 'A dead beaver on your organ.' He fell over laughing, curling up like a fetus, holding his sides.

'I'm still waiting to see your pecker,' she said after a while. He exaggerated his laughter shrilly. It echoed off the high stone walls surrounding them. With a lunge, she pushed him flat, holding him down with one hand like a naughty child. With the other, she ripped at the front of his beltless baggy, urine-stained pants, tugging them down with one quick movement.

He howled as if violated and jackknifed, his hands clawing to cover himself. 'Ya crazy bitch! Ya fuckin' pervert!'

She tugged her T-shirt free from her jeans and throwing off the satin vest, yanked the shirt over her luxuriant red waves. Her breasts fell free, large alabaster globes with aurorae of dusky rose.

His eyes bulged above his hollow cheeks and he went limp, lifeless, as if overwhelmed. 'Christ, I wish I had me some *shitka*,' he said sullenly.

'*Shitka*?' she bubbled and lifted her breasts, cupping one in each hand as if airing them. 'What's *shitka*?'

'This here dope that makes ya 'orny as 'ell.'

'Sounds divine,' she purred.

101

'But better yet . . . ya don' remember nuthin' what ya did. Not a single, blessed solitary thin' . . .'

Her hands fell and she stared at his pimply face. 'No memory?'

'Yeah . . . bit o' bliss that *shitka* is.'

She measured her next words carefully. 'Where can I get some of this stuff?'

'Only one place I know of, an' it's a 'elluva long way from here. 'Sides, I sure ain't tellin' no sleazy slit.'

She mulled over what she had heard very carefully and made up her very determined mind. She was going to get the information out of this little shit if she had to eat him on top of the Eiffel Tower at high noon. She turned on her ample charms, covering her breasts modestly with her arms, speaking in a motherly tone; 'I think you're afraid you have a tiny cock.'

'I ain't either,' he bawled, shrinking away. 'Let me alone fer Chrissakes, an' I'll show ya.'

'Promise?'

'Try me.' As she withdrew, he struggled to a sitting position and sniffed, 'Ya let me suck a bit? On them titties?'

'Try me,' she said easily. 'But you first.'

Deliberately he hesitated, then moved to his knees and parted his baggy sports coat, exposing himself like a flasher in the park. She appraised his flick of flaccid flesh objectively. It hung, uncircumsized, like a tired finger with no nail. The bit of fuzz above looked as if it had been glued on with spirit gum. She raised her gaze up through her long, auburn lashes, her blue eyes soft, luminous. 'I think it's just lovely.'

'Ya do?'

'Perfectly adorable. Certainly your best feature.' She reached out to fondle the tiny, fuzzy balls.

He cooed like a baby and touched a grubby hand to her left breast, squeezing it hard as if testing the ripeness of a melon. 'Ayeeee,' he moaned. 'Ain't that a bit o' 'eaven.'

With trembling fingers he began exploring both of them, holding them in the palm of his hand, bouncing them, weighing them. 'Blimey, that's a chestful,' he whimpered and fell upon them, sucking the nipple of one like a starving teething infant.

Amused by his sudden docility, she cast a thorough glance around and, satisfied they were completely screened and alone, doubled over to place her mouth around the punky prick. Like a toy balloon being blown up, it fattened but did not lengthen.

He continued to slobber between her luscious breasts, his head buried to his pointed ears in softly firm, snow white flesh. His ravaged face looked as though he were in an exalted state of divine visitation. He humped his skinny hips, pumping excitedly into her mouth. She tongued him expertly, pushing back the foreskin, caressing the leeklike bulb, polishing it tenderly.

His jerky, spastic movements knocked her leather carryall to the earth, spilling out its contents. At the sound, he looked down and spotted the ivory dildo of Disa. With a cry of discovery, he grabbed it up, pleading, 'I wanna be fucked right here.' He shoved the ancient incient instrument of pleasure into her hands.

She was wondering how it had gotten into her bag and figured that darling Disa must have slipped it in as a token of her affection. Honey licked one bulbous end of it, tasting the heaveny ambrosia of darling Disa. When it was slick, she pulled his greasy head off her distended nipple and said, 'Okay, sonny, bend and spread 'em.'

He made it clear he did not want to let go of her boob, so she lay flat, pulling him over her, his sharp-angled buns pointed between her knees. Reaching around him, she found his asshole with one finger and with a firm push, thrust the ivory dildo into his animated lower orifice. He moaned through teeth that bit into her nipple, the pain just short of intolerable.

She rammed the long thick bone in and out, noting

that he was jacking on his baby pink peter. The whole situation seemed so erotically bizarre, lying there in the public cemetery, the danger of being discovered at any moment increasing her rising tension, that Honey became quickly turned on. She managed to free one hand, leaving the other reaming firmly and unzipped her jeans. They were too tight to take off without disrupting little Joe's fantasies. So she just shoved a hand deep inside, skimming her bush and zeroing in on her fast-growing clit.

'Oh, Mommy, Mommy,' Joe Scurvy groaned into her full breasts, rubbing his pimply face all over them, his wet, rough tongue leaving slimy trails, like ski tracks across her snowy mountains. 'Gimmie some milk, Mommy, some milk . . .'

'Suck my big titties, boy,' she urged and rammed him a good hard-on, making certain she was not neglecting her own pleasure with her darting digit in her sex ditch. 'Suck them, boy,'

He jerked forward on his knees, farther up on her belly, pushing his tiny hard prick into the soft mounds as if testing the temperature of bread dough. In the deep valley between her mounds, he poked insistently, and suddenly little warm spurts of cum from his flea-flicker prick shot onto her tits, dribbling down them like vanilla frosting on large scoops of vanilla ice cream. Instantly he was upon his own dribble, sucking the cum off her breasts as if it were mama's milk. She hurried to catch up with him, getting off on the boy-sized figure nursing at her hard nipples. Within seconds, she was coming in her jeans, dampening the crotch, lubricating her finger with her own special mixture.

He sat up on her stomach, his pecker fast wilting and pumped her boobs with two fists. 'Oh, Mommy,' he said in a decidedly more masculine tone, 'ya can ask anythin' ya want. Long as I get me my titty.'

She smiled dazedly. 'For starts, mind moving your bony butt? And for seconds, where do I find some *shitka*?'

That night, after filing by cable a surprisingly effective interview and thus meeting her last deadline for the month, Honey retired to the lonely, big bed of her hotel suite, sipping a glass of cold Krug champagne and writing what she had learned from Joe into her daily journal. At last she had something to go on. A slim lead, but it was something. She wanted to call Dirk and tell him but according to his itinerary, he was somewhere over the Atlantic right that moment.

9

DIRK

On the teeming, narrow street of Marrakesh, just off the marketplace, in the sticky heat of the midafternoon sun, he peered up excitedly at the large star-shaped window cut into the thick stucco walls.

It had taken him three full and exhausting days to track it down. Starting in Tangiers with the very villa at which Honey had stayed, Dirk had crisscrossed that city's streets and alleys searching for this very window. But to no avail. It was not until he finally had located a former contact in the area, a native called Yazid, that things had begun to click. Yazid, a wiry, jack-of-all-trades who previously had proved his usefulness on Dirk's photo excursions to the area had looked once at the rough sketch Dirk had drawn of the unusual window and had said emphatically, 'Not in Tangiers. Casablanca. Maybe . . . Marrakesh.'

They had started in Casablanca, the closer of the two cities, but after nearly twenty-four hours nonstop, they were only pooped and more perplexed. Yazid had been cheerfully unfazed and had pressed the search south to Marrakesh. As Dirk was paying him a healthy per diem, plus a promised bonus, Yazid was willing to search for the rest of his life. But not Dirk.

Now the star-shaped window was before him and Yazid was exiting the building to report what he had learned. Approaching with a 'wanting to please' smile, he whispered, 'A whorehouse.'

'A whorehouse?' Dirk repeated and thought, Why the hell would anyone drag Honey all this distance from Tangiers to bring her to this – a whorehouse in Marrakesh? He looked down at this beaming, swarthy guide. 'Did you ask about that Sunday?'

Yazid shrugged. 'Lady wants more cash, *effendi*.'

Dirk did not hesitate. He lurched toward the entrance to the building and strode inside. The waiting room looked like the lobby of any motel in Kansas – lots of plastic flowers, formica end tables and imitation-leather couches. The only distinctive feature was the obese, dark-haired lady sagging one couch with her thunderous thighs. Dirk thought she looked just like the whore, Seregrina, in Fellini's *8 1/2*. The ponderous rolls of her portly trunk were encased in a black dress five sizes too small. Her face would have looked like a truck tyre if it had not been for the layered-on makeup. Her black eyes, like small lumps of coal sunk in a dirty snowbank, regarded him with suspicion and greed.

He turned on his boyish charm, grinning like a young, lanky Jimmy Stewart. The behemoth in black remained stone-faced. Dirk turned to Yazid. 'Ask her if she speaks English.'

Rapidly, arrogantly, the little bantam cock relayed the question in Arabic. Ignoring him, she answered directly to Dirk in a voice of hoarse basso profundo. 'A little.'

'Good,' Dirk sighed. 'That room upstairs with the star window? Would you remember who used it on a specific day?'

108

'One hundred dollar.'

Dirk unhesitatingly peeled off a bill from his fat money clip and handed it over. She held it high and rolled slowly to her feet like an avalanche of dusky flesh in a tight black shift. She wore bedroom slippers of red carpet. They shuffled her thick, fat ankles toward a bead-covered doorway at the rear of the waiting room. Yazid waved Dirk to follow and Dirk did, pushing through the cheap strings of beads and into a surprisingly cool, dimly lit room that reeked of cheap perfume.

She shut the door and rolled past him, her monstrous hips rising and falling like giant waves on a black sea. 'My name is Rah-BEE-ah,' she pronounced heavily and stopped by a large bed covered with a gaudy embroidered spread of shiny threads. Before he could blink, she had peeled off her black shift and pulled off the spread from the large bed. Her ponderous breasts hung to her waist like deflated inner tubes; her stomach was grotesque, layers and layers of rolls of tallowy, coarse skin. Her thighs were mammoth whales and stubbled with black hair.

Dirk stammered, 'Look, I just want information. That's all. No . . . really . . .'

She paid him no heed but moved onto the sheet-covered mattress like a large brown bull entering an arena. With a massive mudslide of brown skin, she fell onto her back, her stomach rising obscenely like an elephantine tumour. Her trunklike thighs rose and parted and she opened herself to him, a yawning black cavern barely discernible in the flabby rolls of stubby-covered flesh.

Dirk cleared his throat, sweating profusely. 'No, you don't understand. No fuck. Just talk, okay?'

'You no fuck, I no talk,' she rumbled.

He moved to her and dropped another hundred dollars onto her sagging monstrous breasts. She took it, crumpled it into a clenched fist and growled, 'No fuck, no talk.'

Exasperated he yanked another C note from his clip and threw it down on her coarse skin, muttering, 'No fuck. Just talk.'

Again she fisted the bill out of sight and spoke in an even deeper tone. 'No fuck, no talk.'

In desperation, he thought of calling Yazid in, but for all he knew the two were in collusion, some horrible pre-arranged joke on the rich American and a split take. Dirk fumed helplessly. This was the most appalling situation he had ever found himself in. Here he was, renowned worldwide for his camera studies of spectacular women . . . and now, having to fuck the ugliest, fattest whore he had ever laid eyes on. Damn Honey and her transgressions . . .

With a low groan of self-pity, he began tearing off his clothes, not wanting to soil anything permanently. He strode to the bed, buck-naked and stepped upright between her gargantuan thighs as though he were stepping into a dinghy. He stared down at the voluminous flabby contours of the terrain below, trying to find something that would turn him on. Rather feebly he began pulling at his wang, stretching it, yanking it, trying to urge some life into it. But as he had feared, ol' Mister Bird of Paradise had a mind of its own. No amount of prodding on his part raised an inch of difference.

With a wave of a thick hand, she motioned him down over her breasts. Almost gratefully he sank over her, placing his recalcitrant cock above her head with some trepidation. Her big mouth opened, displaying dirty, pink gums without a single tooth. Before he could question the health issue, she had sucked in the full length of his spiritless prick and began gumming it, squeezing the blood toward its bulb as though it were a tube of toothpaste.

Much to his surprise, the odd gum-job began producing results. His cock pumped up and offered thickening resistance to her chomping gums. Soon it was his hard ridges against her. She jerked it out of her mouth, spat on the end of it and pushed it away from her.

The moment of truth, Dirk decided, as he positioned himself between the warm, mountainous thighs. He tried pushing aside the heavy rolls of fat covering the entrance to her dark cavern. His whole hand was soon buried to his wrist in sweaty flesh and still he could not find anything remotely resembling a cunt. Boldly his fingers struck pay dirt, a scraggly patch of kinky pubic hair, like a Brillo pad wedged far up the walls of her overhanging thighs. He grabbed hold of it for future reference and using it as a guide, shoved his disinterested cock toward it.

Unexpectedly, the head of his exploring dick slipped inside something warm and wet. As it could have been just an oily roll of fat, he tried determining from her expression if he had entered her waxy womb. She stared back blankly. Fuck it, he decided and blindly began pumping into the crevice of warmth.

Rivers of sweat began forming under and around him, making her slippery to stay on top of. Teeth gritted, he was buried in piles of jiggling, swaying, brown, oily fat. He bounced and bumped, slipped and slid. It was like fucking a rubber raft.

In no time, he sensed it was little use. Coming was far, far away. He groaned loudly, faking a contented orgasm and pulled out of the sweaty folds. She shoved him off, pointing to another door.

Behind it, he found a complete, modern bathroom and eagerly took a hot shower, washing his cock thoroughly and making a note to get a VD shot as soon as possible. He dried off, dressed and entered her room. She sat on the edge of the bed, in her black shift, smoking a thin, brown cigarette. She growled deeply, 'What you want?'

'Who used that star-room on the first Sunday of last month?'

She rolled her massive shoulders into a shrug.

'Do you keep any records? A registry?'

111

She shook her head. 'No records. Snoopy police.'

'Would any of your girls remember?' he pressed. 'Two of the occupants were black. Big blacks, a male and female. The other lady was white with red hair and tall.' He could tell by her flat expression that she did not remember – or chose not to. He asked several more questions and got nowhere. Frustrated for having paid his dues and gotten shafted, he asked if he could see the room. She told him to go on up, but the stairs were too steep for her.

He wearily climbed the three flights of narrow, smelly, dark stairs and opened the door of the only room on the top floor. The star-shaped window – much larger now that he was so close – lay directly opposite on the plain, white-washed wall. The room was exactly as in the video tape. Other than the red-spread bed, no other furniture. He moved to the unique window, noting the angle of the shadows and sunlight. He figured it was about this same time of day that Honey had been abused there. He felt a chill crawl the ladder of his spine. It was like entering the room of a nightmare. Anxious to leave, he turned and stopped short.

In the doorway, a strikingly beautiful young girl of barely twelve stood barefoot, petite and brown in a short, white cotton dress, watching him through enormous, expressive black eyes. Her long straight black hair shone lustrously, her skin was the colour of almonds, her small breasts poked through the front of her dress like tiny buds ready to bloom. She was absolutely pure magic, delicate yet nubile, large-eyed, timidly curious, like a wild fawn.

He stared in quiet admiration, wishing he had brought his camera that afternoon, afraid to move or speak for fear of frightening her away.

Wordlessly, not taking her huge black eyes from his, she entered and silently closed the door. 'My name is Melantha,' she said softly, her voice like melodious wind chimes. 'I was named for a purple lily.' She walked

112

straight to him, smiling fragilely, a mixture of innocent child and knowing woman. 'I speak good English, yes?'

'Yes . . . very well,' he murmured, transfixed. 'I'm Dirk. What are you doing here, Melantha?'

'I work here,' she said simply and floated to the bed, a wisp of dark gossamer on the sun mote air.

Before he could protest – not that he really had wanted to – she had tugged her dress over her head and stood there nude, slender and budding as a tender reed. Her almond limbs glowed with health, her pointed little breasts barely forming, her box, open, hairless, slightly pinker, like a vertical mouth ready to whisper poetry.

He struggled to find his voice. 'What do you want?'

She laughed gaily; it bubbled out of her like uncorked champagne and for a moment she looked even younger. 'You are American, yes?' He nodded, unable to tear his eyes from her tender, childlike frame. She crawled onto the bed like a kitten, and settled down on her sweet little cheeks, giggling softly, 'Come, Dirk. Let's fuck.'

It was an invitation hard to turn down. He found himself sitting beside her, but afraid to touch, as if she were delicate crystal that would shatter.

She smiled knowingly, her black eyes speaking volumes. 'I fuck many men. No American yet. Come.'

'Do they pay you?'

'I work here,' she said with a trace of pride.

'For how long?'

She shrugged, a wisp of a move. 'I live here. Long time.'

He made a mental connection. 'Is Rebilah, downstairs, your mother?'

Melantha nodded and a large hank of jet black hair fell softly over one thin shoulder. He reached up and brushed it back. It felt like heavy silk. He ran his fingers through its thick shiny strands and she watched his face, trusting yet cautious. She took his fingers, running them over her dewy soft cheeks and pressed them down to a sprout of a

113

breast. He could feel her heart beating extraordinarily fast. Like a frightened bird's. His own had lodged in his throat. He outlined her tiny buds, stroking the sharp inclines up to their pointed peaks. Both nipples, surrounded by a wide band of a dark-oak colour, grew visibly aroused, pointing at him, urging him on.

His hand shook and dropped to the red spread. She touched his arm, then a kiss of a soft insect on his lips. 'Am I not pretty?'

'You're sensational,' he admitted mournfully. 'It's my damn conscience.'

'What's a conscience?' she asked, mimicking his pronunciation.

'It's what hurts when everything else feels so damn good,' he mumbled, not remembering where he had heard that before.

'Do not be afraid,' she said in a sing-song tone. 'I'm very good with old men.'

He laughed and let her push him back against the pillows. Slowly, with full concentration, she unbuttoned his sports shirt, which was wringing wet with sweat, opened it, pushed it aside and touched his fair skin – as though he were a new item in her marketplace. He could not bear to look at her face, it was so incredibly beautiful and openly excited. He felt her little hands struggling with his belt. She unclasped it and attacked the top button of his slacks. She reached for the zipper. The rasping sound of opening metal seemed to him unnaturally loud. He held his breath expectantly, frozen with delight as she parted his slacks.

His cock was already standing on end, and poked out energetically, its head a blushing red. She reached under his hips for his pants and he raised up and she yanked them down to his knees. He trembled violently as she clasped his thickness with both hands, like a child with a new toy. She began pulling up and down on it, a look of excitement on her petite, dark face. She glanced up through her long, black lashes and asked matter-of-factly, 'You want to eat me?'

He could only jerk his head feebly. He was so excited he felt trapped on the downward curve of a ski jump. Nowhere to go but rapidly straight off the end. Still moving the skin of his pleased-as-punch prick, she twisted her slender body around to his mouth. His tongue sought its delicate, soft fullness and lightly he traced its length, parting its sweet meat like the halves of a walnut.

Her trim hips vibrated wildly as he stuck his tongue into her tender, tight trench. She tasted of figs and smelled of muskwood. Gripping the small handful of cheeks of her sweet brown ass, he sucked at her delicacy. To his astonishment, he found in its moist recesses an adult-sized clitoris, hard as a belly button. Her pumpings on his ecstatic prick grew more frantic and suddenly he felt her warm, wet mouth close over the pulsating head. Wrapping her small tongue around it, she yanked her hips out of his grasp and scooted around.

In a state of delicious suspension, he watched her tiny sprouting body lower over his harder-than-usual cock. She held her tiny twat open with two fingers and she sat, pushing down on his proud prong with a determined smile. She was so tight, he had flashes of splitting her open. He tensed in agonized pleasure, but she kept feeding her tiny cunt more of his boner until her bony little pelvis – her cunt spread wide and hairless like a fresh-cut peach – touched the forest of his pubic hair. He stared as she began to rise and fall on his extended rod, jumping faster and faster up and down with a growing enthusiasm, as if she had found the best ride at the playground, laughing and jabbering in her native tongue like it was the most natural of everyday acts.

He could not prolong his extreme enjoyment. With a spasm of uncontrolled and violent release, he shot his hot load into the tiny receptacle, filling her to overflowing. Her eyes grew wider with surprise and her rosebud mouth formed a perfect *O*. She stood, pulling off him, and looked down at the stream of heavy white cum flowing down the inside of her brown, thin thighs. With a whoop of laughter, she bounded off the bed, flew across the room, a blur of soft brown skin, and out the door.

Under the star-shaped window, he lay, eyes closed, trying to recover his equilibrium, panting in the hot, stuffy air. Soon she was back with a towel, damp on one end. Carefully, she washed his cock and patted it dry, like playing with dolls, and packed it back into his pants even though it was still stiff as a board. With difficulty, she zipped him up. As she buttoned up his shirt, he extracted a hundred-dollar-bill from his pocket and held it out.

She shook her head seriously. 'Mama say it free.'

'You keep it anyway.'

Solemnly she took it and bent to pick up her dress. 'I listen to you downstairs,' she said quietly. 'I here that Sunday.'

He sprang to his knees. 'Did you see anything?'

'I saw the big blacks. And the wild one with the white skin and red hair. She look very happy. Laugh all the time.'

'Did the blacks bring her here?'

'No,' said Melantha, her dark head shaking slowly.

'Who did? Who rented the room?'

'The little man,' she barely whispered.

Dirk took her hands. 'What little man?'

She looked around almost fearfully and held up a flat palm, circling the air with it, and he recognized the gesture to ward off bad spirits. 'The little man with the big suitcase,' she breathed tensely. 'Big as he.'

'Do you know his name? Where he's from? Have you seen him before? Since?' To each of these questions, he received a negative shake of the head. 'Does your mother know him?'

'No, she sleep that day. I took his money.'

'What currency did he pay in? Francs?'

116

'American dollar. A lot.' She pulled away, tight, reserved. 'I must go. My Englishman waits.' She fled to the door, stopping suddenly, her eyes seeking his like a frightened chipmunk. 'Beware of the little man,' she warned in a hoarse whisper. 'He is evil.'

10

HONEY

She laughed at the antics of her darling Disa, who batted a playful hand at the limp cock of the gyrating nude dancer as if she were swatting a pesky fly. They were in a small, dingy club in the red-light district of Amsterdam, a club that advertised in neon outside, 'live focky-fock' shows. Honey had flown into the city that very morning in a hurried attempt to locate the source of Joe Scurvy's reported mysterious drug of 'wild abandonment but no memory'. The contact whom Joe had named – someone called only Toujours Pret – had not answered her persistent knock and she had had to temper her overwhelming curiosity and impatience, hoping for better luck later that night.

Much to her delight, however, Disa had unexpectedly shown up that very afternoon from her quick trip home to Munich to visit her father. And, as always, delectable Disa was in high spirits, ready for anything, even a little slumming. Now, with much amusement, Honey watched her beautiful blonde lover teasing the young male dancer whose prick had grown considerably harder from all the attention. He pranced away to the small, brightly lit stage and joined a frizzy-haired young woman who wore only a gauzy singlet. Her breasts were oddly shaped, like small, crooked gourds, but her snatch looked definitely edible, for it was shaven clean, her pussy lips heavily rouged, like a red mouth puckered for a kiss.

The young man, whose cock was now a rigid branch jutting from his thin trunk, fell on his knees to tongue the rouged lips. Honey tingled as Disa groped for her thigh under the table. The male performer kneeled and brought his partner's legs up over his shoulders. Quickly he inserted his stone-hard cock into the rouged lips, and soon they were fucking like two dogs in heat, the taped music adding an appropriate love theme from Tchaikovsky.

Honey's eyes drifted to Disa's adorable face – it fairly glowed with titillation, her pink tongue repeatedly darting over her full, lower lip as she observed the frantic coupling of the performers. She and Honey had snorted a considerable amount of extra-fine cocaine in their hotel suite before leaving to tour the varieties of stimulation offered in the wide-open, red-light district. And now Honey recognized on Disa's exquisitely beautiful face a combination of stoned bliss and growing lust. Just like she herself was feeling. Delicious.

The young man on the stage barked in Dutch that he was ready to come. To the accompaniment of a snare drum roll, he jerked his glistening prick from his partner's painted pussy and stood, creaming down on her an almost invisible quantity of white cum as the lights dimmed. The applause in the club was minimal also.

Immediately, the full curtain parted noisily, revealing a blue-lit pit of gooey, brown mud. Into it jumped two young women, their naked, fair-skinned bodies oiled and greased for action. Their pleasing breasts bounced enticingly as their legs sank into the brown ooze up to their calves. Like two ferocious wrestlers, they circled each other in the muck, crouching, arms ready to grab. With a forced cry, they leaped upon each other like two wild-cats in the alley. The larger of the two threw the other headlong into the mud, burying her momentarily.

Disa leaned forward, tense, expectant, her tongue flicking, her perfect breasts rising and falling excitedly under the tight-fitting dress. Her fingers on Honey's thigh inched closer to the rapidly inflaming snatch.

The two pit women were on their feet again, their trim bodies layered with wet mud, covering them from head to toe with a strangely erotic coating that looked like a dark frosting. Their prominently protruding love-boxes stood out like chocolate-covered cherries, their bushes matted and flat with goo. Again they rushed headlong and with a grunt clasped onto slippery limps, falling into the pigpen of mud, threshing wildly about. The larger girl had her fingers jammed into the cunt of the other and, using that for leverage, flipped the other over on her back. An announcer's voice broke out over the loudspeakers inviting in several languages anyone from the audience to join in.

Disa shot out of her clothes before the announcement had concluded. With a clean, swift movement, she pulled her clinging jersey dress over her light blonde hair and kicked off her high heels. To appreciative whistles and catcalls from the rest of the audience, mainly a tour bus of Japanese men, Disa bounced up to the stage and turned with a laugh, her arms flung overhead like a winning prize fighter, displaying fully her statuesque, sensual body, her heavy breasts like globes of honey, her long legs tanned, her golden bush like a fluffy pastry. Giggling, she jumped into the pit.

Honey did not need further enticement – she leapt from the small table and peeled off her Diane von Furstenberg dress, stepped out of her heels, and rushed to join her animated lover, now coated entirely with mud, looking like a lovely gingerbread lady. Rolling with great gales of laughter, Disa latched onto one of the gooey girls. Honey flexed her muscles and ploughed into the warm mud, the nearly all-male audience screaming their aroused approval. The viscous suction pulled her feet in deeper, her full, pale breasts bouncing like basketballs as she struggled to reach the other girl. With a squeal of pretended outrage, she jumped upon the startled performer, whose brown-coated body, though in fighting shape, offered little resistance. Soon Honey was plastered with the warm ooze, which felt strangely primal, primitive and highly stimulating. Wiping the mud from her eyes, she tried to squeeze two fingers up the love crack of the girl. Surprised at her own strength, she managed to force the girl on her back, straddling her in reverse.

Hearing Disa's howl of laughter, Honey felt her lover jump on her from behind, bending her over into the muddy pussy of the girl underneath. Disa, riding Honey, like a horse, tore her off the other girl and fell on her in the brown muck. They grovelled over each other, pressing their excited nipples into each other's slippery mounds, tasting the earthy mixture as they snaked their clean, pink tongues into each other's mouths. They were still threshing about, locked in each other's arms heatedly as the stage lights faded to the sound of raucous applause, shrill whistles and the stomping of demanding feet.

In the darkness, she and Disa were pulled offstage and into a large, white-tiled bathroom equipped with multiple shower heads. There the two athletic performers, plus the two randy volunteers from the audience, washed and soaped the mud from each other, gradually revealing their normal skins with the excitement of miners panning for gold. Soon she and Disa were flat on the wet tiles being scrubbed with willing tongues; their crevices and crannies, cracks and cream-holes were licked and eaten clean while the warm water cascaded over them from the shower heads.

Honey came first, explosively with a hearty howl which set off a chain reaction. The loud echoes of her wild coming bounced off the tiled enclosure and mixed with the increasingly vocal responses of Disa and the two performers. The resulting cacophony of shrieks and screams reverberated so clamorously that out in the club, the Japanese men thought it was a raid and raced for their parked tour bus.

All in all, it was an amusing evening's entertainment, Honey decided as she dropped Disa off at the Amstel Hotel. Disa stood outside the open taxi door, drawing out the good-nights plaintively. She was dying of curiosity as to where Honey was so mysteriously running off to at three in the morning. But Honey gently yet firmly refused to divulge her destination or her reasons for secrecy. She kissed Disa tenderly, promising to return soon, and whispering, 'Keep it hot, darling. I won't be long.'

Disa stared wistfully, longingly. '*La demoiselle éludé*,' she murmured and ran for the hotel entrance.

As the cab pulled away, Honey felt a pang of remorse. 'The elusive lady' was what Disa had first nicknamed her in finishing school as Honey seemed always running off somewhere without her. At the time, Honey liked to respond by quoting Henry Adams: 'Chaos often breeds life, when order breeds habit.' But now, on her way to track down Toujours Pret, she felt that perhaps her life had become a little too chaotic, and she longed to set some semblance of order back into it. But to do so, she was compelled to solve the riddle of the raunchy tape.

Within ten minutes, Honey stood before the address off the Herengracht, the Gentleman's Canal, which the punk Joe had given her. The warehouse-looking building was ramshackle and isolated. Not a light showed from inside. Her attuned sixth sense warned her to be careful. She knocked at the door and it flew open, startling her.

It was so dark inside she could not see who was there. 'Toujours Pret?' she asked hesitantly.

A tiny figure, garbed in a dark robe, materialized and beckoned her in. She slipped inside and almost gagged. The air was thick with the noxiously sweet, heavy aroma of opium smoke. The little figure, gender unknown, motioned for her to follow. Down a pitch black corridor Honey trailed, guiding herself only by the clicking of wooden sandals before her. They passed through an area lit only by the dim, red coals of glowing bowls of opium. The overpowering fumes made her dizzy and she groped past several tiers of hardwood bunks holding zonked-out, reclining shapeless figures.

Through a rear door she was led and outside into the cool, night air of a small, inner courtyard. She filled her lungs, clearing her head. The shrouded tiny figure waved to a small door outlined by glowing cracks of light around it. Honey stepped forward uncertainly and turned to ask a question. The little figure had vanished into the darkness. She took a deep breath for courage and tapped on the wood door with her knuckles. '*Entrez*,' a thin, voice rasped.

She opened the creaking door and blinked in the light as she ducked in. A monklike cell lit by several candles. On a hard narrow bed, sitting cross-legged, lotus position, a Gandhi-like form gazed back at her with bright, inquisitive black eyes. His skull-like head seemed shrunken, totally bald. The old man was of undeterminable age – anywhere from fifty to a hundred beyond that – and wore only a dirty loincloth. His sinewy, yellowish skin looked mummified.

'Toujours Pret?' she asked, instinctively knowing he was.

'Oui,' he croaked.

She felt overgrown and gangling in the small room but a strange sense of calm swept over her, as if in the presence of a Zen master.

124

'Take your things off,' he said abruptly in French.

She was so surprised that she unknowingly replied in English, 'I just want some information if you please.'

'Clothes hinder communication and create barriers,' he replied in her native tongue and sat patiently, as if he had done so forever.

Deliberating briefly, deciding he was harmless, she peeled off her patterned silk dress and folded it neatly over her carryall. His bright, roving eyes studied her openly.

'Come here,' he ordered, a bony hand patting the bed.

She moved barefoot across the cold, stone floor and sank onto the foot of the blanket-covered cot. His intensely clear eyes were on her full breasts as he spoke next: 'Why do you seek me?'

She began timidly, 'I was told you know of *shitka*.'

His bony, sunken face wreathed upward into an odd smile and he cackled loudly, like the rattling of dry canvas. At once he fell silent again, staring at her breasts. His silence made her uncomfortable but she asked again, '*Shitka*. What is it?'

He did not answer, merely studied her breasts with a detached yet significant air. 'Do you know what Toujours Pret means?' he suddenly voiced with a rakish tilt to his bald head.

'Always ready.'

'Oui,' he confirmed. 'Can you guess why they call me that?'

She could, but did not voice her suspicions. 'Why?'

With a swift hand, he threw off his loincloth. His cock was rigid like an India prayer stick; intricate tracings of blue veins figured its sides, the skin leathery-looking, the colour of faded parchment. He cackled again and patted its smooth head like a pet lapdog. 'Always ready,' he intoned religiously.

'Always? You *never* get soft?' she asked, amazed.

'Never,' he rasped emphatically. 'Touch it if you like.'

Brimming with curiosity, she reached out and stroked the side of the hard shaft as if it were a religious artifact. The dry skin felt tissue-thin, and yet its cool hardness felt polished like the toes of saints' statues in cathedrals, rubbed smooth by countless pilgrims. 'How long has it been like this?' she asked.

'Since I was fourteen,' he giggled.

'Why? I mean . . . how come?'

He winked broadly, a crafty fox. 'My secret.'

'It is something physical?' she murmured in awe. 'Mental?'

He leaned closer and whispered, as if sharing a divine revelation. 'A potion. Of rare herbs and fresh newt's eyes.'

She sighed, withdrawing her hand. 'You could make a fortune with that secret.'

'Money brings no pleasure.'

'Not in itself,' she said. 'But it sure as hell can buy a lot of good times.'

He tapped his skull. 'Good times, all up here.'

'Oh no,' she laughed softly and parted her thighs, tapping her fiery red bush with his same rhythm. 'Down here.'

He cackled like a schoolboy. 'Ah yes, the pleasures of the flesh.'

'You don't indulge?'

His cock jerked, bobbing its polished head.

'Is that a yes?' she asked facetiously, liking his spirit.

Cryptically he did not respond but concentrated on her naked breasts with a stoic mysticism.

She broke the heavy silence. 'Can I get some *shitka*?'

'Suck me,' he rasped abruptly. 'And you can, *if* you are clever.'

Without even considering, she fell forward onto his extended shaft, eager to please. Her lips closed around the faded pale yellow, slightly curved head and she inhaled it fully into her mouth. He tasted vaguely of salty

126

fish and the parchment-dry skin was smooth as silk. In her hand, his tiny balls were hairless, like small marbles in a thin leather pouch far too big for them. She worked feverishly, raking his length with her toying tongue, nipping gently at its sabre-curved, swollen tip, slathering it with her warm saliva. In silence, she laboured, with only her chesty breathing making a noise. She could feel his bony fingertips, the pads thick and calloused, begin to squeeze her nipples as though peeling grapes.

The more she sucked on his thin, ancient prick, the more turned on she became. Soon she was panting in heat, the bell-mouth of her pussy opening without being touched, crying out for some attention. 'I want it inside my cunt,' she pleaded.

'I don't fuck anymore,' he explained and pushed her head back down to its appointed anointment.

Disappointed but undeterred, she resumed blowing him feverishly, her own fingers inserting into her wet, pulsating pussy, locking on the extended nipple of her love button, jerking herself off toward never-never land. With her mouth, she tried every trick she knew – and several invented on the spot – to bring him to a climax. She sucked in his small balls and washed them around the inside of her mouth like pebbles from a stream. She repeatedly and heatedly licked the length of the old tool and concentrated on the polished cap and its sharp, little ridges. She sucked and blew, licked and tongue-whipped, teased and tormented until she thought she would pass out from the exertion. But still he did not come.

Her own progress was unstoppable. Finally, after threading the taut tightrope of erotic tension for what seemed ages, she said to hell with it and jumped off. A series of sharp pops lifted her crinkled crack off her finger and brought forth a cry of release from her sucking mouth. She felt the thick sap of her love plant bathe her insides with welcome release. She rose in mid-bloom and panted, 'Aren't you ever going to come?'

He giggled childishly. 'Haven't for forty years.'

She dropped the hard thin cock in exasperation. 'Then what the hell am I doing down here?'

'I could not resist you,' he admitted with an apologetic smile. 'It has been decades since I witnessed such a pair of paradisiacal mammae.'

'A tit freak, huh?' she asked dryly and smiled. 'I'm flattered. Tell me, what good is an always-ready cock if you never come?'

'Oh, I came all right,' he said and tapped his bony skull again. 'But up here.'

'A mind fuck?'

'Precisely,' he uttered and threw the dirty loincloth over his on-guard weapon. 'I climaxed three times before you even touched me.'

'You must have extraordinary mental powers.'

'Everyone does. If used properly.' He straightened his spine. 'So it is *shitka* you want. Why?'

Rapidly she explained – everything. Right down to Joe Scurvy on Morrison's grave. The old man listened intently and when she had concluded asked, 'And you don't remember a thing about the taping?'

'No.'

He nodded to himself, smiling secretly. 'Ah yes . . . *shitka*. A marvellous mushroom. Of the *psilocybe cyanescens* family.'

'A mushroom? Do you have any more samples?'

'Unfortunately that punk cleaned me out.'

'Where can I get some? Where does it grow?'

'That particular species is the rarest. It flourishes only after cool spring rains and more than four hours of warm sun. And only in one tiny area of the world. Northern Lapland.'

'Finland,' she repeated, already making plans. 'Should I look for anything special?'

'Reindeer shit.'

Her eyes flung wide like startled blue jays. 'Reindeer . . .'

'. . . shit,' he finished for her. 'Hence the name.'

She leaped for her dress and began tugging it on. 'I can't thank you enough, Toujours.' Hastily she bent to kiss his withered bony cheek. 'You've been divine.'

'*You* are divine,' he corrected. 'I only proved again how very mortal I am. Come again,' he laughed and patted the hardness in his loincloth. 'We'll never forget you.'

"But he flushed for her, Madeline's name."

She logged for her dress and began tugging it on. "I said leisurely, you scamp." Thomas at Madeline she had to love his without any check. "You've tried them."

"You're doing," he corrected. "I only prize to get her we were such a happy car to work again." he brushed and patted the baby next to the bathcloth. "We'll never forget you."

11
HONEY

Outside of the Hotel Pohjamhori in the city of Rovaniemi, she hesitated in the warm spring sunlight, unsure of where to begin. Her sudden flight to Helsinki and the subsequent journey north over thousands of deep blue lakes to this thriving, cosmopolitan city had left her itchy for immediate results. But now on the edge of the reindeer country, she was uncertain how to press her quest.

As if heaven-sent a handsome vision of a brawny blond youth appeared, smiling boyishly. 'May I help you in any way?' he asked in perfect, overenunciated English.

She gave him a quick once over and instantly liked what she saw. The fair-haired youth, no more than eighteen, looked like a walking advertisement for every rugged, outdoor activity she could possibly think of. Above his scuffed hiking boots and thick white socks that climbed muscular, golden-haired calves, his massive thighs rose like solid tree trunks. His slim hips and tight-cheeked butt were covered by short, tan, lederhosen, creased and

131

appropriately begrimed. The heavy bulge of his fly promised further delights and his well-defined pectorals were displayed to great advantage by a tight, spotlessly white T-shirt. His chiselled face was decidedly handsome. And his sparkling blue eyes studied her every curve with obvious equal interest.

'Can I trust you?' Honey asked with a warm smile.

'Yes,' he said earnestly. 'I am a honest man.'

And horny too, she thought with amusement noticing the way his eyes caressed her tight Calvin Klein jeans and revealing silk blouse. She instinctively decided to trust him explicitly. 'I am looking for what is called *shitka*.'

'Shhhh,' he hissed softly, casting a worried glance around. 'You must not ask strangers for that.'

'You're a stranger,' she teased. 'And I'm asking you.'

'I will tell you the truth,' he uttered directly. '*Shitka* is illegal and causes much grief.'

'Yes,' she sighed. 'I learned that.'

'*You*'ve eaten *shitka*?' he asked, astounded.

'Yes. And I want to find some more.'

His rugged frame snapped to attention. 'I am Lokka and I will take you to *shitka*.'

He had spoken so firmly, with such a take-charge manner, she felt a rush of relief. She smiled. 'I place myself in your very capable hands.'

His handsome, youthful visage bloomed with anticipation. 'You will not be disappointed. I am *very* good.'

'I just know you are,' she murmured.

Within minutes, Honey was on the back of his BMW 500 motorcycle roaring out of the surprisingly modern city totally rebuilt after the Nazis had torched it. Across several bridges high above rushing, white water and through verdant forests, they raced with Honey hanging tenuously onto Lokka's muscular torso. Though he drove his powerful bike full-out on the empty, straight stretches, she soon discovered he was an exceptionally skilled biker and began to relax, enjoying the erotic sensations of the

132

constant vibration between her spread thighs and the touch of his firm, young body.

After a good three hours, Lokka swung the bike off the main highway and onto a narrow road of hard-packed dirt covered by smelly fish oil. The terrain began changing: the pine and spruce trees thinned and the meandering road threaded through deep gorges and high fells carved and left by glaciers. Around noon, Lokka stopped beside a rushing stream in a wooded, narrow valley. 'We will eat here,' he announced forcefully.

She alighted and stretched, raising her breasts up as if to greet the sun high overhead. 'How far do we go?'

He tore his eyes from her awesome treasures and dug into the black saddlebag. 'Several hours more.'

She nodded, not too energetically, already feeling the effects of her long-spread thighs. 'Why is *shitka* illegal?'

'Is it not the same in America?' he asked, fishing out a green bottle of wine to add to the quick snack of cheese, rough, crusted bread and beef sausage. 'Are not some pleasures made unlawful just because they are – pleasures?'

'How true,' she said and accepted an open-faced sandwich. 'But in America we are still under the influence of a Puritanical tradition. Certainly here in Finland the Puritans never landed.'

'The Soviets did,' he said and passed the bottle.

She drank thirstily of the tangy wine. 'The Soviets made *shitka* illegal?'

He nodded, wolfing down his sandwich. 'They send spies to collect it all.'

'Why?'

'Perhaps they don't like anyone else having fun.' There was a trace of bitterness in his tone and he stood, peeling off his T-shirt. His chest was as solid as a granite cliff. 'We will go now.'

'Wait. These jeans are too hot. Let me change.'

He turned his back, tinkering with the brake as she

133

slipped off her tight jeans and wrapped a short cotton skirt around her bare hips. She was positive he was watching her moves.

Soon they were back on the bike roaring across the deserted, odoriferous road, bouncing through the deep ruts. She clutched at his bare trim waist. The combination of the hot sun, the strong homemade wine, the powerful bike beneath created a rising heat in her loins. Shooting over a deep bump, her hands accidentally slipped around to the Lapp's lap. She felt an unmistakable hard-on straining through the leather shorts. She hung on to it, rubbing it playfully, relishing in its size and hardness. Growing bolder, her arms encircling his waist, she managed to unbutton his fly and soon had the sturdy big prick in both hands.

Unbuttoning her blouse with one hand, she pressed her full breasts into his broad, shirtless back. Still he roared the bike on and she felt her thighs growing wet with sweetmeat moisture. The thick, long prick jerked in her hands and still he did not stop. Over hill and dale he sped until she was so hot and bothered she felt she would explode from the tension roaring inside her like the very motorcycle itself.

Finally he slammed on the brakes, screeching to a halt with a cloud of oily dust. 'Off,' he said hoarsely. She crawled off, her knees weak. He swung a leg over one side and stood, revealing his hard-as-oak cock. It bullnosed up like a petrified log, the head the colour and size of a pomegranate. He dropped his shorts, stuffed them in the saddlebag and once again sat on the seat, naked except for his boots and high white socks. He motioned her forward to his front. 'Sit.'

Breathlessly, she hiked up her short skirt, flashing him her bonfire bush, and straddled the bike, facing him. Standing on the foot supports, she raised up and, taking the beautiful proud appendage upright, lowered onto it, feeling its considerable breadth shoving her ardent gates wide. With a sigh of complete contentment, she inched down into his lap, their eyes locking fiercely, her flaming funnel full. She threw her legs over his, kissing him scorchingly, sucking his tongue past hers.

He gunned the still running engine and took off again with a shower of loose gravel. Her arms wrapped around his powerful young neck, her hard nipples rubbing his stony pectorals, her head buried into a broad shoulder, she began moaning in exhaltation, celebrating her euphoria.

Every deep rut of the road added to her ecstacy, for with each jarring bounce Lokka's thick pole jabbed at the top of her inflamed flume. Neither of them really had to move as the swaying, bouncing, vibrating, roaring power beneath them provided more than enough motion for their blood-thickened organs. Suddenly she heard a hearty laugh break from his throat and she looked behind them.

Fast disappearing in the road, a peasant man in an odd embroidered hat stood in openmouthed amazement looking after them. She waved gaily until a bend blocked the laughing Lapp from view.

On and on they raced, on and on they fucked, like a mighty machine welded together for the express purpose of higher transportation. She *did* feel transported – into a region of such all-encompassing rapturous bliss she wanted it to continue forever.

As they reached the top of a steep fell, she began bouncing up and down frantically, screaming over the roar of the bike, 'I'm coming! Holy Lokka, I'm coming!' Down whooshed her sluice juice as the bike plummeted down the sharp incline. Up the other side of another steep rise she and the bike climbed and then down again like a roller coaster of erotic pleasure. She came and came and in his ear groaned sweet endearments to his throbbing meat. She lost track of the number of peaks she traversed by the time Lokka shot his fusillade. She recoiled at the force of his blast, for it felt like a cannon filled with soft, warm buckshot had blasted her innermost interior. He hollered exuberantly, and poured on the speed, propelling them farther into the empty, barren tundra.

Many hours later, the eerie sky a suspended twilight, they reached their destination – a vast treeless plain – and pitched camp in a protected gully. She was anxious to proceed with the task of finding a few of the rare specimens, so she had the lad explain in detail the shape, size and colour of the magic mushroom. He pointed out the clumps of thick green grass indicating reindeer droppings, and anxiously she began to explore.

Wordlessly they fell to searching the seemingly endless tufts of grass and the piles of decaying faeces dumped earlier that spring by the roaming herds. They drifted farther and farther apart on the gently rolling plains and Honey, on her hands and knees, was completely oblivious to all except the minute focus of her concentrated efforts.

'Halt!' a rough voice barked behind her.

She swung in surprise and faced the barrel end of a Russian semiautomatic pistol. It was held by a large, crew-cutted man with a grim, humourless face. He snarled a command in Russian. Her apprehensions shot to the sky, but she said innocently, 'I'm an American. A student. On vacation . . .'

The burly man looked only more suspicious. 'On your feet. Move!' he commanded in broken English.

Warily, she began walking in the direction of his sour wave. She thought of calling for the hearty Lokka, but feared only making matters worse. Frantic, she scanned the horizon, angry at herself for having strayed so far from camp.

With the gun in her back, she was marched down a ravine and into a hollow by a clear, small pond. A simple stone hut nestled in the large rocks looked like a habitat for a hermit. He pushed her inside the one-room, dirt-floored cabin and slammed the door, the pistol still trained on her breasts. 'What you doing?'

She batted her long lashes like a schoolgirl. 'Searching for *shitka*, what else? Back in the States, us kids are wild about them 'shrooms. Heavy shit, you know?'

'*Shitka* all gone. No more,' he growled.

'What's all this then?' she asked, indicating with a sweep of her hand the glass jars lining the shelves above a rustic counter. She could see they were packed to the brim with tiny, dried mushrooms of a definite pink hue, just like Lokka had described.

'For Mother Country,' he said and thrust his gun into his waistband. 'Not for me. Not for you.'

She flashed her most radiant smile. 'What does mother do with them?'

'I not ask questions.'

'My, you do have a lot,' she enthused, moving to the shelves. 'Couldn't I have just a few? Promise I won't tell.'

'You know what they do?'

'Oh yes. I adore them.'

His plain, flat face registered growing interest. 'I never try them.'

'Out here by yourself, I can see why,' she said and took several deep breaths, sampling the clean fragrant air, swelling her breasts provocatively.

The first smile cracked his face and he leered at her full breasts. She lowered her lashes and her voice, 'Wouldn't you like to try some? With me?'

He thought dully and then nodded like a child, before his face fell. 'My leaders want all.'

'Surely they wouldn't miss a few. How many would it take?'

His eyes drifted to the tight crease in her jean crotch. 'Maybe I spare a few. Only for me.'

'And what about me?' she pouted, laying it on.

Another small smile. 'We do as Sami do.'

'The Laplanders? How do they do it?'

'Man eats. Woman drink piss. Both get off.'

She considered for a moment, then smiled engagingly. 'Well, feed me, Poppa, feed me do.'

It was the longest two hours Honey had ever had the misfortune to experience. He had instantly swallowed a small handful of the dried mushrooms and sat, staring at her, waiting for them to take effect, guzzling warm beer to increase his bladder. To get away from his piercing gaze and lustful leer, she slipped outside to take a swim in the cool pond. Though it was late evening, the sky looked like early twilight, yet with an odd greenish tinge. She swam as long as she could, wishing Lokka would appear before she had to go through with her desperate, off-the-cuff plan. She heard a bellow from the cabin, looked and blanched.

His hairy, nude body filled the doorway. One thick hand held the pistol, the other stroked on his already hard cock. Even from her distance, his prick looked like an Idaho potato – wide, squat, dark, and pitted. He growled at her, motioning hurriedly. Reluctantly, she rose from the water and, dripping, scurried for her clothes. His eyes bulged at her bouncing wet curves and his baked potato bobbed. 'Now, now,' he laughed. 'I pee now.'

Trapped, she could only nod. Picking a mossy incline, she lay full out and he stood over her, his legs spread wide. She sat up in a flurry. 'My name is Honey, what's yours?'

'Serge Cyron,' he growled and shoved her flat with a broad bare foot. 'Open mouth.'

'Whatever you say, Serge,' she murmured and spread her mouth to its fullest, desperately trying to think of another stall. Squatting over her, he pushed his grubby grinder down to the appropriate angle and let loose a steady, hard stream of golden showers. It flowed directly into her mouth, and though she tried not swallowing, the duration and the force were too great – she choked down

138

a mouthful in a coughing attempt to breath. His piss smelled acrid and tasted bitter. The hot liquid splashed her hair and face, flooded her white breasts, drenching her upper torso. When it trickled to a halt, she made a mad dash for the pond again, diving in, drinking as much as she could of the cold, clear water, in hopes of diluting the potent drug even further.

Serge was dancing along the edge of the pond wildly like an anxious suitor fast going insane. He roared and thundered for her to come out, his eyes wide and crazed-looking, his squat hard cock like a tumorous growth on his burly, hairy body. She postponed her emerging from the water as long as possible, feeling nothing unusual in her system. In hopes that she had missed drinking enough to get stoned, she climbed out slowly.

He grabbed her roughly and, laughing hysterically, threw her to the ground, falling on top of her, crushing her with his weight. She fought for breath. His thick potato rammed her thighs. She clamped them closed, locking her knees, both incensed at his he-man, macho approach and frightened by the unknown. She slammed the heels of her hands into his shoulders and pushed with all her might. His bear-paw hands grabbed hers and his arms flung wide, carrying hers out too. His beefy chest timbered into her large breasts, flattening them, causing extreme, intense pain.

In savage reaction her gleaming, white teeth lashed out catching an earlobe. She clamped onto it like a steel trap onto a rabbit's foot. Squirting blood, he bellowed hugely and reared back, lifting her – latched to his ear – to a sitting position. Once upright, she forcefully threw her hips to one side, twisted and scooted out from under him – fast enough to slide away to her knees, but not quick enough to miss the thudding fist to her stomach.

She doubled over, gasping for breath, her full breasts heaving like fire bellows. She staggered to her feet and lurched away. She began to run wildly, barefoot, nude, fleeing over the barren knoll of the tundra, suddenly afraid for her life.

She flung a desperate glance over a shoulder – he was lunging toward her like a mad musk-ox in heat, rapidly gaining, his hard cock wildly slapping his beefy thighs, his mouth wide with howls of hideous, absurd laughter.

In spine-shattering fright, she stumbled and crashed, sprawling full-out onto sharp rocks. She felt blood and heard a woman scream far away. Vaguely she thought it sounded like her. Dazed, she struggled to a hip. He was almost upon her. Her heart lodged in her throat. By the time he reached her, she was shrieking with uncontrollable laughter, rolling on her back, arms flung wide, her long legs flapped the twilight air in huge, welcoming circles, her bright red bush beckoning like a landing beacon.

It was the last thing she remembered . . .

Her consciousness slowly filtered to the surface like a slowly ascending escalator. Her skin felt alive with cool fire, a sharp tingle pleasantly invigorating her back and legs, even the soles of her feet. She was perspiring profusely, the air was very hot and dry, searing her nostrils. Eyes still closed, she was increasingly aware of the hard wooden slats under her. And the sound of thrashing in the air. Stinging yet refreshing blows raining on her back. The smell of something sharp, pungent, a natural oil, minty. Her eyes fluttered open. She stared directly into the gorgeous, unforgettable sight of Lokka's pomegranate prick pointed at her with one large eye. She grabbed at it and rolled up.

'Finally,' he muttered and tossed the leafy aspen branch aside. He was nude, like she, his muscled torso dripping with sweat. She realized they were in a cedar-lined sauna. And that Lokka was perturbed at her. He slunk to the opposite bench and sat glumly glaring, his hard pole ignored between his legs.

'My hero,' she mumbled. 'You rescued me.' Her mouth

140

felt extraordinarily dry and she ached all over, inside and out.

'I didn't rescue you,' he grumbled. '*You* found me. When I tried to rescue you earlier, you kicked me in the balls and fled.'

'How rude of me,' she said, trying to grasp at any memory. She sighed sadly. She obviously had been had again by the mind-blowing *shitka*. She forced herself to ask, 'What happened?'

'Are you sure you really want to know?' he asked with youthful disgust and judgment.

'Yes . . . yes, I do. Everything.'

In remarkably graphic details, the hunky young Finn spelled out the torrid outline of her debauch with Serge Cyron. Lokka had seen most of it, for he had had the cabin under surveillance long before she had come out for her first swim. The entire twelve-hour period had been conducted outdoors on the tundra, a rollicking, bucolic, pagan, bestial orgy between nymph and satyr. Lokka said he had lost count of how many times they had fucked, but it was well over three dozen, not to mention all the sucking, shitting, pissing, eating, ass-licking and butt-fucking. Lokka intimated it was a disgusting display, but she detected his hurt jealousy. He glumly concluded with his attempt to sneak her away while Serge was fucking a rock, and how she had ferociously resisted.

Honey was beside herself with a sense of discovery. It had to have been *shitka* that had produced the Moroccan orgy too. She felt exonerated and couldn't wait to phone Dirk. But there was dear Lokka, hung like a horse and horny as hell. She moved to his side and kissed his furrowed brow. 'Dear sweet Lokka. I'm so sorry.'

'*Shitka*,' he spat out contemptuously. 'I wanted to take them with you. I even found a group for us alone.'

'Oh no,' she said with a playful growl. 'Let me take some back with me, but this – you and I in all this heat' – she reached for pomegranate head of his dazzlingly

141

impressive log – '*this* I want to remember. In every lurid detail.'

And she did too, on her flight to Cairo to meet Disa. It was such a savagely erotic memory she came without touching herself – just before she found the next possible clue of the conundrum spread out in the pages of *Harper's Bazaar*.

12
DIRK

'Where the hell are you?' he shouted into the phone, irritated by the late morning, transoceanic call that had so rudely awakened him from a heavy sleep in his New York Soho loft.

'Cairo,' Honey's voice came as if at the bottom of a very deep well. 'I'm here with my darling Disa. We're trying to track down that old couple who were servants at the baron's villa in Tangiers.'

'You haven't told Disa anything, have you?' he asked sharply and rolled over to see who the warm body was next to him. Though he couldn't remember her name, she was pleasantly lovely, coiled nude under the midnight blue, satin sheet like a child in slumber.

'Of course not, Dirk,' Honey replied with equal sharpness. 'She thinks I just want to hire the couple to work for me. Anyway, listen, will you? The reason I called . . .' Her voice faded out in a burst of staccato interference.

'What? I can't hear you!' he shouted and scooted up against the headboard of his king-sized waterbed.

Her voice cut through in mid sentence, '. . . in *Harper's* on page eighty-six.'

'What about page eighty-six?'

'My missing gold waist-chain!' she yelled through the wire. 'I'm positive it's mine. It has the ebony goat-headed clasp and everything.'

He rubbed the sleep from his eyes and asked her to repeat the message. Thickly, his hung-over mind tried to grasp the essentials – a gorgeous young model was wearing the missing chain in an editorial layout of that month's *Harper's* and Honey was insisting that he track her down and find out where she had gotten the chain. 'Did you get all that, Dirk?'

'Yeah, I think so,' he grumbled and slid down to spoon his long frame against the still-sleeping beauty. Honey rattled on excitedly about finding the *shitka* mushroom and how convinced she was that it was the reason behind her sexy transgressions. Dirk, though pleased with her discoveries, had his own pressing needs – a raging morning hard-on urged him to find some immediate release. He pulled the deep blue sheet off the reposing beauty and started stroking her surprisingly large ass, soft as a field of snow.

'Dirk? Dirk!' came Honey's faraway voice. 'Let go of that girl and answer me dammit!'

He chuckled at her astuteness and flopped on his back, gently rocking on the firm waterbed. 'Gotcha, Honey. I'll call the photographer who did the layout and get the name of the model.'

'Do more than that,' Honey urged. 'Personally find her and ask where the hell she got my belt. Okay, Dirk?'

Sleeping Beauty had awakened and rolled over, displaying tender young breasts that rose from her torso like vanilla sno-cones. He was sucking greedily on one and barely heard his sister's annoyed shout from the forgotten receiver. 'Right, Honey,' he mumbled, his mouth full. 'Catch ya later, okay?' He slid the receiver off the rocking bed and returned to his breakfast of vanilla sno-cones and hot pussy lips.

Sometime later that day, Dirk finally reached by phone his photographer pal who had taken the *Harper's* shots. As they chatted amiably, Dirk dug out the issue from the stack of current magaznes littering the glass-and-chrome coffee table in the living-room area of his spacious, sunlit studio-loft. Idly he thumbed to page eighty-six and stared in admiration at the stunning, lithe, honey blonde girl who, bare-breasted, modelled a long, flowing beach-skirt. 'Who's the chick in the sarong?' Dirk asked casually. 'I've never seen her before. She new on the scene?'

His friend laughed. 'Yes, you could say that. She's not a professional model.'

'She should be,' Dirk praised. 'She's got something.'

'That's what I told her. She goes by the unlikely name of Sweet Dew.'

'Sweet Dew? Jesus, why a handle like that?'

'Beats me. But if you're interested in using her, she'd be tickled pink. You can find her at a club called "Promises" in the Village.'

'What she do there?'

'Dances mainly. But I got to warn you, buddy. She's not what she seems.'

'What the hell's that mean?'

'You'll see,' his friend chuckled and rang off.

Shortly after 9.00 p.m., Dirk showed up at his reserved table in the tacky little club Promises and settled down to what he thought was going to be a typical evening in search of one more magical face. Honey's missing waist-chain was almost incidental to his being there. Once he had glimpsed the young model on page eighty-six, he had been hooked and now awaited her in the flesh.

145

The lights dimmed, the recorded music began – a disco version of Debussy's 'Afternoon of a Fawn.' Onto the small dance floor, Sweet Dew, in person leaped with the athleticism of a seriously trained dancer. Wearing only a skimpy, doeskin bikini, her tawny skin glistened with oil; her honey blonde waves caressed her strong shoulder; her dancer's legs were long in proportion to her trunk with well-defined, but not overly exaggerated, muscles and tendons. He was fascinated by her breasts – nearly perfect, round mounds almost too large for her trim frame.

But it was her face that still captured him – the features were strong but definitely sweet, innocent, like a cherub. Her generous mouth had a distinctly sensual turn and her limpid sea green eyes were full of a knowing awareness. He was so taken by her magic that he barely criticized her dance. Her movements were on the jerky, awkward side, with not enough flow or follow-through.

Sweet Dew's routine evolved energetically into a modified striptease. Her strong, graceful back to the patrons, she slowly peeled off the top of her brief costume, danced a few measures with a peek-a-boo style and ultimately displayed the perfection of her finer points. They were exactly as Dirk had imagined – bright pink nipples marking perfect bull's-eyes on the circular targets. Soon, with an exaggerated, flirtatious manner, she wriggled out of the bottom half of her bikini, revealing first her ass with its firm, hard globes of dancer's cheeks and then her bulging box, which remained covered by a tiny swatch of flesh-coloured material.

Dirk was pleased by the ripe fullness of her love mountain, which balanced the same qualities of her bouncing breasts. She bumped and ground with traditional efficiency until abruptly the music ended and the stage lights blacked out. Dirk pushed his chair back to go meet the enticing package. He reached the stage door before remembering he had forgotten to note if she were wearing Honey's chain.

146

In the cramped, backstage area, her dressing-room door was wide open. He tapped lightly on the doorjamb and strode in expectantly, more interested in the dew of Sweet than the chain of Honey. The tiny room smelled heavily of theatrical makeup and the sweat of many previous performers.

In the triple dressing-table mirrors, Sweet raised her sea green eyes to his and he felt a sharp stirring in his balls. Her limpid, expressive eyes held the promise of mysteries to be revealed. Her bare shoulders were covered by a long, ratty Japanese kimono of a pale pink pattern and she was freshening up her eye makeup. 'Well, hello stranger,' Sweet greeted with a husky, throaty voice.

'Hi,' Dirk said, turning on his laid-back, winning charm. 'I enjoyed your act.'

'My pleasure totally,' she purred and swivelled on the stool to face him. She raked his lean, long frame with her knowing eyes and smiled approvingly. 'My name is Sweet Dew.'

'I know. I'm Dirk. Want to have a drink someplace?'

The mesmerizing combination in her green eyes of innocence and carnal knowledge deepened. 'How 'bout my place? It's nearby.'

'Sounds great,' he enthused, congratulating himself, 'How much time before your second show?'

She stood, languidly reaching for a cloth street coat, her kimono falling open, the glitter of a gold chain encircling her trim waist. 'More than enough time . . . for whatever it is on your mind.'

Her apartment turned out to be a small, railroad flat above an all-night deli off of Bleecker. Furnished with an assortment of early Salvation Army, the short, narrow, main room was comfortable and strictly feminine. On the peeling plaster wall above the day-bed couch, a large black and white poster of James Dean held the place of honour.

147

Tugging off her outer coat, Sweet swept the skirt of her kimono into the back kitchen and shortly returned with two glasses full of ice and a bottle of Kentucky Bourbon. 'It's all I have,' she apologized and poured three fingers into each glass.

'Anything's fine,' he said and settled back onto the couch, sipping the bourbon, unable to take his eyes off her incredibly evocative face. 'I couldn't help noticing your waist-chain. It's really beautiful.'

'Isn't it though?' she said and parted her kimono to finger the delicate single strand of twenty-four carat gold resting gently on her slim hips.

'Mind if I look closer?'

'Be my guest,' she breathed and tossed the kimono off her shoulders. Her bare, round breasts were still filmed with the oil of her routine and she raised the shiny orbs as if to allow access to her waist area.

Though his eyes remained on her impressive breastworks, his fingers touched the black goat's-head-clasp of the chain. He remembered Honey telling him that Humboldt – a Capricorn – had designed the chain himself – cast it in his own image, she had joked. 'It's quite unique,' Dirk said with a constricted tone.

'It's my favourite piece of jewellery,' she said huskily and one of her hands fell softly on his jean-covered thigh.

'Mind telling me where you got it?'

'First things first,' she voiced sexily and promptly squeezed the hard lump in his lap.

His boner had crept up on him so slowly he had not even been aware he was hard until she clasped it. Now, with her strong, sturdy fingers rubbing it diligently, he was all too aware that he wanted to fuck this chick silly. *Then* he wanted to photograph her – itching to do her face and figure the justice it so warranted. 'Okay, I'm easy,' he joshed. 'First things first.'

'How 'bout some noshes before the main course?' she

quipped and unzipped him completely. 'Just lean back. This first course is all on me.'

He took her at her word and fell back against the cushions, feeling her cool, hard hands pulling his hot, thickened member out of his jeans and stroking it assuredly. She fell to her knees between his sprawled thighs and began yanking down his jeans. He had to slip off his handmade Texan boots before she could tug his pants over his feet. Throwing the jeans to one side, she held his cock upright and studied it carefully as though uncertain where to begin. 'From your height,' she said, looking up with her openly aroused face, her wide lips parted, moist, 'I thought you'd be bigger.'

'Not the size but the stamina,' he offered.

'Makes no diff to me,' she said with genuine enthusiasm. 'I love all cocks. Each has its own personality. Yours is sort of piquant yet perturbed.'

'Well unperturb the damn thing before it gets pissy.'

She growled a chesty laugh and latched onto his hard cock with her warm mouth, wrapping a slick tongue around its engorged head. Skilfully, with the expertise of one who practises frequently, Sweet proceeded to suck and blow, lick and nibble at his pulsating prick, paying special attention to the bulging ridges on the underside of its bloodred cap. Within minutes, she had him so primed he felt poised on the edge of a giant precipice, ready to leap headlong into ecstatic oblivion.

He pushed her off his ready-to-explode cock. 'My turn for hors d'oeuvres,' he rasped and pulled her up beside him on the sagging day-bed. Eagerly he leapt upon the shiny mounds like a dolphin at feeding time. Her perfect, round tits were surprisingly hard and it did not take him long to figure out by their feel that they were artificially enhanced by silicone. Regardless, she was a delicious mouthful and he sucked at the elongating nipples with the increased fervour of a man obsessed by big tits.

Every time his hand slipped to her barely covered

snatch, she pushed it away and he grew frustrated trying to reach his ultimate goal. Finally in exasperation, he grumbled, 'You on the rag?' Cause if you are, big deal. The best meat's always bloody and raw.'

Without responding, she writhed passionately under him and sought his lips with hers. He engaged her briefly in a kissing and tongue duel, but his objective was still farther south. His prick throbbed with unreleased tension and he longed to ram it into her toaster.

Trailing a wet tongue down her throat, across her round, hard breasts and over her flat stomach, he scooted to press his profile into the scant, flesh-coloured material covering her protruding box. Tangible waves of heat poured from it like from an open oven. She slipped a hand under his face and, cupping her mound, pried apart the thin strand of cloth covering her heated trench.

Like a small, rosy croissant, its lips curved invitingly and he plunged his tongue deep inside. She tasted like some sort of ripe melon – perhaps a honeydew, he mused to himself – and he probed the furled edges of her tasty twat. Briefly, he wondered why her hand still covered all of her box except for the delicate rosy slit. Wanting desperately the full meal, he forced her annoying hand away and tore off the thin strip of material, exposed her fully.

What greeted his eyes was more than a surprise; it was fucking mind-blowing. A small cock, hard and pointed like a dog's, lay flat on the dark blonde bush just above the dewy trench. No balls, just a little dick. 'What the fuck!' he exploded and reared in confused consternation.

'Please, don't stop,' she – or he – pleaded in a whimper. 'A freak of nature, that's all . . .'

'You were born this way? With both a cock *and* a cunt?'

Tears flooded the sea green eyes. 'A thin membrane covered my cunt,' Sweet cried. 'I had it surgically cut two years ago.'

'How were you raised?' he asked after a moment of

trying to temper his confusion and not trample on her sensitivity. 'Boy or girl?'

'A boy,' she sobbed and wiped her eyes. 'But I knew I was a girl. Always.'

'Well, I'll be damned.'

'Does it turn you off?'

He thought for a moment – or rather, his smaller head thought for him and urged him to action. 'Always a first time for everything,' he mumbled agreeably and rose to his knees, bringing his insistently hard-up hard-on to her tiny, semireal twat.

Gingerly, he shoved his stony prick into the rosy pink opening. Though a snug fit, his cock went in easily and soon was mantled in moist, musky hot meat. He began pumping, trying to ignore the hard lump of the extra little cock pressing into his stomach. Gradually his hips picked up speed and he felt her love cave milking his driving, ramming rod like the genuine article.

Sweet wrapped her well-muscled dancer's legs around his waist and matched athletically every movement with one of her own. The springs of the day-bed creaked their heated rhythm and soon Dirk had forgotten all but the warm juicy tightness surrounding his loaded cock.

Sweet's little dick came first, squirting a warm load against his belly. Then he came, joyously, enthusiastically, flying off the end of the precipice and rocketing into blissful paradise. He collapsed onto the firm, round tits and panted for breath. Whatever she, he, or it was beneath him, the fuck had been well worth it. In spades.

He pulled out of her and with amusement, eyed her now-limp little lump of goose-flesh just below the gold chain. He flicked a finger over the dick and up to the thin metal strand. 'Where did you say you got this?'

'I didn't,' she said warmly and slipped out from under him. She checked the alarm clock on the portable TV set and frowned. 'I've only a few minutes.' She darted up and across the small space, ino the adjoining bathroom. 'A friend gave it to me,' she called out, unseen.

'Who?'

'A beautiful lady named Koka.'

'Koka what?' he asked, wiping his cock on his shirt-tail.

'Just Koka, I guess,' Sweet said and came out looking radiant. 'Never knew her last name.'

Dirk stood and began pulling on his jeans. 'What's she look like?'

'Spectacular, really. Tall, muscular and –'

'Black?'

Sweet's green eyes widened. 'Yeah, how'd you know?'

He shrugged, grinning, and tucked in his shirt as he slipped one foot into a standing boot. 'Lucky guess. You know where I might find her?'

'Why?'

'I'd like to get one of those chains for a friend.'

Sweet tugged the cloth coat over her kimono. 'Koka is impossible to find. I tried."

'What do you mean?'

'Well, I only met her once. At the club. We spent the night here. She gave me the belt. Split. That's it.'

'You've never seen or heard from her since?'

'No. Koka just blew into my life and out,' Sweet said softly and kissed him on the cheek. 'But I'll tell you one thing: if she ever blows back, I'll let you know. She'd dig you too.'

13

HONEY

A fluorescent school of darting angelfish nibbled at her braless, pale breasts. Gracefully she finned through their midst, scanning the astonishingly clear depths for a sign of Hum. Some of the sea had seeped into her mask, partially obscuring her vision, but she could read the dials of her wrist gauge. She had only another fifteen minutes of tank oxygen. A giant tortoise paddled lazily by, looking at her through beady eyes, old as Methuselah.

Suddenly, meaty hands grabbed her hips from behind, ripping at her bikini bottom. She choked with laughter into her mouthpiece and wiggled free – minus the bottom. Hum waved the material at her like a bullfighter and she charged, her arms close to her side with powerful kicks of her fins, her red hair trailing behind like fiery seaweed. Her head butted harmlessly into his healthy gut and he latched onto her full, ripe breasts as though they were doorknobs and he was trying to open

153

her up. In their acquatic cavorting, Hum managed to slip out of his trunks and they floated free. Through the sun-drenched waters, his thick, extended cock ploughed toward her like a mad sea snake.

Resting her thighs on his, she raised her half-opened clamshell to his erect sea-cock and, maintaining a sweeping motion with her arms, held her torso upright with little effort. His powerful legs treaded water furiously until he was fully inside her. Once the hard snake was safely bedded, he stopped kicking and let their grinding hip movements propel them haphazardly in the rays of sunshine and the towering, belly-dancing kelp.

Their sensually heated underwater ballet was a passionate powerful clash of strong bodies, but because of the tropical water, it was almost languid in movement, a slow-motion gravity-free fuck. Her face mask fogged with lusty heat and the fires of her loins bucked her hips spasmodically. Streaming bubbles of exhaled air exploded from their nostrils and rose like translucent balloons.

Rocketing to the heights of passion, Honey felt the trembling walls of her love-trench suck in his hard cock as though trying to absorb and swallow it totally. Poised on the verge of coming, she was suddenly aware that she was sucking a dangerously thin amount of air into her lungs. Instinctively, she broke out of her trance and checked her gauge, signalling Hum she was out of oxygen. She took a huge lungful and slammed her pelvis repeatedly into his until the kaleidoscope of orgasmic colour exploded before her eyes. She wrestled free of him just as he came – a geyser of milky cum shot a trajectory of white trails, like tiny, long-plumed fish in the blue green water. Still coming in waves of heightened bliss, she drifted upward toward the bright sun.

They broke surface together, ripping out their mouthpieces and gasping for pure, sweet air, panting from their thrilling exertion. Weakly she swam for one of the pontoons of Hum's private helicopter and clung to it in the gentle swell, gathering the strength to haul herself up. Hum, ever the gentleman, was by her side, unstrapping her heavy tanks and handing them up to the outstretched hands of his young, uniformed pilot. together they pushed and pulled her up onto the light rolling pontoon.

On her stomach she lay on the hot metal for a long while, luxuriating in the abundant supply of fresh air and the bright sun warming her fair skin. Clambering up beside her, sputtering like a beached whale, Hum threw her short robe over her bare ass and she, only then, remembered that she was totally nude and that he did not like his employees to see her so.

Climbing into the chopper, tying the belt of her robe, she wondered again why she had been so suddenly summoned to his vacation retreat. Without warning, Hum had sent his private Lear jet to Cairo to fetch her. Why? Whatever the reason, she hoped it had nothing to do with that damned video tape. She knew that Hum would never forgive her if he happened to see a copy of her flagrant transgressions.

The short flight back took less than six minutes. Throughout, despite the spectacular vista of the blue green Gulf of Mexico and the Yucatan peninsula on the western horizon, Honey's concern about Hum's unusual silence continued to fester. Usually her presence alone would create in him a boundless energy and enthusiasm for everything, manifested by gargantuan appetites and a talkative, gregarious sharing. Now, however, he sat in a glum silence, staring at the approaching tip of his private peninsula on the island of Cozumel as if he were landing on top of a sewage plant. Honey was usually thrilled by the sight of his sprawling white beach and the tidy red-tiled roofs of the hacienda compound surrounded by towering date palms. But this time, Hum's withdrawn mood tempered her own.

155

Under the swaying palms, they dined that evening on the terrace overlooking a wide expanse of Hum's beach and a setting sun that fired the sky with rich purples and golds, a sunset befitting royalty. She had decided to wear one of Hum's favourite dresses – a filmy, apricot-toned, Grecian-styled gown by Halston that left little to the imagination. Exposing the healthy swell of her snowy breasts, its gossamer softness clung to her every curve. As usual, she wore nothing underneath. Hum sat across the intimate table in white dinner jacket and crisp black tie, his larger-than-life figure every inch the successful, influential, bullish publishing emperor that he was. Tonight, however, his magnetic, high-voltage energy was still being short-circuited and she greatly missed the main ingredient that made him so damned irresistible.

'What is it, Hum?' she asked finally, unable to stand anything unspoken between them. 'What's on that magnificent, awe-inspiring, cradle-of-genius mind?'

His bushy greying brows collided, either with surprise or distrust of her teasing, playful tone. 'Did I indicate something?'

'Hey,' she murmured genuinely, 'I'm tuned into you remember? You're my main channel. And I sure wish you'd share more, right now.'

He waited for one of the Mexican houseboys to refill his after-dinner glass with his favourite 1955 Taylor's Port. Then he eyed her strangely over the rim, his craggy face reserved. 'Honey, I want you to come back to work. Immediately after we leave here.'

Her concern fled, replaced by a wash of disappointment. 'Hum, you gave me a month . . .'

'I'm aware of that fact,' he said. 'But I am taking half of that back.'

'Why?'

'You chose not to share with me why you wanted an

156

unprecedented month off and I choose not to share with you my reasons for asking you back.'

For a quiet moment, she fought the burst of temper that bubbled up in her chest. She desperately needed the two remaining weeks. Especially now that Dirk had reported hearing of a giant black lady name Koka. Their mutual quest seemed on the verge of a major breakthrough. She could not abandon it now. Even for the man she worshipped more than any in her life except for her father. But how to tell him without seeming intransigent or ungrateful?

She ran a finger around the rim of the Baccarat crystal wineglass. 'Hum,' she began in the brisk tone used strictly for business – very similar to his telephone voice, 'is there a special assignment you want me to handle?'

'Nothing special,' he admitted freely. 'I just miss having you around.'

'I'm not a toy,' she flared. 'I resent being categorized as "something" you like having around.'

To her surprise, the craggy plains of his rough-hewn face dissolved into a broad smile, rather than the matching fire they so often enjoyed in their occasional duels. He leaned forward confidentially. 'How would you like being categorized? Protégée? Partner in life? Mistress? Perhaps, wife?'

'You've never given me that latter option.'

'How forgetful of me,' he said and pulled a small, black velvet box out of his white dinner coat. With typical lack of fanfare, he handed it to her.

Uncertainly, she flipped open the lid and blinked back the rush of tears. Inside was a huge diamond solitaire, at least twenty carats. Emerald cut on a simple platinum band, it glittered like an icy glacier under powerful searchlights. 'It belonged to my great-grandmother, Annabelle,' he was saying seriously. 'The Hamilton side. My father presented it to my mother when he proposed. As I'm giving it to you now.'

'Hum . . . dear sweet Hum,' she murmured, so overcome with conflicting emotions that she was unable to respond more articulately. The topic of marriage had never been broached by either side before, and its sudden appearance on the evening's agenda completely confused and disoriented her. Of course, she had entertained occasional fantasies about their eventual union, in five years or so. But as Hum had steadfastly extolled the virtues of bachelorhood to all, including her, she had never considered such passing thoughts as having any basis in reality. Now Humboldt Harrison Hamilton, one of the world's most powerful men, was waiting for an answer and she did not know how to respond.

'I'm deeply touched,' she voiced and her vivid blue eyes sparkled mischievously, 'but you're the one who always quotes William Allen White: "My advice to the women of America is to raise more hell and fewer dahlias." '

He grimaced, as if perturbed at the pointed relevance 'Aren't you going to put it on?'

She hesitated. 'I'm afraid once it's on I'll never want to take it off.'

'And rightly so. Put it on.'

His tone had expressed a direct order and her desire for independence quickly bristled, fighting against her romanticism, which wanted to acquiesce. She snapped the lid shut. 'I just can't . . .'

'Why in God's name not?'

She looked up at him through lashes moist with barely controlled tears. 'Because I don't know what strings are attached.'

'If you don't know that by now –' He stopped and yanked his beefy torso back into his chair. 'I've never proposed in my life,' he grumbled, a raw chunk of his hurt nakedly exposed.

She squeezed one of his large, soft hands. 'And I've never even considered accepting before.'

'I'm perfectly aware that I'm only one of dozens who have asked for your hand.'

'Oh, Hum,' she blurted out. 'I'm not saying no.'

His shrubby brows raised. 'But you're not saying yes.' For a long period he sat silently, leaning back in his rattan armchair, stroking his determined jawline thoughtfully. Eventually his stern, paternal countenance softened into that of a forgiving, patient lover. 'As your boss,' he began with mock authority, 'I demand you come back to work. Or face the wrath of God.'

She laughed freely in release. 'I'll compromise. I'll be back at my desk in *one* week.'

For a moment, his expression hardened and she thought for a moment she had pushed too far. Then, like a cloud withdrawing from her sun, he brightened. 'Compromise accepted.' He stood, reaching automatically for a long Havana from the teak humidor on its special stand. 'Come, Honey, my dear. I've sent all the servants to their abode and arranged for a little surprise.'

Gathering the long skirt of her apricot-toned gown, she rose like a Grecian goddess, statuesque, regal, and classically beautiful. She laid a hand gently on his offered arm and they started up the tile walkway, threading through the lantern-lit, lush foliage. Night-blooming jasmine intoxicated the balmy night air.

As they entered the huge hacienda by a fountained atrium, she said playfully, 'Knowing your extraordinary good taste in talent, I am agog with anticipation.'

She was not one whit disappointed.

A mother-daughter contortionist team. Petite, brown, pretty, and double-jointed. Wearing only smiles, their flexible, girlish figures assumed the most unnatural of positions. Human pretzels of astounding professional skills. Just watching them made Honey's joints ache. And her V-kettle began to steam.

Their hairless pussies were hued a burnt umber, the two sets of small, flat breasts identically formed. Mother and daughter looked more like sisters – each about fifteen. Their limber youthful limbs soon were glistening with perspiration, which added a lustrous sheen to their earth-coloured skin. Their lovely faces were luminous and childlike, free from any concerns except to entertain. Their foxy black eyes conveyed knowing pleasures and a willingness to explore. With each unique contortion – either in tandem or solo – they each flashed welcoming smiles from every one of their luscious sets of lips.

Soon Honey was wildly beside herself with desire. She knew that Hum was watching her heat grow, studying her with his detached sense of amusement and his own arousal. Knowing that her Sapphic excitation turned him on heightened her own increasing passion. Side by side they sat on the red velvet couch at one end of the luxurious, Spanish-decorated living room. At the other end, under the illumination of two glowing hurricane lamps, mother and daughter flowed effortlessly from one impossible position to another. Honey could not stand it one more second. She jumped to her feet and quickly dropped her Halston gown as if it were an unnecessary beach towel. Already barefoot, and now gloriously nude, she kissed Hum on the lips and darted to join the twisted duo whose lips beckoned.

The mother was bent over backward, clutching her ankles, her brown thighs wide, her umbered lips high in the air. Honey turned her back to the outstretched knees and flipped over into a back-bend, catching her weight with both hands on the tapestried carpet. She lowered her head and brought her mouth in line with the mother's unfilled taco shell. With a zestful cry, she buried her inverted face into the moist, heady darkness and sucked in the loose lips that hung like soft moss from the petite frame.

Soon the daughter had joined the happy configuration. Standing on her head between Honey's legs, she balanced on her elbows, and with her small brown hands lowered Honey's hips until the bright red bush was over her mouth. The girl's quick brown tongue demonstrated the same limber dexterity as the rest of her arousing performance. It did not take long before Honey's knees were quivering with sympathetic vibrations to her vaginal stimulation. She could not hold her bent-over-backward position. With a soft groan she collapsed, pulling down both mother and daughter.

Into a warm pile of tangled limbs, bouncing breasts and spread cunts, they fell, sprawling on each other like precocious kids in a sandbox. Their mouths groped momentarily, like sucker fish out of water, before attaching to another's puckered pussy. This time, the profile of the mother was upon Honey's fire-engine bush, and Honey tongued the daughter's moist ripening wet twat, which tasted like *café au lait*. Through the daughter's spread legs, Honey could see that the girl was eating out the mother's available box lunch. It was a trio of tortuously ecstatic twats that thundered toward being a triumvirate of triumphant cunts.

Honey was so lost in bliss that she did not hear the telephone ring, or Hum's annoyed answering, or even his calling her name sharply. Eventually his bark brought her to consciousness enough to raise her head to see what was so damned urgent.

He waved the phone receiver, growling as he stuffed his fast-dwindling cock back into his dressing robe. 'A cable. For you. Marked urgent.'

Flooded with disappointment, she lurched away from the dazzling duo and half stumbled to his side. He handed her the receiver with the grim expression of a man sorely put upon.

She put the receiver to her ear, said, 'This is Honey Wildon,' listened to the one word telegram, 'Snatch,'

161

and hung up. 'I'm sorry, Hum,' she said, gathering her resources. 'I have to leave. Immediately. Would you have Denny warm up the chopper?' She started for the master bedroom suite to change.

'Honey,' he voiced harshly, not used to being walked out on. 'What is it? For God's sake, what is it?

'Dirk wants me,' she said without stopping.

'Well, *I* want you!' he shouted. 'Stay.'

She tossed over her shoulders, 'Sorry, Hum. Blood is thicker than diamonds.'

14

DIRK

He threw open the door to his Soho loft and frowned at the somewhat dishevelled sight of his sister. 'It's about time,' he snapped and whirled back into the living-room area, leaving her unkissed and unwelcomed in the doorway.

She slammed the door behind her and stormed after him, a sudden red squall in the desert. 'What kind of greeting is that?' she railed, her bright blue eyes shooting sparks. 'After busting my ass to rush here? I had to change flights four times, couldn't get a cab at Kennedy, had to *hitch* a ride with some jerk who tried to molest me in the tunnel, and I *walked* the last eleven blocks! And for this? I could have stayed the weekend with Hum in paradise.'

'Well, why the hell didn't you?' he asked snidely and plopped onto the grey velour pillow-couch that formed a giant square *U* in one corner of his spacious loft.

She towered over him, flushed with anger, even her red hair looking more fiery in the pools of bright light from overhead. 'Because you sent for me! 'Snatch,' right? Our code for 'drop everything and come immediately. Right? So I did. Fast as I could. And you welcome me as if I had –'

'Aw, can the shit will you?' he growled, cutting her off. 'I've just about had it with you, Honey. Up to here.' He dragged a pointed finger across his neck.

His grey blue eyes were so coated with rare animosity she hesitated, a growing unease filling her chest cavity. 'Okay, Dirk,' she said with barely controlled sarcasm. 'What have I done now? That so upsets your delicate sensibilities?'

Glowering, he shot to his feet and, silently fuming, stalked off the Persian carpet onto the polished, tongue-and-groove oak floor, toward the photo studio section of the lengthy, floor-through loft. She tossed her carryall bag onto the glass-topped coffee table and followed, her eyes sweeping over the huge blowups of some of his more famous feminine studies adorning the high white walls.

One in particular caught her eye. A new colour photo with sultry sepia overtones. It was of the precious-looking model who wore the gold waist-chain in *Harper's*. But she was not wearing it in this photo. She lay on her stomach, arching upward, staring directly into the camera with a wistful, faraway look in her sea-green eyes. Her round, perfectly formed breasts rested lightly on her crossed arms like two large peas on a pod. Honey thought it was an exquisite portrait – sensual, erotic, Sphinx-like. She made a note to ask Dirk to introduce her sometime to the delectable creature.

Reluctantly, she tore her gaze away from the bewitching presence Dirk had so magically captured and entered the long, narrow, enclosed darkroom equipped with every conceivable device and gadget used in the processing, developing, enlarging, and reproduction of his photos. He stood rigidly before a wire line above the mixing tanks. On the line hung twenty or so recently developed and enlarged black and white glossies. In disgust, he waved at them. 'Someone anonymously mailed me a roll of film. I'm sure you'll recognize the recorded event. It's a real doozy, Honey. The *National Enquirer* would have a fucking field day with them.'

Warily she moved to them. Her mouth fell open and an icy cold gripped her intestines. 'Oh, my God . . .' She groaned in genuine pain and spun away. Each of the photos revealed a step-by step progression of her erotic encounter with Joe Scurvy on Morrison's grave. In precise detail, the expertly taken shots clearly showed her reaming Joe's pimply, skinny ass with the large white dildo and her own hand-in-her-jeans masturbation. Sick to her stomach, she fled from the darkroom.

He found her curled tightly in the centre of his unmade king-sized waterbed. Over her head, a large, brick-arched window offered a night view of the World Trade Centre towers. Two of the largest erections in the world, he mused bitterly, and poor Honey failed to find the humour in it this time. She was weeping into her hands, her shoulders heaving convulsively. His bitter anger fled and he felt a sharp pang of remorse and a deep tug of pity. Quickly he crawled onto the rocking bed and gathered her into his long arms, cradling her like a baby. For a long while, he let her sob onto his shoulder, patting her back softly. 'There, there my Honey,' he kept repeating, her tears tearing him apart.

She raised her wet-streaked face. 'Someone's out to get me, Dirk,' she cried. 'And I'm scared. Goddamn, am I scared.'

He held her tightly. 'I'm here. With you all the way.'

'Who?' she moaned. 'Who could be behind this? And why? And why, for God's sake, are they sending *you* this stuff? Like they're toying with us.'

'I was hoping you'd have a clue by now.'

Plaintively she shook her rich red waves, and tears started once more, flowing unchecked down her pale sculptured cheeks. 'We're no closer than when we first started.' She clutched at his thin, long frame with renewed desperation.

'There's an old English proverb,' he began, overly conscious of her soft, full breasts heaving into his chest, 'that goes, "every path has its puddles." You've chosen a certain path for your life, and twice now you've stepped into rather messy puddles.'

Defiantly she pushed back. 'I've been leading my life exactly the same since I was twelve. I fuck with whom I want and when I want. Why *now* all of a sudden is someone recording my activities? Drugging me, dragging me off in broad daylight, following me? What'll they do next?'

'You draw up that list I suggested?' he asked, trying his damnedest to concentrate on her unusual state of mind, rather than her usual frame of body. 'The enemies you might have made? The people in power you've alienated? For whatever reason, careerwise or personally. Anyone seeking revenge? Or curtailment, or suppression of a planned interview?'

She kept shaking her head from side to side like a metronome beating a funeral dirge. 'Dirk, I've tried, honest to God I have. But it's useless. I can't think of anyone. Not one solitary soul who'd do this to me. You know I hate hard feelings – I always clean up messy affairs. Smooth things over. And as far as professionally, hell, your guess is as good as mine.' She wiped her eyes struggling to control the helpless welter of emotions ranging from paranoia to a deep righteous anger at being violated. 'Idi Amin reportedly screamed for my head after that piece I wrote. And Castro supposedly was livid for my pointing out his macho-pig behaviour toward his mistresses. Damn, Dirk, it could be anyone, From Julie Andrews to Nixon. Anyone that I've done a column on. Even the ones I went easy on – someone's nose could be out of joint by my slightest reference.'

166

Dirk rolled over on his front nodding seriously, trying to conceal the raging hard-on. 'The way I figure it, kiddo, is this,' he began, all business on the surface. 'If it were done for professional reasons – to destroy your credibility with Hum or with your readers – this junk would have been sent to Hum himself. Or the editors, or Board of Directors for *World News*. Not me, right?'

She agreed, sitting up to rearrange her heavy breasts in the skimpy, blue stretch halter, cupping them with her palms to place them properly. His eyes followed her movements as she spoke, some of the usual spark surfacing.

'That makes it even harder then. Harder to think of who personally is that pissed with me. And harder to take, too. Even thinking that some former or present friend – or lover –is out after me . . .' Again tears welled in her bright eyes and she blinked them away determinedly. 'I'm a good person, Dirk. Aren't I? I don't hurt anyone intentionally. I'm not petty, or mean, vicious, vindictive, bitchy, driven – I'm always careful of stepping on innocent people's toes. Sure, I mean, hell, my hot temper burns people now and then. But I'm always quick to make amends . . .' Her voice broke again and she threw herself on him, pleading, 'Hold me, Dirk, please . . . I feel so . . . so damned threatened.'

He wrapped his lean frame about her, and for a long while they just lay there, in the semidarkness, Honey searching her mind for answers, Dirk trying to stem the flow of his overly heated libido. Memories plagued him of how, as kids, she had used to play with his young bird of paradise. And how she had let him explore fully her budding pussy, fingering it, sticking things in it, licking it – the first pussy up close in his whole life. The only one he had never forgotten.

They had both been so young then. Everything they had done together seemed so natural, merely an extension of their deep love for each other. Then their parents

167

had been killed on a business trip and Honey had swiftly, mysteriously ended all such intimacies. Ever since then he could not be with her for any length of time without conjuring up those wonderfully arousing memories. Like acid etchings, they had stayed indelibly engraved in his mind, teasing him, tormenting him, frustrating him.

Like now, on the king-sized bed, with her voluptuous body softly entwined around his hard frame, he was finding it damned difficult to deal with her tearful upset because his furnace was raging so deep, deep within him.

He kissed her forehead tenderly, then her perfect aquiline nose, then both her sculptured, priestesslike cheekbones and her graceful jawline which completed the lovely oval of her face, her alabaster throat which smelled faintly of jungle gardenias, even the lobes of her ears hidden like pale pink seashells beneath the burnished red masses of hair.

Unexpectedly, her luscious, soft lips sought his mouth and they kissed fully. His heart flip-flopped and began hammering extraordinarily fast. He pressed the length of his full-blown bird into her warm thigh and groped a hand awkwardly, like a fumbling teenager, for her full breasts. He could feel her breath quicken as he traced her teasing nipples under the stretch fabric.

Suddenly she gasped and pushed away, rolling to the far side of the big bed and rising to her feet with one hurried motion. For a moment, she swayed uncertainly, as if gathering her composure, before saying in a hoarse, husky voice, 'I love you, Dirk, totally. You know that. More than anyone in the whole wide world. But not . . . not that way.'

He shrugged boyishly, in spite of the disappointment flooding the fires of his furnace. 'What's a little incest when you're in love?'

She laughed throatily, the tension broken, and tossed her red mane like a frisky colt. 'Incest is the only taboo I haven't broken, thank you,' she said with a lilting chuckle.

'And believe me, if I ever cross that bridge, it'll have to be you, won't it? You're the only family I've got.' She flounced with exaggerated coquetry around the closet partition and into the kitchen area.

'It's a pity,' he said dryly and pushed up to trail after her, 'that Mom and Dad didn't have any close relatives. You could have gotten over this hurdle with someone else. And come to me unhindered by such atavistic notions.'

'Atavistic,' she murmured mockingly. 'My Dirk, you *have* been hanging out with more erudite folk.' Her well-shaped ass was projecting toward him as she bent into the refrigerator. 'Hell, Dirk, I've seen more food in a refugee camp.'

He laughed heartily and slapped her firm cheeks. 'C'mon on. I'll treat you to dinner at Luchows.'

She rose, sparkling like a bubbly burgundy. 'Now *there's* brotherly love.'

They tore to the famed German restaurant on Fourteenth Street in Dirk's new toy, a bright red Ferrari Daytona, its twelve cylinders powerfully roaring them through the nearly empty streets as if lower Manhattan were their own private racetrack. They had a grand time, considering recent events, and drank many tankards of dark, strong beer, laughing a great deal, recalling happy moments from their close childhood in the San Francisco Bay area. They even shed a tear or two over their departed parents. Upon their return, Dirk carefully parked his favourite car in the underground garage of the converted warehouse which housed his loft ten floors above and, arm in arm, feeling light-headed and expansive, they took the elevator up to the top floor.

As they emerged, a slight figure stepped out of the shadows of the dimly lit hall, speaking quietly in a deep, mellow voice: 'Hi, Dirk. Sorry to show up like this without phoning first.'

It was Sweet Dew, the hermaphrodite, looking embarrassed but breathtaking in her beige cloth coat. 'Hi, Sweet,' Dirk greeted warmly, giving her a kiss on the cheek and unlocking the door. 'Meet my sister, Honey.'

'Call me, Honey, please,' Honey said, drinking in the sight of the delectable creature. 'I recognize you from Dirk's study. Mesmerizing, really. So inscrutable.'

'Oh, I'm scrutable, all right,' Sweet said and laughed shyly. 'I think you're terrific too, Honey. I never miss your column. You should be on TV, you know? You're so beautiful you'd be a big star overnight. Way bigger than Rona or Barbara Wah-wah.'

Honey trilled a pleased laugh. 'Oh, save me from that hubris. I cherish my even limited anonymity.'

'Okay, you two,' Dirk said pointedly from his open door, distinctly feeling left out of their gushing mutual admiration society. 'C'mon on in, have a nightcap. Or two. Or three . . . what the hell . . .'

He kept the music low-keyed – jazz mainly, a lot of Stan Getz and Buddy Miles – and the liquor flowing freely, scotch on ice for himself, vodka and tonic for Honey, bourbon and water for Sweet. They also indulged in copious amounts of excellent whiff and some super Indica bush from Thailand. Throughout, Honey and Sweet were getting chummier and chummier, each laughing with great gales of hysterics over everything the other said, sharing intimate details of their personal lives as if old friends, and raping each other with their eyes – in general, becoming more and more turned on by the other's tantalizing presence.

With a growing realization that he was the odd man out, Dirk sullenly watched the two beautiful beings coiled so closely on one section of the modular couch. Honey so fiery red, all soft curves and rounded femininity, and Sweet's lithe, firm limbs, her honey blonde hair like a halo of soft gold. Their body language alone bespoke their mutual and heated regard. it was not long before Honey impulsively kissed Sweet on the lips. Sweet reciprocated passionately.

Dirk's bird leapt to attention. With a firm resolve that surprised him, he forced himself to stand and moved out of the warm circle of light focused down on the intimate seating arrangement and the torridly embracing couple. Distracted, he drifted to his workbench at the far end of the studio and began fingering his various cameras absently, especially his favourites: the Nikon F-3 and Hasselblad 500 CM. Every few seconds he would sneak a glance in their direction and then reluctantly tear his gaze away, refocusing on the expensive, top-of-the-line, state-of-the-art gear spread out like a collector's showcase before him.

He thought briefly of signalling Honey somehow, giving her fair warning she was embracing a genuine freak – a beautiful one to be sure, but still a freak. But he decided to let nature take her course. Honey would find out soon enough for she had skinned off her own tight jeans and was stripping Sweet's thirties-styled dress over her honeyed hair.

As Sweet's perfectly formed, round breasts bounced into view, Honey's excited ooh's of approval drifted back to Dirk, and his hands began to tremble. Honey was skimming down Sweet's panties. He waited tensely for the expected discovery. It came with unexpected exclamations.

'How divine!' Honey cooed excitedly and stroked Sweet's little hard dickie. 'Something for everyone! You damned lucky person you. I'm positively green with envy!' With the quickness of a tiger in heat, she fell upon the tiny, distended appendage and sucked it fully into her mouth.

Dirk's own angry bird leapt in his faded jeans. In extreme frustration, he grabbed his Nikon and screwed on a 250 mm telephoto lens. From his end of the huge, open loft he began focusing it on the writhing nudes on his couch under the warm, bright light. Sweet had slipped under Honey and was lapping at the slitted trough in the fiery red fur. Concentrating fully on the image in his viewfinder, he composed a terrific shot framed by Sweet's firm raised thighs and snapped the shutter. While the film automatically advanced, he stepped closer, admiring the highlights on Honey's pale, full-cheeked ass. *Click*. Another dynamic shot. Now lowering his camera, he ventured closer, zeroing in on Sweet's fast-licking tongue catching it in mid-lick, just at the clit level. Snapping one shot after another he moved closer to the dikey duo.

They bounced off the couch and rolled onto the predominantly deep maroon Persian rug that he'd picked up for a song at ten grand in Quandahàr. Their bodies formed a vivid pattern of pale flesh on the dark background, their lusty embrace not breaking for an instant. Dirk ran softly back to his bench for a 135 mm lens and replaced the 250 rapidly, returning to find the sexy sixty-niners unchanged in their interlocked position. Only the heat had been turned up. Each was now moaning deeply, their bodies taking on a lustrous sheen from their perspiration. Their mouths and tongues worked furiously. Dirk aimed for some exciting close-ups of Honey's tongue alternating speedily back and forth between the small cock and the shallow trench in Sweet's sand-covered playbox.

With the distanced eye of the seasoned professional, Dirk continued his shots, lying flat for one, standing over and shooting down for another, backing away for a wide angle, rushing close for an especially tasty tidbit. The objectivity of his eye, however, was not shared by the one-eyed monster straining at his fly. His hot bird was so insistently demanding, he finally yanked it out and began beating on it with one hand as with the other he focused and shot, his film advancing speedily, allowing him up to six shots per second.

172

Sweet had climbed on top of the much larger, fuller-figured Honey and now lay between the raised knees, sucking at the large pale globes of Honey's beautiful breasts. Dirk crawled behind Sweet's pert dancer's ass and aimed directly into Honey's ripe, rosey snatch, catching in the lens Sweet's little hard prick dipping into the full-petaled cunt. The sight of Honey's incredibly succulent pussy snapped something in Dirk. He forgot the camera, left it on the rug, and scooted forward on his knees, his erect bird of paradise winging directly to the precious vital areas like a Geiger counter to precious metals. He slobbered spit on the bulging head and once it was thoroughly lubricated, posed it like a lance, aiming not for his first choice, nor his second, but for a close, also-ran third – Sweet's deep pink rectum.

With an uncontrollable lunge, he rammed his quivering cock into the tight target, bringing a squeal of shocked but delighted surprise to Sweet's lips. Honey buried underneath, did not know what all the squawking was about but she felt the added weight above her and correctly assumed it was butt-fucking Dirk. It pleased her knowing that her baby bro was not left out from enjoying this heavenly erotic creature who had so much going for her.

With growing fervour, Dirk pumped away in the tight asshole, relishing in the sense of fucking the fucker fucking his sister. The tight buns of Sweet slammed excitedly into his burning groin and he reached around, grabbing her tough silicone titties. Nearing a gigantic climax, he fell onto her back and she, in turn, collapsed onto Honey which pressed Dirk's hands between their smashed-together breasts, smothering his hands in boob-flesh. With a joyous growl, he began bombarding heavy loads of creamy cum into the stretched-to-straining anal canal. Looking down over Sweet's shoulder, he could see by Honey's vacantly transported gaze that she was nearing her own nirvana. He pulled his still-shooting bird out of

173

the hot, tight buns so Sweet could more freely hump Dirk's first choice. Squirting his last hot drops onto the muscled cheeks, he heard Honey's explosion rip from her throat, like the sound of distant eruptions down a deep mine shaft. It rumbled to the surface, building into a shrill shriek like a warning siren and he felt Sweet's hips quake with Honey's thrusting, bucking climax.

'I beat you both,' Sweet giggled shortly and immediately expressed a desire to fuck Dirk, who said, 'thanks but no thanks.' While Honey teased him about his 'fragile' masculinity, he walked into the bathroom to wash his cock. And to yank the roll of film from his Nikon, exposing the whole roll to the harsh bathroom lights, regretting deeply that he would never see some of the most erotic shots he had ever taken.

It wasn't until they were all in the king-sized bed – Sweet in the middle again – ready to drift off to sleep, that she remembered why she had come to visit Dirk in the first place. 'I heard from Koka,' she said apologetically. 'Meant to tell you earlier. Got sort of sidetracked, you know what I mean?'

Honey snapped on the bed lamp, asking, 'Where is she?' At the same instant, Dirk queried, 'You going to see her?'

'Koka wrote from Sri Lanka,' Sweet explained. 'Where's that?'

'Tip of India,' Honey said hurriedly. 'Formerly Ceylon.'

Sweet nodded, her green eyes sad. 'She wants me to come visit. But I can't.'

'Why not?' Honey asked.

'No bread,' Sweet sighed. 'You've no idea how little I can make dancing.'

Honey snuggled close to her newfound friend. 'Sweet? How'd you like to fly first-class to visit your beautiful black lady?'

'Would I!' Sweet exclaimed, sitting up. 'When?'

'How about first thing in the morning?'

Dirk raised to one elbow. 'You going too, Honey?'

'If Sweet says yes.'

'Yes, yes, yes,' Sweet raptured and hugged them both close. Over Sweet's shoulder, Honey winked broadly at her brother, who could only shrug a 'well you asked for it, now you've got it' gesture of resignation. Honey laughed, disappearing under the down comforter with Sweet, making it real hard on Dirk.

15

HONEY

The heavy, grey rains fell in sheets on the small, old Morris Minor taxi, making it impossible to see much of anything on the short ride from Katunayake International Airport into downtown Colombo, largest city of Sri Lanka. 'Monsoon season,' the wizened driver said dryly.

Honey had to explain what that meant to Sweet. But then, she had been explaining just about everything since they had left Dirk's apartment thirty-two hours earlier. Everything but the truth of why she was so desperately anxious to meet Koka. Honey did not know how Sweet would handle the truth. Sweet was a dear creature who had so much going for her she didn't really need to be too quick on the uptake. What she lacked in the mental area she more than made up for in genitalia. Honey adored her, felt close and protective, like an older sister. She did not want to unduly upset the kid or put a terrific trip in jeopardy by explaining the real purpose behind the quest.

And so far it *had* been a terrific trip – even the tedious

177

hours in the Bombay airport waiting for their hastily booked flight connection. Sweet was a great travelling companion – patient, warm, affectionate, able to go with the flow. Between the three of them – the two cunts and a cock – she and Sweet had been having a ball.

The moment they were shown into their booked suite at the five-star Lanka Oberor Hotel, Sweet flew to the phone to surprise Koka with a call. Honey tipped the bellboy generously and waited until he had withdrawn before attacking the dish on the mouthpiece.

She had the sweet thing's clothes off before the hotel operator had even made the connection. 'It's long distance,' Sweet whispered excitedly. 'It's ringing . . .' She jammed the receiver between her shoulder and ear to free her hands. Swiftly she unbuttoned Honey's leaf green silk blouse and slipped a cool hand inside, cupping generous breast as if appraising the weight.

'Hi, is Koka there?' she asked suddenly and withdrew her hand. Honey quickly tore off her own clothes and pulled the pliant phone-talker down onto the couch, eager to get at the wondrous *cockunt*, as she had dubbed the dual organs.

Her head wedged between the firm, dancer's thighs. Honey licked Sweet's entire perineum, from asshole to naval and back down again, barely hearing Sweet's disappointedly leaving a message for Koka to call as soon as she returned. Sweet left the name of the hotel and their suite number and hung up. Instantly, she was straddling Honey's face, kneeling, jackrabbiting up and down on Honey's stiffened tongue, stabbing her clit, jabbing her little prick, the size of a pink snail, into Honey's sculptured cheekbones.

Soon Sweet was eating Honey's sweet-meat sandwich and started coming shortly thereafter. Honey watched enviously the paroxysms of Sweet's ecstasy, jealous that the lithe firm dancer was able to have vaginal, clitoral and penile ejaculations. The lucky little stiff! Bringing off

178

those three at once created such a euphoria for Honey, she came like a clap of thunder and showered fluids like the monsoon raging outside their open windows.

The rains were still pouring several hours later as their hired chauffeur stopped the black limousine in front of Koka's address in the small town of Kandy, high in the mountains. Ducking from the pelting torrents of tropical waters, Honey and Sweet ran lightly through the puddled path and up the steep, wooden stairs leading to the plain, clapboard box-styled cottage isolated on a steep bluff.

Under the eave of the overhanging porch, they shook the water from their hair like two bitches caught in a sudden shower. Honey noticed the excited flush on Sweet's cheeks as she knocked, and was aware of her own tension and anticipation.

The black giantess herself answered the door like an African princess, wearing a long, batik gown of browns and golds. From her height of well over six feet, she looked radiantly down, her short-cropped hair hugging her scalp like a tight-fitting wool cap. Her large, soft eyes grew even larger at the sight of Honey.

She whooped melodically and swooped Honey into her strong, muscular arms, babbling with obvious joy. 'Honey! This is outrageous! Where? How? Sweet, you imp, you. You arranged this? How did you know?'

Sweet blinked in astonishment. 'You girls know each other?'

'You mean, *you* didn't know?' Koka swooned and Honey caught a faint British accent for the first time.

Honey, still under one strong, protective wing of Koka drew Sweet close. 'I'm sorry I kept it a secret,' she said gently. 'Yes, Koka and I have met before.'

Koka roared with laughter, her Amazon frame shaking. 'What an understatement, Honey. Please enter. We must get you out of those wet things.'

Honey found herself being whisked inside to a cozy,

firelit sitting room. She was puzzled by the unexpected reaction from the large lady of the video tape. There were no tensions, no projected fears of retaliation, or harboured suspicions on the part of Koka. It was plain from the effusiveness of her welcome that she dearly treasured Honey. She was clucking over them both like a mother hen, hurrying the damp dresses off their moist limbs as if her only thought were to make both of them as comfortable as possible.

Strangely, Honey did relax, basking in the rays of warmth that Koka projected and forgetting – momentarily at least – the pressing questions she still would have to ask at a later time. The more she observed the statuesque Koka, the more she found to like. While Sweet rattled on a mile a minute, telling about their whirlwind adventurous trip, Koka moved about the two-room cottage barefoot, with a feline grace, head held high, the trailing sleeves of her gown following like a pack of trained gold and brown butterflies. Graciously she administered to their needs, providing two short 'happy' coats from Japan and brewing a pot of tea on the open potbellied stove. Pulling on the short robe over her nude full figure, Honey caught Koka eyeing her openly and felt a distinct flutter between her thighs.

On an arrangement of brightly coloured, mirrored pillows from Afghanistan, the trio sat, sipping the hot strong tea. Honey quietly studied the giantess. There was an air of refined dignity that indicated education and intelligence; Koka was soft-spoken and articulate, and the exquisite taste of her simple surroundings clearly demonstrated a fine eye for beauty – a slender, black vase held a single pink rose bud on a white Chinese lacquered tea table; a collection of Oriental fans, ranging from minutely carved ivory to colourful tissue-thin paper, spread across the wall above their heads. The constant drumming of rain on the roof, the crackling fire, the coolness of the mountain air, all contributed to the cozy atmosphere.

180

'Koka,' Honey asked after a spell, 'where are you from originally? I can't place your accent.'

The beautiful, broad, black face pulled into a mock grimace. 'For shame, Honey. Don't you remember? I told you practically everything about me in Morocco.'

'I'm sorry . . . I don't recall.'

'Too much weed,' Sweet giggled. 'Eats the memory banks.'

Koka patted her hand affectionately. 'I'll tell you again a thousand times, Honey. Anything you ask.' She leaned back, her mighty breasts filling the tight bodice of her gown. 'I was born in the Bahamas. Educated primarily in England. An advanced degree in archaeology from Cambridge. That's why I'm here in Sri Lanka. I'm assistant to the head man at the digs near Dalada Maligawa.'

'The Buddhist temples of the fifth century,' Honey said with real interest. 'I've read about them. How fascinating.'

Sweet's sea green eyes looked befuddled. 'I never knew that, Koka. I thought you said you were some sort of jock.'

Koka laughed liltingly, ladylike. 'I am . . . or was. I used to throw the javelin. Amateur, strictly. But I did place fourth in Moscow.'

'You've given up athletics?' Honey asked.

'Only certain kinds, luv,' Koka said and winked, catlike. 'The indoor sports are so much more – how should I put it – rewarding?'

The overwhelming desire to see Koka in the flesh surfacing abruptly, Honey untied her sash-belt, allowing the robe to fall open. The healthy fullness of one breast slipped palely into the firelight. 'Well ladies,' she said huskily, 'do I dismiss the chauffeur for the night? Or should we head back to the city for a night out?'

Koka smiled knowingly. 'I took the liberty of sending the driver back some time ago. In the city, as the majority of the population is Buddhist, the night life is decidedly tame.'

Sweet parted her own robe casually, as if seeking more air for her tits; they popped into view as though helium filled. 'Sure as shootin' we'll find more action here.' Sexily wagging her bare, tight buns, she crawled to Honey eyeing her nose to nose. 'Wouldn't you agree, you pretty pussy, you?'

'You cocksucker,' Honey growled playfully. 'Go strip that black bitch. I want some dark meat for a change.'

Picking up the cue, Sweet obediently dog-walked to Koka and barked bravely, 'Didja hear that you big black bitch? I want you out of that dress by the time I count to five. Or I'll whip your black ass red. Understand?'

'Yeah-us, mas'ser,' Koka drawled and crawled with exaggerated laziness to her feet.

Sweet started counting; 'One . . . two . . .' Koka was hung up on a button on the back of her dress. "Three, four, five," Sweet finished in a rush. Spying a curved sword in a tooled leather scabbard, Sweet grabbed it from the wall and whipped out the blade. Brandishing both above her head, she advanced menacingly on the towering black beauty. Koka struggled free of her dress and dropped it, displaying her bountiful goodies.

Honey's breath caught in her throat. The video tape had not done the lady justice. In the flesh, Koka was truly magnificent, like an African queen carved out of lustrous ebony. In the firelight, her deep black skin rippled like that of a panther; muscles and tendons were graceful yet undeniably powerful just under the glowing surface. Her bush was full, thick, like the foliage of the deepest jungle. Her legs were immensely long, sleek, her womanly hips high, as were her breasts, which jutted out from her torso like huge polished black pearls.

Sweet threw the gleaming sword into a corner and, slapping the leather sheath into one palm, sneered effectively. 'On your knees, you slow, clumsy cow. I'm going to whip you good.'

'Oh, no, no,' Koka whined in a high-pitched charade of Liza crossing the ice floe. But she dropped to her knees, facing Honey, who sprawled open her pale thighs, displaying her bright red pelt like the fur of a baby fox.

Sweet raised high the scabbard and brought it down with a solid *thwack* on Koka's bare buttocks. 'Bloody hell!' Kola exploded. 'That really hurt, you two-bit cunt.' With a mighty heave, she crashed a broad shoulder into Sweet's legs, tackling and driving her into the pillows next to Honey. Easily she sat on Sweet's belly and folded her arms across her bouncing black breasts, intoning dramatically, 'Too black for heaven and yet too white for hell.'

Honey identified the quote quickly: 'Dryden. From the 'Hind and the Panther,' Right? How does the rest –'

Koka's strong arm snaked out and hooked Honey's startled head, clamping on a modified hammerlock and twisting her neck just to the point of danger. 'Don't condescend to me, you honky trash,' she hissed into Honey's upended ear. 'Now suck me, you pile of pale shit.'

'You contumely cunt, let go of me,' Honey snorted and struggled valiantly to pull the muscled arm from her throat.

Her struggles were useless. Like handling a rubber doll, the ebony giantess forced Honey's head sideways and flat onto Sweet's rib cage a few inches from the inky foreskin between her magnificently muscled thighs. 'Let's see if you remember that,' Koka growled, 'you fucking forgetful bitch.' She shoved Honey's nose into her pitch black fur, burying it deep into the coffee-coloured layered lips.

Honey inhaled deeply the musky odour of coconuts and slid her nose up the moist channel. It bumped into the biggest clit she had ever found – bigger than Sweet's pink prick, it rose from the mocha-coloured reef like a proud beige lily, stately and majestic as Koka herself.

Honey could not believe she had forgotten such a wonderful unique feature of such a gorgeously unique person. With a lusty roar, she impaled her mouth upon it, inhaling it fully, flicking the bonelike tip with her talented tongue.

'I'm feeling excluded,' Sweet wailed and wiggled beneath Koka's hips. 'For cryin' outloud, give *me* something to eat!'

Koka's strong thighs lifted her up from off Sweet's midsection and Honey's head followed the upward movement, her mouth firmly attached to the most titillating clit she had yet to discover in her many adventures. It so fascinated her, she was only vaguely conscious that Koka's large hands were moving her ass around, bringing it over Sweet's honey-coloured head. Only when Sweet began her own lingual digs at her already-dripping pussy did Honey realize that she was receiving tremendous satisfaction in two of her three ports of call. Sweet promptly inserted a wet, stiff finger up Honey's asshole satisfying the third area of gratification. Honey quickly filled with pumping juices.

Koka began caterwauling like a mare stuck in quicksand. Suddenly Honey's mouth was being washed out with a thick, sweet pudding of deliciously creamy cum. The enormous quantity filled her mouth to overflowing. Sweet was crescendoing beneath them and picked up the speed of both her swollen tongue in Honey's twitching twat and her reaming finger in Honey's aroused anus. Sweet spit her mouthful of pearly cum onto the thick jungle bush, then tongued it off, licking her lips, savouring the tasty, sweet treat like a gourmet cook. Gradually, Honey eased into one of the gentlest, most satisfying and lengthy orgasms of her life. It seemed to roll on forever, lifting her up, soaring her into blissful space like on a cloud white hang-glider.

They slept curled together on the mirrored pillows before the dying embers. Each of their bodies – ebony black, honeyed gold, and pale alabaster – was truly a work of art. Each was clothed in her own special beauty – from the firm trimness of Sweet, to the soft, voluptuousness of Honey, to the reposed strength of the giantess Koka. Dirk would have had a field day with his camera, Honey mused before she fell asleep deeply, exhaustedly, contentedly to the sound of the hard-falling rain.

In the morning, she eased awake with both her face and her loins burning fiercely. A shaft of bright hot sunlight lay across her pillow, and Koka's black-cropped head bobbed between her thighs, savagely sucking her inflamed pussy. Sweet slept on beside them, unaware of the delectable doings of the dexterous duo.

Wanting another round with Koka's fabulous clit, Honey awoke in a flash and scooted down to seek out its satisfying length. With the firm conviction of knowing what she liked, she wrapped her tongue around the abnormal appendage and teased the hard nail unmercifully. Koka's mighty arms pulled Honey's frame over, pressing their full breasts together in friendly greetings, their black and white globes equally matched, melting and mashing together, their hard nipples smashing into soft, buoyant flesh.

Koka, on her back on the carpet, swung around to bring her face up to Honey's. They kissed with increased fervour, tongues inserted, sweeping the roof of each other's mouth. The large black hands pushed Honey's hips down so they were cunt to cunt, bristly black bush to silky red. Honey could feel the throbbing head of Koka's giant clit probing into her unfurled twat and then gasped with extreme pleasure as it landed on her own love button.

They ground and mauled their clits together and Honey felt strangely small lying on the giant, hard-coiled muscles. The tantalizing turmoil building in her feverish pussy swept her unrelentingly over the dam. She burst. Losing herself in the jubilation of the joyous morning treat, Honey came and came again, pounding her clit

185

against the hard, stubby pencil, rubbing her juices into Koka's healthily squirting squawk-box. It was a sensational way to wake up.

After showering together, they sat nude, drying off in the warm sun on the wood steps of the back porch, sipping strong black coffee and watching the mists rise from the deep, lush valley below. As far as Honey could see there were green, tropical forests, rugged mountains, blue skies and fleecy white clouds. It was so incredibly beautiful, as was her partner, that Honey felt at peace and very secure. She decided it was time to tell Koka the truth about their wild torrid Sunday afternoon in Morocco. Quietly she began, telling of her inability to remember anything about that afternoon and of the video tape's implied threat, of her discovery of *shitka*, even of her fears of exposure and ridicule.

The exquisite black face listened attentively, sympathetically and when Honey's narration had dwindled to silence, Koka pulled her close in a sisterly embrace. 'I had no idea,' she said softly. 'Kola and I were positive you had entered into that scene with full awareness. Willingly. Even eager. You were so damned hot and beautiful we couldn't believe our good fortune.'

'Kola?'

'My twin brother,' Koka explained with a sidelong glance. 'You poor dear, you don't remember him either?'

The mouth-watering image of the black stud's enormous thick cock, like a burnt log, filled Honey's mind. 'Only from the video tape,' she murmured with a smile, then grew serious again. 'Do you know who arranged that afternoon?'

'Kola said that *you* had. I wouldn't have done it otherwise.'

'And the little man who taped it?' Honey asked, remembering Dirk's report from Morocco. 'Where might I find him?'

186

'Kola might know.'

'Where is your brother?'

'In Spain. Working on a film.'

'What is he? An actor?'

Koka laughed heartily. 'To be sure. A ham since birth.'

'A black ham,' Honey mused and hugged her new friend. 'Do you think you could wire Kola I'd like to visit him?'

'I'll do better than that. I've a four-day holiday due me. I'll take you there personally.'

'Terrific!' She smothered the broad face with grateful kisses. 'Now let's go in and wake that little bitch up.'

Laughing, they pranced nude into the cottage and leaped upon the warm pile of Sweet.

16
HONEY

Kola turned out to be an even more magnificent hunk of man-flesh than Honey had dared hope. A true fraternal twin to his equally-as-stunning sister. His mammoth bulging muscles, tightly packed into a baby blue leisure suit, the white of his sports shirt worn wide over his lapels, Kola met them at the Madrid airport and hustled them into a gleaming white '76 Cadillac convertible for a hair-raising ride through the crowded streets and out into the rustic, dry countryside.

As he raced the car up toward the mountains, Kola waved his giant hands expansively, his handsome, broad face as animated as a child's, explaining his small but vital character of a runaway slave in the spaghetti western being shot. Everything he said had so much enthusiasm behind it, and he talked for so long, Honey did not have a chance to ask what was plaguing her. Besides, the bewitching bulge of his basket was so captivatingly monstrous, she had a devil of a time keeping her mind out of his pants. He also kept handing her jay after jay of such heady Afghani Cannabis Ruderalis, she was reeling by the time they reached their destination, the tiny town of Cuenca.

Following a winding canyon road along the river Jucar, Kola pulled the Caddy to a stop and waved a hand upward. 'Casas Caplgadas,' he rumbled. The three of them craned their necks, following the sheer stone cliff far above to the multistoried, doll-like houses poised over the abyss as if pardoned momentarily from plunging to their doom.

'Your film is Italian?' Honey asked, dizzy from looking up in her stoned state. 'Shot in Spain? About the Old West?'

'Yup, reckon you're right there, ma'am,' he teased.

Honey shook her Titian waves. 'Where in the Old West was there a place like this?'

Booming a laugh, he started the car. 'Dramatic licence.'

'More like flights of fuckin' fancy,' she said dryly.

Proudly, boyishly, Kola showed them around some of the locales in the tiny cliff-village being used for the film. The whole cast and crew had gone into Madrid for the bullfights, leaving the constructed set-fronts of a typical western street deserted and windswept. The desert mountain air was tinted with pine and pitch. And it was hot. 'This is more like it,' Kola observed as they trudged through the dust. 'At least, my impressions of what the Old West was like.'

'Like my impressions,' Honey quipped. 'All from the movies.'

Kola stopped before a set of swinging louvred doors straight out of 'Gunsmoke.' 'Just yesterday we wrapped a scene of mine in here. I'll show you what I had to do.'

They followed him into a large, naturally lit room decorated not as a saloon but as a plush bedroom of a fancy bordello – red flocked wallpaper, a crystal chandelier and

190

an enormous antique bed with filigree brass head- and foot-boards. Kola, eyeing the big bed, straightened her bodice. 'Was this scene X-rated, brother?'

He rolled his eyes wickedly. 'Not the way it'll be shown.'

Honey knew an opening when she heard one. 'Kola, do show us what you had to do.'

Enthusiastically he tore off his leisure jacket and stripped off his shirt. His firmly packed muscles rippled like torrents of black water, dazzling Honey with their definition and power. 'My character,' he began, all energy, 'escapes from a chain gang and takes refuge in this whorehouse. The madame is in cahoots with the villain – who's after me – and I . . .' He paused, flashing an ingratiating grin at his sister. 'Koka, you play the madame, okay? You enter through that far door.'

'Sure 'nuff, boss,' she replied and sashayed out.

'Honey, you play the whore with the heart of gold.'

'Tra-lah,' she trumpeted. 'What's my motivation?'

'You try to help me by –'

'Honey! Come here a sec!' Koka squealed.

Honey hurried into the small, adjacent room. Koka had found a rack of costumes, and was slipping out of her clothes. Soon she was wiggling into a tight Merry-Widow corset over net stockings, while Honey, who had doffed her travelling ensemble, was tugging on a revealing short chemise over her bare, bosomy torso, wrapping a large, red feather boa around her neck. In appropriate costume, they emerged giggling, arm in arm, vamping like a couple of street tramps.

'Well, *all* right,' Kola drawled, raking his eyes over their scantily concealed breasts. 'I guess I'd better get in costume, too.' He began unfastening his belt.

Trying to be nonchalant, Honey watched in fascination as he shucked off his baby-blue tight pants and stood in his even tighter, white jockey shorts. His bulky soft bundle of black goodies was clearly outlined under the thin cotton

191

material and his colossal thighs were like carbon pillars. Making certain he had their undivided attention, he beamed a smile and punched the white shorts off his narrow hips, dropping them and shaking them free with his feet.

His Cyclopean cock, even though semi-soft, was the most glorious Honey had ever seen. Thick, titanic, coal black, it hung under his kinky pubes like a slab of smoked bacon on a furry meat-hook. His gonads swayed heavily, the size of tennis balls, and she had the undeniable urge to begin swatting at them.

Koka smirked at her brother's bareness. 'And you told me they'd cast you for your acting talent.'

He chuckled, pointedly staring at Honey's hardening nipples beneath her thin chemise. His whacking prick jumped a notch. 'All kinds of talent, sister.'

'Okay, Kola,' Koka japed, 'what's this scene you had?'

As if at the very thought his elephantine cock jerked to half-mast. 'I'm hiding in the bed of the goodhearted whore, and we're getting along splendidly when the evil madame appears.'

'Oh, shit,' Koka grumbled. 'Another heavy? I played *that* last night.'

'*And*,' Kola said, drawing it out to gain centre stage again, 'the evil madame tries to detain me until the villain comes.'

'Goodie,' his sister camped. 'I was hoping I got to bash you up a bit.'

His ponderous prick had reached the top of the flagpole and bulged out at them like an average man's fist and stiff forearm. 'Woman,' he roared to his sister, 'get your buns in the other room. This scene is rolling. Right now!' With a forceful wave of an inky muscled arm, he motioned Honey on top of the bare mattress. Willingly, breathlessly, she climbed aboard. His voluminous peter visibly throbbing, the plump veins pumping away, as he waited for his sister to saunter out. She flippantly flipped her black-muscled cheeks under the tightly cinched corset and left the room. 'Okay,' he barked. '*Action!*'

With a belly dive, he leaped upon the bed. His heavy landing *crashed* the antique bed to the floor and busted bed-springs. A cloud of choking dust mushroomed around them. Over their gasping and coughing, spewing and sputtering, Koka's burst of unrestrained laughter filtered in to them. 'Shut your fat mouth, sister,' Kola shouted in the dusty air. '*Action!*'

Honey was beside herself both coughing and laughing at the same time. At once she felt his enormous hands grab at her soft breasts like panicked lobsters. She winced – he definitely did not know his own strength. In return, she groped for his big balls, but could not get both of them in one hand, so settled for giving one hulking testicle an equally determined squeeze – if he were a lobster, she was at least a crab.

He howled in displeasure but loosened his grip on her full tits, immediately replacing his hands with his lips. His generous mouth around a breast, he sucked it in, almost swallowing it. She clamped onto his mighty cock, finding she could not get her fingers around its entire thickness. The thundering skin was so hot and hard it felt hewn from fevered marble. She measured its gigantic length with a hand-span and had to add a second before she touched the moisture oozing out of the nickle-sized slit of the pachydermatous head. When she tried to suck it, even with her mouth stretched open to its fullest, her teeth scraped the thick skin and she was able only to get the corpulent crown inside. The only action she could give him, without abrading him raw, was to undulate her tongue under the bulbous ridges.

By the time the dust had settled in the hot dry air, Kola had lifted her up like a child and turned her hips over his face. Into her steaming petals, he injected a stiff tongue that seemed the size of a normal cock. Like a jackhammer, she jerked her passionate pussy up and down on the hard meat of his tongue.

He yanked it out of her tortured twat and croaked, 'You're the hottest cunt in the whole damn world. I'm going to lick your humpy ass.' His slippery clapper slid up to her asshole, reamed her thoroughly and then slathered the full cheeks of her soft ass.

Everywhere he put his beefy warm tongue, she felt electrified. Both fists around his burning black log, she pumped furiously. His tongue was back into her juice-sluice and her chiming clit responded to its flutter like a tuning fork, vibrating her entire body, and raising the pitch of her crotch to C above high C.

At once, she felt herself in the air again. He pushed her up by her hips, held her aloft, deftly swung her around like a dripping mobile and set her fiery bush down on the iron of his one-legged stool. She leaned back into his raised thighs and with her feet flat, she kissed her full-flowered pussy lips to his fist-sized head. Caution thrown to the heated wind, insatiable lust driving her on, she squeezed down on it, inch by inch, lowering herself, wanting to get as much as possible of the mighty instrument into her demanding, hungry cunt. Stretched to the verge of discomfort, she felt the steel-ribboned sides of the massive prick scraping and pushing at the walls of her love trough like an overly inflated dirigible. Its magnitudinous meat reached the top of her chomping channel and ploughed onward, forging a new canal, pushing up into her empty stomach cavity. She froze, literally ready to bust a gut, and rose up a bit, easing the annoying thickness down to bearable levels.

Reaching below her filled-to capacity twat, she felt to see how much of his stout pole she had been unable to cram inside. The unswallowed length astonished her. Several inches remained outside like a long line at the box office for a standing-room-only hit. Infused as she was with his quivering strength, she felt giddy, the voracious-

194

ness of her vaginal victory vomited her into a swirling vortex. She did not need to move a centimetre, for his throbbing cock, which seemed to be panting inside, whirlpooled her into a whopper of a climax. So tightly was her pussy mouth plugged, there was no room for escape for the fluids she so healthily gushed. With some alarm, she felt her barricaded tunnel pump past its limit.

Dizzily she raised her hips to pull off the plump plunger. A giant sucking sound erupted as his long, fat tool uncorked completely and a thick shower of her sticky cum baptized his cock for the second time.

'You black bastard!' his sister screeched in character, and jumped upon them like an enraged mountain lioness. Caught in the middle of thrashing hard limbs and muscled blows, Honey weakly rolled free, still panting from her magnitudinous coming, her pussy already sore, feeling devoid and depleted.

The mock fight of Koka and Kola evolved rapidly into an all-out sibling battle. Their powerful, sleek bodies slammed into each other, their muscles bunched and released, their black skin shone with the sheen of sweat. Koka proved surprisingly strong against her brother, her agility even greater, her long, strong legs coiled like pythons around his trunk, her glistening, sinewy arms fighting fiercely for advantage, her shapely breasts heaving.

With amazement, Honey watched the two evenly matched Herculean giants wrestling furiously beside her. She did not dare join into their roughhousing for fear of being severely clobbered. With a grunt of great power, Kola flipped his sister onto her back and fell between her legs. His hard cock poised for an instant like a trained seal, then with a mighty thrust plunged to the hilt inside Koka's commodious canal.

Honey's mouth fell open. Koka's kinky-covered cunt had swallowed the horrific hard-on as easily as a baby devouring gumdrops. The brother and sister were now

195

bucking and humping with so much force and power, Honey was thrown from the mattress onto the dusty floor. She leaned her chin on the bouncing edge of the bed and watched wide-eyed. Like a clash of Goliaths, the two thundered to a finish, roaring their mutual climax as if in their final death throes. At the last instant, Kola pulled out his ebony swagger-log and shot huge snowballs of cum the entire length of Koka's long torso. They splattered and broke on her chin, like eggs, dripping onto her bountiful black pearl treasures.

'Bravo! Brava!' Honey cried and applauded wildly deeply envious of their incestuously arousing behaviour. 'Cut! Print!'

Later that night, on a breezy terrace, after a scrumptious dinner of spicy lamb stew and over many glasses of *resol* – a local liqueur made of pure spirits, coffee, cinnamon, orange peel essence and sugar – Honey told Kola the truth about their Moroccan ménage à trois.

He shook his handsome head with obvious surprise. 'I was told when I was hired that *you* had arranged the entire scene. That you wanted to make some lover jealous.'

'The little man with the big suitcase?' she asked quickly. 'Did he hire you?'

'No. He just showed up with his equipment and set to work. Never said a word, did he, Koka? Honey, you were already in the room when we arrived.'

Honey stared from one to the other of their strikingly handsome faces, her pulse beginning to pound, her keen nose for the essence of a story beginning to twitch. '*Who* hired you then?'

He hesitated and caught his sister's eye apologetically. 'I've been supporting myself off and on by doing fuck films.' His sister stopped toying with her glass and began to watch his face impassively. He smiled uneasily and continued. 'I'd done a few for this one guy. Couple hundred bucks a day, tops, got it? Then one day, he calls and offers me two grand. But I had to provide a black chick and pay her.'

Koka's nostrils flared. 'You bastard, you gave me five hundred.'

He ducked his head, a guilty lad. Honey blurted out. 'So who the hell is the guy? The dude that hired you?'

'The King of Pornos,' Kola responded. 'No lie, that's what he's known as. Evidently he's some cracked mega-millionaire who digs fuck films. He puts up his own money and has made them by the hundreds. For his own pleasure first. And then, when he's tired of them, he dumps them on the market and screens a new batch.'

'Where is he?' she asked tensely. 'What's his name?'

'I don't know where he is. I've never seen him personally. Out of the blue, wherever I am, he'll phone. He tells me how much, where and when. That's it. The money's wired to anywhere I want.'

'His name then? His name!'

'Won Fat Hi.'

'Chinese?'

'Who knows? On the phone, he sure sounds Western to me.'

'How far west?'

'L.A.'

She nodded abruptly and swept to her feet, a beautiful bundle of fiery red energy. 'Excuse me. I must phone my brother.'

offers are two-a-pant. But I tried to persuade asked, chide
and pay her."

Kate's mouth firmed. "You bitch-I, you gave in-live
birthday."

He ducked his head, a guilty look. He a... blamed Yuri.
"So who the hell is the guy? The GRU that hired you?"

The King of Potholes Kah responded. "No he, that's
what his... known... Evidently he's some cracked rich
millionaire who dies look think. He puts up an own money
and has made them by the purchases. For his own profit
first. And then, when he's rid of them, he dumps them
off the market and scoops a new batch."

"Where is he?" she asked tensely. "What's his name?"
"I don't know where he is. I've never seen but personally. Out of the line, wherever I am, by the phone. He bills
me line much, where and when. That's all. The money's
wired to an overseas I want."

"He came about his name?
"Won PU Tz.?"

"Won?"

"Wing maybe? On the phone, he sure sound Wasem"
he said.

"Huy Phu er?"

She nodded numbly, and swept to her feet, a bundled
bundle of leaving energy. "If it me on, I must phone the
brother..."

17

DIRK

It took Dirk forty straight hours of excruciating persistence to track down the King of Porno. For over a full, frustrating day, Dirk had spun his wheels, getting nowhere fast, checking and rechecking, calling, hassling in person, even bribing in a few cases, every New York dealer, distributor, director, producer, performer – anyone who had been or was now involved in the underground pornography market. His many legit contacts around the world also had been unable to come up with even so much as an educated guess. Dirk had persevered, however, both for his own and Honey's peace of mind.

Then – bingo! Pay dirt. An anonymous male had called, wanted five grand delivered to a specific locker in the midtown YMCA, promising the address of Won Fat Hi. Dirk, at the end of his tether, begrudgingly had complied with the demand and had returned to his Soho loft to sit by the phone. Within an hour, the caller had phoned back, thanked him for the prompt delivery and had relayed the sought-for address. Within two hours, Dirk was on a direct flight to Bangkok.

Wringing wet now – both from the excessive humidity and heat as well as from a serious attack of nerves – Dirk alighted from the taxi on a quiet, residential canal in an exclusive section of the city, and strode purposefully toward the high, brass-bound, massive, teak gates set in the tall masonry walls surrounding the estate. Ignoring the sign printed in several languages warning against unsolicited visitors, he pulled the rope and heard in the far distance the answering *bong* of a muted, heavy bell. He waited.

Shortly, a tiny peephole opened and a pair of femininely enticing eyes, bewitching in their blackness, peered out. Slipping his printed card in through the slot, he said, 'I'd like to speak with Won Fat Hi.'

She read the card and voiced in a hushed tone, 'One moment, please.' The peephole closed and again he waited

Close to twenty minutes later, a small doorway in the heavy teak gates opened. He ducked inside. A lovely Thai girl of no more than fifteen, dressed in a traditional long gown of pale yellow silk, gazed up at him with friendly curiosity and whispered, 'This way, please.' He followed the vision in pale yellow, her jet black hair bound back in a tight bun, through a luxuriant, tropical garden ablaze with vivid blooms and towering stand of bamboo. Already he felt cooler. The canal glimmered through a stand of coco trees. A series of large, dark tea houses came into view, connected by walkways covered with blooming wisteria. Through an open doorway they entered the central house, larger than the rest, and the lovely, black-eyed girl disappeared, leaving him alone in the breeze-cooled entry.

For close to a half hour, he studied the intricate detail of an antique Oriental tapestry that stretched at least thirty feet along one wall, before another young vision of beauty, perhaps a year older, wearing a long, peach-coloured silk dress with puffed butterfly-wing sleeves, appeared and smiled. 'This way.'

They moved through several large, elegantly furnished rooms abounding with priceless Oriental antiques and finally into a smaller, Western-appointed, denlike room. A UCLA banner hung over the Panasonic stereo unit. 'Please wait here.' Like the former black-haired, will-o'-the-wisp, she withdrew silently.

He lowered his tall frame into the comfortable, leather Chesterfield and again waited. This time for a shorter period. The far door opened and still a third young woman, even more breathtaking than the last, entered, announcing quietly, 'Won Fat Hi.'

The King himself strode in, looking like he had just stepped off the links of any American club – wearing a white-knit Lacoste shirt, double-knit, dark blue slacks, white patent-leather Gucci loafers, and a red Brooks Brothers fibre belt. He was perhaps fifty, with balding grey hair and a small, round, Oriental face with thick glasses that made his eyes look larger. 'Mister Wildon,' he said without a trace of accent. 'My pleasure.' They shook hands vigorously and Won Fat beamed. 'Want a drink?'

'No thanks. What I'd like is some information.'

A tiny hand waved away his request, a diamond pinky ring flashing. 'First pleasure. Then business.' Won Fat poured a healthy gin and tonic for himself and came to sit opposite. 'I am deeply honoured, Mister Wildon. I have been an admirer of your art for years.'

'Thanks.'

'I wonder if you'd be so kind as to sign your last book for me?' Reaching behind him to the bookshelves, he pulled out the large, coffee-table-sized collection of pictorial studies.

'Delighted,' Dirk said and signed the inside cover with

201

a nearly illegible signature, adding above it, 'With Thanks for your Warm Hospitality.'

That seemed to please the little king. As he thumbed through the photos, they chatted briefly about inconsequential matters, such as Dirk's choice of camera or lens or who a specific model was and where did he find her. At one point, Won Fat looked above his glasses slyly. 'May I ask? Is it true you have slept with each of these women?'

Dirk smiled cagily. 'My lips are sealed.'

'But not your fly,' Won Fat chuckled and Dirk laughed. He had been expecting a gross, uncouth man not this epitome of Oriental correctness and good humour.

The hall door opened quietly and in came two more delicious dark-eyes creatures in long silk gowns of pale green and powder blue, floating forward with pounded brass trays layered with edible treats and delicacies. Leaving the trays on a mosaic tea table, the girls slipped out but not before exchanging sultry glances with Dirk. He followed their exit with aching eye and low balls. 'You certainly have a bevy of your own beauties, Won Fat.'

'Please, call me by my real first name. Attaporn.'

'Attaporn?'

The round face grinned broadly. 'A very common name here in Thailand. I changed it when I was in your country. Four years at UCLA. A bachelor's degree in economics,' he said proudly.

'Is that a fact? I went one semester to USC, across town. Before getting kicked out,' Dirk said, nibbling a rice and fish concoction wrapped in a strip of banana leaf. 'But then, I was kicked out of every school. Seventeen in all.'

'For what reasons?'

'Little bit of everything. At USC it was for "incorrigible and promiscuous behaviour." '

Attaporn laughed merrily. 'Rebel without a cause?'

'Oh, no. I had a cause. Still do. Beautiful women.'

'Ahhh, yes. I myself share that cause. A worthy one to be sure.' He munched thoughtfully and then, 'What brings you to me?'

Dirk hesitated. 'I have a sister, Honey. Terrific lady. Through no fault of her own, against her permission, she ended up in one of your video tape productions. She's going through a personal hell because of it. Me too. So I'm trying to find out why. That's all. Why was it done? I understand you arranged it.'

The enlarged eyes in the gold-framed glasses remained unreadable. 'Is Honey Wildon, the journalist, your sister?' As Kirk nodded, Won Fat leaned forward. 'A very talented family. I am a faithful reader of her column. In fact, I am a true fan.'

'Thank you. But I'd like –'

'Pardon me, why do you feel *I* had anything to do with this affair?'

'Kola – the black actor – said you'd hired him.'

Won Fat stood slowly, as if suddenly tired. 'You must forgive me if I do not continue this discussion at the present time.' He pushed a small button by the door. 'Your needs will be attended to. I must see to mine.' He withdrew quickly.

Almost at once, another young woman, older than the others, all of twenty-one and incredibly more beautiful than the last two, glided into the room with a gracious smile. 'This way, please.'

Dirk was led by the stunning vision in a long, pale rose silk dress to the rear portion of an adjacent house and into a room that opened through wide-sliding panels onto a garden of absolute perfection. A white lily bloomed near an ancient bronze bell. A bamboo wind chime tinkled intermittently. In the centre of the room, the floor of which was wooden slats, there was a large, wooden tub of steaming water. 'Please remove your clothes,' the beautiful Thai woman said. 'I will fetch the others.' She slipped out.

Not certain what was up, but definitely interested in whatever it was, Dirk struggled out of his damp clothes and stood waiting, nakedly anxious. A panel door slid back and all six of the lovely, fragile, graceful young women came into the room in flowing robes of flowery embroidered silk. Wordlessly they looked at him as if he were a visiting dignitary. He grinned back, trying to control the stirring interest of his long-dormant shlong. With a rustle of falling silk, the mesmerizing young women emerged from their robes and revealed six beautiful, slim bodies – like a holograph illustration of the varying stages of womanhood. Almost exactly alike in size and colouring, they were so perfect, so enchanting in the delicate femininity, he had difficulty breathing. Their breasts, though small, were like soft blooming orchids and the black triangles between their legs were like patches of welcoming moss on riverbanks. His bird began to raise its pesky head to take its own look at them.

Moving delicately as a team, they hung up the robes and led him to a three-legged stool. They brought forth wooden buckets of warm water, which they poured over his head. Next, the delectable beings produced large bars of brown, rough soap and, each taking a different section of his long frame, began soaping him thoroughly. Enchanted by the soft touch of their small, diligent hands, Dirk luxuriated in the sensual scrubbing, the sweet smell of honeysuckle from the soap and the delicate features of each of the precious girls. The one in charge of his groin casually pushed aside his now full-grown bird and lathered his pubic hair and balls before stroking his hard length with a gentle scrubbing action. He was urged to his feet and bent over, while still another washed his ass and cleansed his anus.

Soon he was covered from head to toe with the sweet-smelling lather, and buckets of warm water were thrown on him as if cooling down a racehorse. His bird bobbed and bounced under the force of the falling water. Once rinsed, he was led to the tub. Slowly he eased himself into the deep, steaming water.

Next, the sextet of magical Eurasian beauties fell to washing and lathering each other, their soft voices giggling and chattering in Thai. Up to his neck in hot water, he grinned from one to another of them, drinking in their tantalizing beauty like a man parched in the desert, surreptitiously tugging on his boiling bird. Soon, one by one, they were rinsed and climbed into the tub, ringing the inside edge like a garland of exotic flowers. As much as he yearned to reach out under the water to touch and fondle – just one of them would do – he forced himself to refrain, not wanting to offend his host. Certainly not before he got some answers.

They soaked silently in the tub; the heads of the six beauties floated above the surface like black-capped water lilies, each a stunning beauty, each a face he would have given anything to photograph – even more to fuck. Just when he thought his cock would pop from so much hidden hand-jive, the young women started climbing out, flashing so many split-beavers, and he had to close his eyes for fear of being rude with his pointed, heated staring.

Once outside the tub, they rubbed him down with large soft towels and tugged him gently into another room. This one was almost completely dark and blessedly cool after the steaming tub room. As his eyes grew accustomed to the darkness, again he felt their gentle hands on every portion of his anatomy – they were rubbing musk oil into his skin, which began to tingle with warm fire. His hard prick was the last to be rubbed and the small hand that anointed his bird-head with oil lingered longer than necessary to complete the simple task. Just to be friendly he jerked his cock up and down in her hands and heard a soft giggle.

Again he was tugged forward and laid on a bed covered with cool, white silk. He felt the bed give and dip as all six climbed on. He lay very still, with baited breath, intoxicated by the sweet aroma of his own oiled skin, and anticipation . . .

Softly he felt their hands begin to touch and probe his body, exploring every inch of it in the dark as if in Braille, their gentle exhalations the only sound. Except for his heart, which hammered so loudly he was certain they would hear. One was clasping his oiled and ready prong as if about to peel a banana. As soon as the soft lips touched his panting prick, he reached out in the darkness to grab whatever his hands could find. Soft, pliant but firm young flesh greeted his every grope. With the fingers of one hand fondling a pair of small fresh breasts and his other hand searching the soft folds of unmistakable pussy-lips, his entire body reeled with erotic sensations.

Over his grinning face a pair of slim hips lowered, bringing a set of moist magnolia lips onto his mouth. Blissfully he lapped at its tender entrance. Even his bare feet were not being neglected, for each was being rubbed against soft pussy fur. He wiggled his toes, relishing in the springing softness, probing like an armless doctor. Soon he had a tight little cunt wedged firmly on each big toe, and his thumbs had slipped into juicy sweet-meats, like Little Jack Horner. Even his tongue had a hard on and poked into the delicious depths of the one on his face.

His pumping cock was the last to be enveloped by a warm tiger lily. Gingerly one sat on its oiled and saliva-slicked head and shoved it in with astonishing grace. With a joyous vengeance he set to work – his hands, his feet, his mouth and his cock all lost in the darkness of hidden, hot-house, horticultural exotics. He felt as though he were one giant prick inside one enormous wet, writhing pussy hole. This has to be heaven, he thought ecstatically just before his overly stimulated senses took over completely.

Dirk was so energetically fucking and sucking, toeing and thumbing, he was completely unaware that the lights of the room had begun to dim upward gradually, ever so gradually. His cock felt like an electric eel, ready to discharge its high voltage. Time inched on with the warm, heady moisture from overheated pussies increasing on and around him. Until, one by one, with soft modest moans, he sensed the girls coming. His buried toes and thumbs were given a hot bath not unlike the one in the tub room. He waited, grittily holding off his own electrical discharge until the one over his mouth trickled her tasty cum in to his throat. Then with the eagerness of the long-denied, he slapped his hips hard, driving his long hot eel into the little love cave, and exploded with such force he thought his balls had been blown to smithereens.

Only when his eyes fluttered open was he aware that the room was abnormally bright.

The reason for the brightness was not revealed to him until he had rejoined Won Fat Hi some time later. Refreshed, relaxed, dehorned and fully dressed in clothes that had been dried and pressed, Dirk had been ushered into another room of the large teak house, where his host sat before a large, blank TV screen. 'Did you enjoy your nap?' Won Fat, a.k.a. Attaporn, asked.

'Greatly. Thanks.'

'Care to see an instant replay?' With that, Won Fat turned on the set and Dirk stared in sickened amazement at the video-tape image unreeling before him. From several camera angles, including an effective high, over-head shot, the entire episode with the six fucking beauties had been captured with glowing colour and precision detail. Dirk squirmed watching himself surrounded and servicing the luscious lovelies. His white body looked like a newly-split rail fence holding six, bouncing sparrows.

Won Fat let it run to the last drop of cum and shut the tape off. 'Not bad, Mister Wildon. If you ever decide to do this professionally, let me know.'

'Then you *are* the King of Porno,' Dirk said angrily.

'I admit nothing,' the Oriental said mysteriously. 'Obscene material is forbidden in Thailand.'

'What was that then?' Dirk asked defensively. 'A Buddhist ritual?'

A slow, inscrutable smile creased the round face. 'Merely my daughters' ablutions.'

'Your daughters?'

'Lovely, are they not? Their mother was Japanese. Even lovelier.'

'I'll be damned.'

'Yes, you most likely are.' Won Fat fell silent. When he spoke again, his voice had lost its veneer of politeness. 'If any harm or damage comes from the information I am about to impart, I will see that this tape is reproduced a hundred thousand times and distributed to every adult theatre and motel in the world.'

In spite of the sudden, mushy lump in his stomach, Dirk shot back, 'Won't that be embarrassing to you *and* them?'

'It would never touch us. We never leave this compound. And *will* never.'

Dirk studied the little man, weighing his limited options. Like Honey, his fun and games ended abruptly at exhibitionism. Finally, he sighed. 'Okay. I promise no harm will come from it.'

The enigmatic smile returned. 'Excellent. The answer you are seeking does not reside here. I only provided Kola as requested. I had no idea – believe me – why his services were requested. I merely returned a small favour by delivering him. If I had known your sister was to have been a victim, I would not have become involved.'

'Who set it up then?'

'The director. A man of great talent. Perhaps even a genius.'

'And his name?'

'Angus Snead. He lives in north Scotland somewhere.'

'By chance is this Snead . . . a little man with a big suitcase?'

208

Won Fat nodded stoically. 'Yes. Mister Snead *is* a dwarf. A very talented dwarf.'

'Thank you, Attaporn,' Dirk said genuinely, and stood. 'I promise I am only interested in who's behind all this.'

'Revenge is not becoming to anyone.'

Dirk paused by the door. 'Yes . . . but it wasn't your sister. Besides, I'm just sick of unanswered questions.'

'The most important questions of life are always unanswerable.' Won Fat said, and rose. 'Good day, Mr. Wildon. I will be following your progress with great interest.'

'Give your daughters my best.'

Behind a thick lens, one large eye winked. 'You underestimate yourself, Mr. Wildon. You have already given them that.'

18
HONEY

Uncertainly, she pulled the rented Triumph coupé off to the side of the twisting, narrow road and stopped on the brow of a windswept hill. Under an ominously grey sky, the bleak moors stretched unwelcomingly. Beyond, Cape Wrath jutted out into the angry sea like a blunted prick. Again she checked the map picked up at the Inverness Airport, trying to determine if she had missed the exit. She had already driven through Tongue; far behind was Wick. What lay ahead, she did not know.

Ten minutes later, not having passed or seen another vehicle, Honey located the lopsided sign that read: SNEAD − NO ADMITTANCE. She steered into the rutted, bumpy trial and followed it, unaware that she was chewing the inside of her cheek. Rounding a bend between two barren knolls, she hit the brakes.

On a windy, sheer cliff, the isolated stone house loomed large and forbidding. Its many-spired chimneys stabbed into the turbid grey sky like unlit candles on a funeral cake. Straight out of a gothic novel, she thought, Walpole perhaps. An involuntary shudder passed through her.

For the first time since landing in Scotland that morning, she began to have second thoughts, especially about not waiting for Dirk's arrival. She had promised she would – but that was before his flight connection in Athens was fouled up. Sitting there now behind the wheel, staring into the distance at the home of the little man with the big suitcase, she considered turning, racing back to the airport to wait for Dirk.

But time was so short. She had given her word to Hum, that she would be back on her column that coming Monday. Three days to accomplish what so far had been impossible. The solving of this bewildering and bedamning problem. And she *had* to. Or she feared she would go mad from the uncertainty of what might happen next. Like the proverbial sword of Damocles, it hung over her head poised, ready to fall. And each day, her nerves frayed more. She hated that in herself. That weakness. And that *had* to change, if nothing else did.

She slammed the shift into gear and slowly approached the grey-stone buildings that stepped down the hill. A large one, she discovered upon passing, had once been a barn; feeding troughs still lined the outside. She parked in the weed-grown area in front of the main entrance and shut off the engine. Nothing stirred about her. No dog or animals. Not even a flower pot of vegetation to indicate someone called this home. She got out, pulling tighter her sable mink coat. Shrieking icy wind whistled as she moved to the front door deeply recessed into thick stone walls. She pushed the door button. Hearing nothing, she pressed it again.

With terrifying suddenness, the heavy door flew open. A beefy, buxom blonde with short-cropped hair and sagging, middle-aged face wiped her nose on the back of a square hand and smeared it on the leg of her baggy men's overalls. '*Ja?*'

'My name is Honey Wildon,' she said as forcefully as she could. 'I've come to interview Angus Snead for my column.'

'*Du bist eine grosse dumkopf*!' the dikey blonde hurled and slammed the door with a horrendous *crash*.

Honey steeled her spine and pressed the door button again holding it in for what she hoped was a rude and pushy length. Again the door flew open, but only partway. She stared across, expecting the big blonde but had to drop her gaze to waist level to view the little man himself.

Wearing a thick black turtleneck sweater and paint-smeared pants, he peered up at her through deep-set, piercing black eyes. His pinched face sported a trim Vandyke beard of mottled grey and black like his Prince Valiant haircut. He had the sour expression of a testy billy goat. 'I am Angus Snead,' he announced grandly, his voice both harsh and resonant, the Scottish brogue stripped to a light lilt. '*You* are Honey Wildon.'

'I am,' she said. 'I'd like an interview.'

'Why?'

'Could I explain out of the cold?' she asked, smiling down at him with her most winning smile of warm pizzazz.

'I do not like visitors. Of *any* kind.'

She leaned over, fighting the urge to kneel. 'I strongly believe it is time for your genius to be known to the world.'

In stony silence, he stared eye level at the crotch of her dress visible through her open mink coat. A thin, devious smile cracked his beard. 'If you insist.' He spun on his heel and vanished into the darkness.

She followed, shutting the door, cutting off the chilling wind. It seemed, however, even colder inside. His little stocky figure was disappearing fast down a dimly lit hall toward an open lighted doorway. She hurried after him, her eyes sweeping the gloomy interior. It was virtually empty of furnishings or personal touches. Like a mausoleum, she thought.

She discovered him standing at the far end of an enormous high-beamed room, the length of which was hard to judge, for Snead was so small anywhere he stood. With two large, worn, tapestry wingback chairs flanking him he warmed his hands before a fire in a mammoth stone fireplace and watched her entrance icily.

Head high, she moved toward the welcoming fire, aware of his intense dark stare. It was cold, detached – a technician's stare. She hated him for taping her in Morocco, but her smile lost none of its charm. 'Have we met somewhere before Mister Snead?' she asked innocently when she'd reached the chairs.

His deep-set eyes bounced off hers and away. 'Have we now?'

'I'm asking you. You keep staring at me as if I should remember you.'

That seemed to throw him off guard for he swung to the nearest chair and pulled himself up into its seat, much like a child clambering into his daddy's chair. He sat hunched against one frayed arm, the pointed, scuffed toes of his black leather flamenco boots tapping together. 'If you don't remember me, I don't remember you.'

She held his challenging gaze. 'I only know your films.'

'Now which ones might you be talking about?'

She stalled, taking a seat in the matching arm chair.

'*Mondo Whacko, Blues for a Scarlet Woman, The Sins of Bo Peep*,' she listed, trying to recall even more from the limited bio her assistant Carla, had been able to dig up back in New York.

He dismissed her efforts with further taps of his toes. 'And which one might it be *you* think was my best?'

She took a wild stab in the dark. 'Undoubtedly, *Mirror, Mirror on the Ceiling*.'

The pointed toes ceased moving and a dubious grin

formed. 'Why might you now select that one? It is over seven years old.'

'It was your breakthrough film,' she improvised impassionedly. 'It transcends all conventional, traditional forms of the entire genre. And it catapulted you into the same realm as Fellini, Kubrick, Kurosawa.'

A steely glint burst to life in his dark, embedded eyes. 'Ay, to be sure. It spills bile into my gaul to consider the total lack of recognition I have received in this filthy obscene world. I have dedicated my life . . .' He thumped his chest like a war lord. 'My life! To the perfection of my craft. Every waking moment of every single day, I am driven, possessed, to elevate by art.' He slid off the chair and began pacing up and down in front of the roaring logs, which were as big as he. His little arms began waving about as if any moment he would launch into a dance to match his Spanish boots. 'My gifts! My talent! My vision!' Abruptly he whirled to her, his pinched face filled with rage. 'And what do they call my art? *Fuck films*!' he shrieked, his eyes bulging in their deep sockets.

He grabbed the arm of her chair and stood on his toes, his tone a tightly controlled whisper with the force of a shout in its bilious anger. 'My work should be on permanent display in every major art museum in the world! And the moralists dare call it pornography! I will tell you what pornography is. Forbidden fruit! Today it is not God telling man what is forbidden. It is *man* telling man. Do not partake of that . . . that is evil. Well, I will tell you what I think of that. *Bullshit!*'

His tirade had so stunned her that all she could do was stare back into his beady, enraged eyes. He was mad. Not in what he said, but in his manner of saying it. Stark raving bananas. She pushed to her feet to seek an avenue of escape.

'*Liebchen!*'

The powerful woman's voice spun Honey around. The Teutonic blonde, wearing a rough, green tweed suit that

215

looked like a broad expanse of unmown lawn, was lumbering toward them in her heavy brogue shoes, carrying a wooden tray with a steaming glass tankard and three cups. As she approached, her hard-set, dour expression eased, and when she spoke it was directed again at Angus but in a softer tone. '*Liebchen, bitte, bitte*, do not exert yourself. Conserve your strength, *mein Schote*. You film tomorrow, *ja*?'

The little man transformed instantly. His angry, hypertense, vitriolic façade faded into that of a worshipful, doting child. His eyes followed her arrival with glowing love and caressed her ample frame as if she were Venus herself. 'Gerta,' he said in a soft, mushy tone. 'Have you met our guest? Honey Wildon, this is Gerta. Gerta Routabusch.' He fixed a starry gaze on Honey. 'Fraulein Routabusch is my muse. Her every action is an inspiration.'

'How touching,' Honey murmured, noting the distinct chill that Gerta's presence had brought on. Displaying no emotion, the pear-shaped dirty blonde drew up with one heavy shoe a cracked leather stool and sat, balancing the loaded tray on her plump knees, her hefty haunches overflowing and drooping on either side of the stool like collapsed bread dough.

'*Haben Sie* mulled wine?' she asked Honey gutturally. With square strong hands, she lifted the glass tankard and began pouring a purplish, steaming concoction into the mismatched, chipped mugs.

Honey hesitated. 'I really should be going.'

Angus Snead reached for a full mug. 'And my interview?'

'I'm intruding. Could we arrange a future date? Soon?'

'Nonsense,' he said jovially and tossed his long, square cut hair. 'Now is as good a time as any other. From tomorrow on, I will be creating for nine months straight. My crowning masterpiece, an epic based on the life of Gore Vidal. Is that not so, Gerta?'

216

'*Ja*,' she replied and thrust a steamy mug to Honey.

Still standing, Honey accepted it and held it in both palms, blowing as if to cool it, inhaling the fumes deeply, testing its smell. Spicy with citrus and nutmeg. A growing unease coursed through her nervous system. She did not trust this odd couple as far as she could spit. Perhaps even less. 'Well, perhaps a few preliminary questions . . .' She dropped onto the edge of the chair seat. 'Do you always use film as your medium? How about video tape?'

The veil of suspicion once more dropped over his dark eyes. 'Why do you ask?' he voiced and sipped his brew.

Honey waited until Gerta took a sip before, 'Curious, that's all. Would you say there are advantages to using tape?'

'I have mastered every visual medium,' he said sourly. 'It makes no difference at all. I create art regardless.'

She raised the cup and took the tiniest of sips. It tasted like an overly sweet burgundy with lemon and spice tea. 'Do you need a crew for tape? Or can you handle it solo?'

'I do not need assistance for any of my art,' he grumbled and took a slug of the hot wine.

'Except for the performers, of course,' she said.

'Naturally.'

Honey glanced at Gerta, who sat silently like a large green toad on a small lily pad, her face frozen. Honey smiled sweetly and, fighting a small yawn, turned to the tiny man in the big chair. 'Do you work only for yourself? Or do you accept outside producers?'

He eyed her strangely. 'A true artist creates for himself.'

Another pesky yawn forced up her throat and she covered its disturbing emergence with the back of a graceful hand. 'But are you for hire? I mean, could I, for instance, pay for you –'

'No,' he growled, interrupting. 'Not for hire.'

A wide shuddering yawn broke from her mouth. Her hand felt too heavy to raise. 'Are there . . . no excep-

217

tions?' she barely got out. Her head was reeling and she was having difficulty holding her eyes open; only her strong will kept her going.

'No exceptions. Ever,' came his voice from far away.

She tried keeping him in focus, her alarm skyrocketing. 'Why . . . for god's sake . . . why . . .' The mug slipped from her hand unfelt and crashed unheard. Blackness descended like a drawn curtain. She slid off the chair and collapsed into a tidy heap on the unswept floor.

In short order, Honey was hauled by Gerta to the modern, fully equipped film studio in the converted barn. There she was stripped and chained spread-eagled on her back to a mattress of straw. The bed rose like an altar in the middle of a set decorated as a medieval torture chamber. While Snead fussed with his extensive array of equipment, banks of lights, snaking cables, and several movie cameras of various designs and functions, Gerta changed into costume in the wardrobe room. She came out, tottering on stiletto heels of high black boots, in a short, black leather skirt, her bare, beefy torso covered only in front by a large, pewter breastplate. On her head, she tugged a helmet of metal spikes with a metal nose flap, and a black leather half-mask.

'Perfection, my dear,' he murmured in admiration. 'Again you fill me with inspiration.' He reached up and took one of her thick hands, kissing the back of it with a formal little bow, clicking the heels of his boots together. 'We must be quick. Before the drug wears off. Places!'

The set's lighting was chiaroscuro in its effect; deep shadows cut by thin bands of cold light, adding to the illusion of a dank, dark dungeon cell. Honey's pale voluptuous body lay pinned on the high bed like a rare, exotic insect stuck on a display board.

'Rolling,' Snead cried crisply and ducked behind the mounted camera at the foot of the set. 'Action!'

With Gestapo force, Gerta strode into the camera

range, cracking a large leather whip in the air. Blocking the camera's view of the victim, she turned her broad, bare back and lashed out at the bed, hitting deftly on either side of Honey's quivering full breasts. Gerta dropped the whip and, from one side of the bed, pounced on the snowy mountains, mauling them roughly, pinching the nipples hard. Snead zoomed in with the telephoto lens for a close-up of the thick, pink fingers crushing one dusky rose teat. The mask of metal and leather slipped into frame; a fat, coated tongue toyed with the rubbery nipple. Like a tiny telescope, Honey's dusky flesh began to rise and Snead zeroed in with an extreme close-up of the extending, aroused nipple.

'Next!' he shouted and dashed to the second camera off to one side of the set and climbed the stairs to its viewfinder, reaching it just in time to catch in medium close-up the spiked helmet descending on the bright bush of fire. In profile, he filmed Gerta spreading open Honey's legs and leaning low over one pale, satiny thigh, prepared to lick the unseen gash.

'Next!' he hollered and jumped to the floor, scooping up his hand-held Aeroflex and turning it on. He stood at one end of the raised bed, and, at eye level, shot directly into the valley of fire, catching Gerta's thick tongue slicing open, like a dull knife, the furled leaves of the deep rose pussy. In his viewfinder, Gerta's chubby pink fingers formed a V and straddled the slit, pushing wider the tender sweet-meat and displaying the pinker, inner petals, moist and succulent.

Smoothly, Snead bellied onto the bed and slid forward, the pricklike telescopic lens erect and level with the tantalizing twat. Gerta's thick finger had been jerking the off-screen clit and the whole, deep pink valley was tremulous, like an earthquake beginning to ground-swell in intensity.

Not losing focus or frittering the delicious image so perfectly framed and lit, Snead splayed his elbows to rest on the white flesh of Honey's lower thighs and, thus steadying himself, he began extending the super-long telescopic lens, zooming in for a micro-close-up, catching in minute detail the undulating ridges of the rippling rose flesh.

'Now,' he croaked, his lens inches from the glistening portal to paradise. On cue, Gerta slipped a metal prong device between the luscious moist lips and yanked open the handles. Like the parting of the Red Sea, Honey's twat leaped open. In perfect micro-focus, Snead captured the duskier inner walls of the trembling trench. 'Wider,' he commanded, his voice vibrating like the very flesh before his long lens. With a gruff growl, Gerta forced the lips wider, the metal digging deep into the rose-coloured flesh on either side, the whole cunt now assuming a diamond-kite shape.

'Good,' he cried and pushed the long lens to the very mouth of the yawning, rose canyon and into the moist writhing flesh. And then withdrew, allowing the light to flood the pulsating love canyon. Again he plunged back into the inky moistness.

A harsh buzzer broke the panting stillness of the cold, lofty studio. The small dark head with the square-bangs shot up behind the camera, a frozen look of black humoured surprise. 'Who is that?' he hissed.

Instantly Gerta let go of the metal spreaders and careened off the bed, wobbling on her spike heels to the heavy-lined drapes. She parted a crack and spied out through a small window onto the front of the house. '*Ein mann* at *der* door,' she reported in a tense whisper. '*Mit ein* camera bag.'

At once, the two of them sprang in to frantic action, the dwarf leading the way.

19

DIRK

The heavy door finally flung open and a dwarf-sized man with a weird pageboy and a pointed beard smiled darkly up at him. 'Yes?'

'I'm looking for Honey Wildon,' Dirk said, realizing that this was the little shit who had defiled his sister in Morocco.

'Who?'

'Honey Wildon, the journalist. Tall, redheaded, beautiful? You haven't seen her?' It took every ounce of his reserve to refrain from smashing the small smug mug.

The bangs shook sadly. 'No one of that description has shown up here. Do come in, though. I'll ask my housekeeper.' He stood aside and waited, like a stubby fireplug, for Dirk to enter.

'Whose rented car is that next to my Jag?'

'My housekeeper's,' the dwarf replied and shut the door behind them. 'Please, this way,' The little legs carried him rapidly down a long, dark hallway.

Dirk followed, not liking anything about the devious-acting half-pint or the floomy, drafty abode in which he dwelled. Halfway down the hall, the little man in black ducked inside an open doorway. Dirk moved to it with the determination of a man hell-bent on getting to the bottom of things. He entered a dimly lit old-fashioned kitchen. Snead was nowhere to be seen.

'Come in,' the lilting deep voice said and he appeared from behind a marble countertop. 'My housekeeper is down in the barn tending the animals. She left some mulled wine. Care for some?'

'No thanks. Look, I'm concerned about my – '

'Have some,' Snead interrupted cordially. 'It'll take the chill off.' Reaching up, he grabbed the half-full carafe and carefully poured some of the purple liquid into two mugs. He spoke in a breezy manner, but the underlying ego was unmistakable. 'I am Angus Snead.'

'I know. I've heard about you.'

'From whom?' Snead asked and held out a full cup.

'Won Fat Hi,' Dirk replied, watching for a reaction.

'And who might that be?' Snead asked, unreadable.

Dirk waved the cup away, irritated by the evasive maneuvering of the little asshole. 'Get off it, Snead. We both know what your game is.'

'Do we now?' he asked sharply and gulped from his cup. 'And what might that be now?'

'Fuck films.'

'*Fuck films*!' Snead shrieked, his cheeks turning as purple as the brew in his cup.

'Including one with my sister.'

The tiny deep-set eyes blinked twice. 'Sister?'

'Honey's my sister. And I know she was coming here.'

'Are you positive now you do not want any warm wine?'

'Damn right I am, I want my sister, you half-baked peanut.'

'Now, Gerta!' the dwarf shouted, looking past him.

222

Dirk whirled just as the frying pan hammered down on his skull. Fireworks blazed before his eyes and then a deep, black void. He collapsed on the stone floor like a broken bag of oats.

When he regained partial consciousness – before he could even pry open his eyes – he was dimly aware of several factors at once: his head throbbed like a mother-fucker, he was coughing from warm liquid being forced down his throat, his arms and legs were immovable, and someone was sucking his cock. Rolling his head from the cup, nearly blacking out from the resulting pain, he spit out as much of the sweet warm stuff as he could and struggled to open his eyes. A blinding light struck him and dizzily he squinted down at the short-cropped blonde, with shoulders like a Steeler linebacker, swallowing his semi-hard-on. He caught a glimpse of a dungeon cell, his own naked body, the heavy chains holding him flat on the rough mattress – and the instantly recognizable, softly rounded, pale figure of his sister, chained beside him like an appeasing sacrifice to the gods.

His neck was wrenched roughly by strong little arms covered in an itchy, black wool that smelled of stale sweat. Again a cup of liquid was forced to his lips. He sputtered, coughing and spewing it out, but not before some of the warm brew slipped down his throat. Eyes welded shut, head reeling from aftershocks, Dirk tried figuring out what the hell was going on. His mouth was being pried open and still more liquid poured in. Filling his mouth, he pretended to swallow, but held it in the back of his throat.

'That should do it,' he heard Snead mutter and felt the itchy arms relax on his neck.

Dirk waited until the little man's feet hit the floor before rolling his head toward his sister, as if passing out. He let the damned brew dripple out of the side of his mouth. He feigned unconsciousness, the heat in his cock growing by the constant attention. Once he pretended acquiescence, his ol' bird lurched upward into the warm abrading wetness of the enveloping mouth. Linebacker or not, the mouth sucked up a storm.

Breathing as if in a deep sleep, he listened to the unseen, intense preparations involving a lot of equipment, plus hurried, unintelligible whispers. At one point, Snead hissed, 'Turn his face, camera front.' Thick fingers gripped his chin, jerked it upright, and a pillow was shoved under his head, propping it up. Next he heard the little dictator cry, 'Places. Rolling. Action!'

The *whip-cracked*, the slashing *hiss*, and the sharp slicing blow on his shins made him jump with intense pain. Another *crack* and the blow fell next to his hips. He fought to appear impassive. A heavy, cold metal weight fell across one thigh and again the mouth was on his cock head, a rough thick tongue licking it like an ice cream cone. In spite of his nervous state, the old bird began to fly. Soon it was as rigid as an angle iron.

'Next!' came Snead's hoarse cry, and Dirk felt his left wrist being unsnapped from the bracelet. That arm flopped over his chest. Soon the same cold strong hands were unlocking his left ankle, and he was rolled over on his side. His hard bird pushed into the warm, pliant flesh of Honey's thigh. It came as no surprise, but with some misgivings, that he felt Mister Bird flutter bravely against the satin-skinned warmth. To force his mind off the frustrating encounter, he began to count backward from a hundred.

At eighty-nine, his left arm was thrown across Honey's bouncing big breasts and with a hard, powerful jerk, his 'at-attention' body was pushed farther onto his sister. Like a flak-hit bomber diving into a forest fire, his bird-head grazed over the top of silky pubes and crashed into the softness of her bush. As the bubble of his cock-pit buried deep into her mons veneris, it almost exploded from the soft landing and the sheer tactile ecstasy.

'Get her legs open,' came Snead's sharp voice and Dirk sensed movement and again the cold strong hands. They gripped his left ankle and powerfully flipped his leg over Honey's. He now lay nearly flat on top of her, straddling her soft thigh, his face brushing against her luxuriant windswept hair, the soft mountains of her breasts squishing into his pounding chest, his spasming bird smothered beneath him on her sweet belly. All of his sensations and awarenessess, however, were centred and focused on a very small portion of his left thigh – which rested on the moist lipped entrance to her portal to paradise. To make it even harder for him, he could distinctly feel her ribboned petals undulating on his thigh like the hot lips of a hungry dolphin. Frantically he started counting backward again, willing his attention to other matters less at hand.

He was doing fairly well, with the heated burning sensation of his thigh fading nicely, when abruptly he was pushed and pulled by two pair of hands and at once found himself directly between her legs, her full breasts smashing beneath him, the length of his rigid bird laying full-out on the softest, juiciest bird nest his hardness had been lucky to find. He about swooned with the delirium.

'Raise his hips. I'm in close-up,' Snead commanded from off to one side and Dirk could hear again the soft whirring camera. The bed sagged as the big blonde climbed up and stood astraddle his legs. Chubby, cold fingers gripped his hips and pulled his midsection up with a breeze into the air. 'Perfect,' Snead whispered. 'I'm zooming onto her cunt now. Ready his cock. Don't worry. You're out of frame . . . now!'

His hips were held by one beefy, bare arm under and around his waist, while a free hand grasped his hard prick at the base, near the balls. A thick thumb pushed down on his cock, lowering the battering ram into an appropriate angle for breaking and entering. Gradually his hips were lowered and the sensitized head of his aiming bird kissed

225

the moist petals of his sister's twat. The succulent fantasy
to which he had been masturbating since long before
puberty was now within a hair's breadth of becoming a
steaming, stunning reality. His brain spun crazily, like an
out-of-control merry-go-round in a Hitchcock film. His
whole body began to tremble violently.

The grip of the powerful, bare arm holding his weight
tightened and he felt himself and his bewildered but game
bird of paradise being lowered into the succulent opening
of the tender sweet meat. For a frozen instant and the
space of an eternity, he was motionless in body and head.

Suddenly, with a howl of enraged frustration, Dirk
reared upright, throwing off the arm that gripped his middle. Ducking a shoulder to the mattress, he rolled off
Honey to one side, his long legs scissoring out, the chain
of one leg clanking loudly, and caught the thick neck of
the startled beefy blonde. He clamped his thighs around
her throat and locked his legs tightly.

'*Liebchen*,' she gurgled helplessly, struggling with her
large hands to force his legs apart.

Dirk raised his head, seeking out Snead. At the side
of the bed, the little man, mouth working furiously but
silently, jumped up and down like a bouncing marionette.
Dirk bucked his legs, snapping the blonde's head upward
and ordered, 'Unchain me, you little turd, or I'll break
her fat neck.'

'Don't hurt her.' Snead whined and darted to the foot
of the bed to release the remaining ankle bracelet. He
flew to the wrist holder and unlocked it with a large skel-
eton key.

Dirk jerked his limbs free and indicated his slumbering
spread-eagled sibling, growling, 'And her.' Quickly the
dwarf, abject panic painting his pinched face grey, raced
around the bed, unfastening Honey's chains.

Suddenly the blonde in the metal-pointed breastworks
wrenched, shoving up at Dirk's legs with a mighty thrust.
Her head popped free. Scrambling to her knees, she

226

growled like a she-bear in heat. Snead screamed, 'Get the bastard, Gerta!'

Dirk lashed out with his feet, slamming them into the hard metal just under her funnels and driving her backward off the bed. She fell out of sight with a loud *clunk* and a soft groan. He jumped up and lunged off the raised platform, landing on her broad hips before she could get to her feet. He flattened her like a snowbank. Her chunky arms clamped around him in a bear grip, pressing his chest into the sharp points over her tits. With a painful cry, he brought his knee up hard, slamming it into her big, bare belly, knocking her grip loose.

He slipped aside and struggled to his feet. Snead was charging with a wooden stancheon, bangs flying, head lowered as though he were going to pole-vault him. As the end of the staff approached, Dirk grabbed it, reversed the momentum by shoving it hard and lifted the still-gripping little man off the floor, swinging him around in the air like a pennant. With a whimper, Snead let go and sailed into a painted flat of the set, knocking it over with a clatter, momentarily stunning him.

Gerta squalled as if wounded herself and leaped like an insane woman onto Dirk's back, pulling at his hair. Buckling under her considerable weight, he whirled backward and crashed her into a solid stone wall. He heard the *whoosh* of air being knocked out of her and as he stepped away, she slid off his back to the floor like a melting block of ice.

Dirk did not wait for her to revive. He bent, grabbed, and with a tremendous head-bursting effort, threw her over his shoulder, hustling her back to the bed. He dumped her onto it, facedown. She lay gasping for air like a channel swimmer, her leather skirt high over her flabby pink ass, her thighs like hoghocks. In a flash, he had her chained next to the still-inert Honey.

He found Snead in a daze trying to pick his little ass off the fallen flat. Dirk grabbed him by the scruff of the neck and the seat of the pants and, like a truant schoolboy, lifted him clear of the floor. Tiny arms and legs flailing the air, a squealing Snead was carried to the bed, thrown between Honey and Gerta and promptly chained tight.

Dirk sagged against the side of the bed, panting, holding his head, trying to quell the quakes rumbling within. He stared at the long, auburn eyelashes of his beautiful sister willing them to open. 'Honey,' he rasped. 'It's me, Dirk.'

The lovely lashes fluttered and she tried to locate him. 'Oh, Dirk,' she whispered groggily and the corners of her mouth curled up. 'What a party, huh? Whose the hell was it?'

Moved deeply, he could only clutch her hand and offer his thanks to the powers that be.

It took close to an hour to awaken her enough for her to understand and grasp what had happened. After the third cup of strong black coffee and the fourth generous line of snow which Dirk had laid out on the marble countertop in the kitchen. Honey was hopping mad, her bright blue eyes shooting incandescent sparks, her high-boned cheeks flushed with bright colour, her soft womanly body – nude under her fur coat – firing with a restless energy. She bent her tousled Titian locks over the last cut line and snorted it fully. She rose, her exquisite profile a perfect cameo, and tossed her fiery mane of hair. 'Okay Dirk, you've damned good reason to be pissed at me. I was impetuous and foolhardy. Stupid, vain . . . oh shit. I was totally fucked up to come here alone. I thought you'd be stuck in Athens. Oh, hell, Dirk, I'm sorry, really.'

'You sure aren't selling me. You're sorry, my and you're sorry. I've never seen you madder. Spitting fire Honey, spitting fire. And that don't say jack-shit sorry to me.'

'Dammit, I *am* mad,' she erupted. 'But not at you dummy. At those two horror stories down in their

228

playpen. Trussed though they be, I would dearly love to beat the shit out of them.'

She looked so damned cute all fired up, sitting there on the highstool, the mink barely covering a stretch of silky white leg, he couldn't help himself. He laughed. 'Well don't let *me* stop you. I'm not against a little kink for Chrissakes. But those two gave me the willies. Still do. What the hell are we going to do with them?'

'We still don't have any answers yet.'

'You want to make him talk?'

'Damn right I do.'

'How do you suppose going about it? I doubt the little fart will sing anything but Götterdämmerung.'

'Very good, Dirk,' she kidded dryly. 'You know, that Valkyrian fraulein *is* his muse. He told me himself.'

'One's man muse is another man's moose.'

She arched an auburn brow disdainfully. 'Dirk, learn to fold a winner, huh? Now shut up and let me think.'

'Bossy bitch.' But he fell silent. He knew that when Honey put her mind to something, she usually came up with a fucking gem.

Within ten minutes, they were back in the dungeon set and Honey's raunchy scheme was put into action. Dirk hauled the chained but docile Gerta to the end of the bed where he tied her kneeling on the floor. Honey, over the thrashing protestations of Snead, undid the dwarf's belt and tugged his trousers past his knees, exposing his flaccid snake, coiled in his black pubic hair. Even in repose, it was nothing to be ashamed of size-wise. But he reacted as if he had been stripped in Buckingham Palace, screaming hysterically and blushing vivid red. After washing his cock thoroughly with soap and hot water, she proceeded to place her mouth over the end of his prick, which because of his frame's shortness looked all that much bigger. She began to suck with a determined diligence. As she worked her magic she shucked off her fur and lay aside him nude, her weight supporting one elbow, her heavy breasts falling free, brushing onto his bare hips with each sway of her head, her bright bush pushed hard into his bony shoulder, inches from his writhing head.

With all the expertise she could muster, Honey sucked and slurped, pressing under his balls on the stem of the stubborn prick. While her mouth sucked his uncut snake, Dirk held Gerta's head, forcing her to look directly up the short legs of her lover and into the delicious pink mouth working on the sallow-skinned member.

In due time, but still surprisingly fast considering the circumstances, Honey had the prick standing on end, practically barking for attention. Snead began moaning as though the soles of his feet were being set afire. And Gerta started crying for his agony. Again and again, Honey brought his throbbing stiff peter to the brink of climax only to pull off at the last instant and let it quiver unattended, cooling it down. She was maddeningly patient.

Soon Snead was screaming for release, his black hair matted into sweaty strands, his hips twisting to force her to bring him off. His prick kept growing fatter and fatter, redder and redder, until it looked like an overcooked sausage ready to burst. Snead seemed on the verge of madness, his deep-set eyes rolling back into his skull, his face drained of colour, like a dirty sheet. 'Oh God, oh God,' he groaned. 'Please lady, I beg you. Finish me off. Please, I beg you . . . let me cum . . . can't stand . . . oh . . . ohhhh, help . . . '

Dirk hurried to Snead's side. 'Why'd you make that tape?'

'No . . . noooo . . . oh God, please . . . '

'Talk you asshole or she'll eat you till the cows come home.'

'No . . . you can't do this . . . ' Snead cried, his cock now the colour of a lobstershell. And Honey's talented lingual application pestered his swollen peter unrelentingly.

Dirk leaned to the ashen-hued skull. 'If you don't tell me, I'll fuck Gerta in the ass and Honey will film it.'

'No! No!' Snead shrilled. 'I'll tell . . .'

Honey's head rose from her self-appointed task and Dirk leaned over the little head. 'I'm waiting you gob of shit. *Why?*'

The cracked, parched lips parted, panting, 'Money . . . my Vidal epic . . . my masterpiece . . . completely financed.'

'Who hired you, then?' Dirk growled, and for emphasis Honey trilled her tongue along the rim of the dwarf's dancing dick.

Moaning in defeat, Snead started whispering. Dirk leaned close to catch the words. A cloud of pain darkened his face. Slowly his eyes sought out Honey's and he stood. 'You're not going to like this, Honey. Not one damned bit.'

20

HONEY

In a state of cataclysmic shock and numb disbelief, Honey dragged herself to Hum's European retreat, arriving near noon at the large Bavarian-styled chalet, high in the Swiss Alps near Gstaad. Dirk had wanted to come with her, but she had refused, insisting that this was a matter entirely between her and Hum. But now that she was there, she found herself wishing that Dirk was along, for she did not feel she had the strength or determination to go through with it alone.

In the upstairs den off his bedroom suite, she found Hum on the phone, talking business – per usual. Dressed only in a velour robe, he displayed enormous gusto, pacing the length of the phone cord like an animated bear on a short tether. With a start he saw her and froze, obviously delighted at her unexpected arrival. Into the receiver he barked a quick, 'Goodbye,' and hung up, coming to her with open arms. 'Honey! What an enchanting surprise.'

He wrapped her close to his bulky velour-covered body, towering over her, making her feel small and helpless. She fought the threatening tears and returned his fervid kisses. Through his robe, he ground his hardening rod into her upper belly. In spite of her previous resolve, she began to melt as he pushed the familiar buttons as only he could do. Like an express elevator, she shot to the upper floors of physical desire, her delta of love beginning to twitch and that all-too-familiar itching-that-begged-to-be-scratched burst irritatingly to life.

She forced herself to deal with realities beyond the moment and pushed away lightly, giving his bone-hard cock a friendly squeeze through the tented robe. 'I'm famished, darling. Could we eat first?'

'Yes. You, me and me, you.'

She arched one brow. 'Substantial fare, to be sure. And part of me would be full, that's for certain. But once we start, luv, I for one won't want to stop. And I'll perish before supper.' She tossed her mass of red polished hair and kissed him on the cheek, a friendly but 'my mind is made up' kind of peck.

His craggy, rough-hewn face puzzled momentarily and then the tough city-editor mask fell into place. 'You're due back at your desk first thing in the morning. Per our agreement.'

'Yes, boss,' she said, mockly meek. 'I'm booked to New York on tonight's red-eyed express. We have exactly – ' she checked her Piaget diamond-clustered watch, a previous birthday gift from Hum – ' . . . figuring an hour's leeway . . . exactly nine hours.' She flashed him a radiantly ethereal smile. 'Enough for two damn good solid meals and one serious, seven-hour fuck.'

'Honey,' he admonished sternly.

She attempted a laugh. To her it sounded tight and foced. 'You old fuddy duddy, I can say "fuck" when

234

we fuck, but when we aren't fucking, I can't.' She picked up the phone receiver on his neatly organized desk and smiling at him like a mischievous little girl, punched up the kitchen line. 'What do you want to put in your stomach, Hum?'

She slipped the dried *shitka* mushrooms into his *fine herbes* omelette when he was on the phone inside. Out in the warm early summer sun, they sat at a table covered by a red-and-white checked tablecloth on the deep balcony, before a railing full of baskets of hanging red geraniums. As Hum concluded his leisurely brunch, Honey, who had been too tied in knots to be hungry and so had dumped her full plate over the side when he was not looking, began eyeing him closely for some sign of his impending wild abandonment. She recalled that it had taken Serge Cryon, the KGB spy in Lapland, close to two hours to come onto the mushrooms. But she had given Hum twice the amount of goodies and was hoping it would hit within an hour. She figured she could play this hideously difficult game of pretending nothing was amiss for another hour. But not one minute longer. Any moment she felt she could slip into a catatonic withdrawal to escape the overwhelming pain tearing at her insides.

'Honey,' Hum began expansively over his last cup of coffee, 'have you given any more consideration to my Cozumel proposal?'

'Yes, I have.' She toyed with her fork but kept her serious blue eyes on his. 'I won't marry you, Hum.'

His bushy greying brows collided with disappointment. 'May I ask your reasons for reaching such a negative assessment?'

She tore her gaze away, looking out over the geraniums at the surrounding evergreen-covered mountains and valleys. 'I've never been here in the summer, do you realize that? All the times skiing, when it's covered by snow. A few times in the early spring. But never now. I like it better with snow.'

'I would prefer a direct answer.'

Her head spun and the fire leaped to her bright blue eyes. 'Would you now? Well, I can appreciate that. I'd like some direct answers myself.'

As if tickled by her outburst, he combed a large hand through his thick, greying hair, his adoring gaze twinkling.

'Do I amuse you, Hum?'

'Enormously. I don't know what I'd do without you.'

His sentiment was so openly expressed, she felt a tugging ebbtide of sadness pulling at her. 'And I you, Hum . . . and I you.'

The *shitka* kicked in right on schedule. It was apparent first in Hum's ordering up from the wine cellar a ridiculously rare and expensive bottle of Glenfiddich Scotch, a gesture so out of keeping with his character – he rarely had anything stronger than coffee in daylight – that she knew something was brewing inside his normally moderate thinking processes. After downing nearly the whole bottle himself, he proposed a hike in the woods and made a big to-do about getting her outfitted with the proper attire culled from the staff of servant girls that ran the chalet on a year-round basis.

By the time she and Hum had begun tramping along – in boots, shorts and light, flannel plaid shirts – climbing the steep wooded trails of the sun-dappled forest, Hum was robustly laughing up a storm. His booming, raucous, boyishly alive roar bounced off the high peaks like the yodel of an abominable snowman. With whoops of childlike wonderment, he delighted in even the most common of sights – the sunshine through a cobweb a speckled snail on a lichen-covered rock, or an arched sword of a fern fanning in the gentle breeze.

He raved about the clean, pine-scented air and went

236

on at great length about moving the entire headquarters and staff of *World News* out of the polluted air of New York and into the mountains near his family home of Hillsprings.

But it was when Hum started grabbing at her tits and clamping a hungry paw on her snatch, that Honey knew for certain that he was past the point of no return. She blessed the Finnish stud Lokka, with the big pokka, for supplying her with the precious mushrooms, and made a point of staying at least an arm's distance in front of the fast-growing-horny Hum.

Leading the way up the isolated mountain trail, she had just entered a sunny little meadow dotted with white daisies when she noticed he was not behind her. Calling out for him, she backtracked, her concern growing. Suddenly he leaped out from behind a tree, stark nude, his thick, stiff peter like a nut-bearing log between his legs. His eyes glazed and a wickedly lusty smirk altered his maturely handsome face. 'Fuck,' he cried and lurched at her. 'Now!'

She whirled and ran. He caught up to her within two steps. His hard cock slammed into her back first, then his beefy trunk. She struggled helplessly in the massive arms which crushed her breasts. The next thing she knew, he had torn off her shorts, pushed her head over and, from behind, rammed his impatient hot poker into her totally surprised twat. She screamed with the sudden pain. He laughed uproariously and butted his hips into her soft cheeks, forcing her head lower by one strong hand on the base of her neck.

Inside her dry trench, his hard-driving cock felt coated with coarse sandpaper, ripping at her tender walls still raw from the Teutonic blonde's administrations. She bit her tongue, enduring the slaughter, waiting for the lubricants to flow, knowing it was only a matter of time.

Within seconds, the scraping eased and she felt the wings of her love-dove flutter and take flight. One of

Hum's big mitts mauled her breasts, tearing off her shirt, tweaking the small cones of dusky flesh until they too were ready for flight. Pressing into her back, he lifted her completely off the ground and she hooked her boots behind his knees. As she hung suspended from him like a salmon impaled on a fish-spear, his rampaging prick plunged into her pressure cooker. Within moments, she found herself flung forward, her hands catching the dirt-needled trail, his pushy prick still tightly wrapped in her gripping goulash. He held her thighs and walked her forward, like a wheelbarrel, his strokes never faltering.

Next, he folded her over on her shoulders, bending her in half, her full hips erect in the air. He leaned over on top of her, supporting his weight on his hands behind her, fucking his hard plunger down into her enflamed cunt. Sharp pine needles ground into her bare shoulders and she thought her neck would break from his heavy weight bouncing into her with so much unrestrained power. The reverse angle of his cock in her cunt filled areas long untouched and she writhed under him, gyrating her hips, grunting from the exertion and uncomfortable position, her full breasts cramped beneath the thighs of her jackknifed body. The molten maze in her liquifying lust-tunnel continued to increase, driving her mad with fulmination.

Then with a wrench, Hum flung himself into a shoulder roll, pulling her over on top of his now-prone body. His cock stuck in her throughout the upheaval as if afraid to leave the dark. She ended up sitting on his joy-stick, facing away from him, balancing herself by using his chunky thighs as pillows. He bucked her into the air repeatedly, the force of his thrusts so strong she flew up his greased pole, almost to the point of dislodging and then, by the weight of gravity, slid down the humping phallus. Like a pussy puppet, she bounced up and down, a gutsy growl bursting from her open mouth.

Much to her shock, from around the bend of the path, a troop of knickered boy scouts began approaching, led by an elderly preacher-looking man. Hum, who was too blinded by lust to care, even if he had seen them – which he had not – kept humping away and Honey was in the throes of such ecstasy she could not have stopped even if she had wanted to. To the passing audience of the frozen boyish faces, she began to scream her joy. 'Holy shit! Motherfucker, I'm coming! Jesus H. Christ. I'm coming!'

Without breaking formation, the entire troop of a dozen pre-teens trudged by single file, mouths open, eyes wide. The elderly scoutmaster, however, was having an apopleptic fit, his scrawny bare legs stiff with fury, his face the colour of his bright purple socks, his arms batting the heads of the scouts back into place, away from the tawdry, tacky spectacle in their paths. As they disappeared up the trail, Hum, who had been watching with profound fascination their sturdy young legs going by, raised a triumphant echoing cry: 'Hot Mother of God! My cock's coming in your fucking cunt!'

Before Honey could finagle Hum back down the mountain into the huge brown and white chalet, he had his bear-like way with her several more times – taking her roughly in the daisy-filled meadow like a lusty shepherd. There he laid his thick pole between her snowy bosoms and as she jiggled them like jelly, he pumped between them singing at the top of his lungs the fight song of his alma mater, Yale, *'Boula-boulah! Boula-boulah!'*

In a large crevice between two giant boulders, Hum felt driven to fuck her mass of red fire hair, his plentiful cum adding a special white highlight to her gleaming dark waves. In a hollowed tree trunk of a dead tree, he was compelled to fuck her toes, laying his thick prong between two rows of Honey's layered feet. The amount of his steaming thick broth had not diminished from his previous ejaculations – in fact, Honey was positive his boisterously bouncing balls were churning out extraordinary amounts of love pudding, as if the *shitka* had increased even his bodily fluids.

In total amazement, she watched him, at the rear of a farmer's pasture, tackle and rape a frightened ewe sheep. The squealing squawks of the terrified animal were topped by Hum's inhuman sounds of deliriously crazed enjoyment. He was like a fucking machine, all grit and gristle, his six-four, 240 pounds skewering the small ewe as though lamb shishkabob were on the menu for their evening meal.

In the chalet's lower pantry, to the bewildered amusement of the kitchen staff across the open hallway, Hum was transported to fuck one of her armpits. With humiliated forebearance, she sat on the floor, nude except for her borrowed boots, watching the staff watching their master fucking her armpit. She clamped her arm tightly to her body, strangely aroused, and flashed the red fire of her bush, hoping to drive the servants away. The girls left. The dishwasher, a gangling youth, stayed to beat his cock under his white apron, winking at her now and then as if they were in on some absurd joke.

After a lengthy detour on top of the grand piano in the vast lodge-like living room, fucking to the blasting sounds of his quadrophonic speakers blaring Musorgski's *Great Gate of Kiev*, Honey eventually got him upstairs to his own suite. As he robustly fucked a stack of folded towels in the linen closet, she found her carryall and took out the transistor tape-recorder and set it on the bed's end table, behind a vase of pink, blue and white sweet peas.

Hearing lumbering footsteps and a thudding as he crashed into a wall, she bounced onto the large feather bed, threw her legs wide over her head and, with her

240

hands under her pale cheeks, spread welcomingly her glorious, swollen, but still dewy gates of paradise.

As he stumbled into the room, he caught sight of the flaming bush set like a glistening ruby amidst the soft ivory of her cheeks and her air-dancing legs. He roared like a tanker entering home port and full-steam-ahead clambered onto the bed, his rigid prong like a ship's rudder, and slapped his head forward under her raised legs, perfectly placed to begin lapping at the lustrous lips the colour of deep rose. With his nose, he slit open her slit, his tongue following closely behind like a tidying damp mop.

She reached around the sweet peas and switched on the tape recorder. 'Hum,' she began with a professional tone.

'Hmmmmmmmmmmmmm?' Hum humped into her tasty snapping turtle.

'Listen to me, Hum. I want an answer to just one question.' His greying head bobbed, stoking the glowing embers of her sorely abused twat once again. To get his attention, she clamped her thighs around his ears with a tight grip. He bulled his neck up freeing his head and looking at her questioningly, his lips dripping, making him look all the more like a foaming madman. She lowered her legs. 'Listen, will you? Can you understand me?'

His head nodded but his eyes crossed.

'Why did you have that video tape made of me?'
'Huh?'

'That video tape? When I was in Morocco,' she said with rising anger, trying desperately to get to his bedazzled brain. 'The one you sent Dirk in Beverly Hills? That fucking tape!'

He stared hard at her as if trying to comprehend, then burst into a laugh that grew quickly into hysterical, uncontrolled waves of howling, gut-busting laughter. He laughed so hard he fell from between her legs and collapsed onto the bed beside her, holding the sides of his beefy, bouncing belly, rocking back and forth. With each uninhibited, raucous rumble, his hard cock drooped a bit, as if the object of the humiliating laughter. Tears streamed from his eyes, his rough-hewn face dissolving into red putty, and his barrel chest quaked as he gasped for breath to continue.

She was not amused and sat up on her haunches. 'Hum, dammit, answer me! Or I'll walk. Swear to God I will. This minute!'

Still howling, he flopped a large hand to hers, gripping it mightily. She pounded on his chest with the other angrily. 'Damn you, Hum, answer me. Why? What the hell did you do it for?'

His laughter ceased as abruptly as it had begun. His head rolled and he looked at her with astonishingly clearheaded eyes. 'Bravo, Honey!' he cried and his peaceful peter jerked alive once more. 'Congratulations, super sleuth! How on earth did you ever find out?'

His jovial, devil-may-care attitude confused and angered her even more. 'It sure as hell was the toughest assignment I ever faced.'

'That bastard Snead, I presume?' Hum asked and stroked absently his tumescent cock.

'You son of a bitch, what difference does it make *how* I found out? What matters most is *why* you did it in the first place?'

'Because I love you,' he chortled.

'So you had me drugged, abducted, degraded – that's love? Boy, are you ever fucked up!' An errant tear slid down her sculptured cheek and, infuriated by its sudden appearance, she slapped it away with a palm.

Still flat on his back, he raised his now brassy brazier and waved it stiffly at her. 'We *both* love you, see?'

'A hard cock is not love, Humboldt. A caring heart is.'

'I have both,' he said, a petulant child. 'My heart

242

cares for no one but you. No one. On this whole fucking planet.'

'You sure as hell have a weird way of showing it.'

'My heart and my cock want to fuck you.'

'As Dirk says, tough titty.' She swung her long legs off the bed and stood, reaching for her dress.

Rolling his hefty bulk to his knees, he crawled to the end of the bed, a plaintive, pleading tone to his rough-timbered voice: 'Where are you going?'

'I'm splitting, Hum. We're through.'

'Unfair, Honey, unfair.'

Her head snapped back on her long neck and she nailed him a hard glare. 'You dare talk about fair? You hypocritical shit, you.' She threw the dress over her upraised arms and tugged it down over her pale breasts.

He watched them disappear as if his ship had sailed without him. 'Ah, Honey, don't leave me. I just wanted to curtail your fucking around so much, that's all. I was jealous, can't you see?'

She cinched the belt tighter around her trim waist, accenting even more her hour-glass figure. 'So you have me defiled and recorded, the tape sent to Dirk. Why, for God's sake, Dirk?'

'Because,' he cried heatedly, his thick hard peter bouncing, 'Dirk means more to you than me. I've always known that. I'm not blind. He's the only one you would have ever listened to. I figured getting him involved, he'd pressure you to stop fucking everything that moves.'

She stared closely at the handsome face she had loved so dearly. She had to bite her cheek to steady the rage roaring through her like wildfire. 'Humboldt,' she muttered tightly, 'you are a dumb asshole. Even Dirk could not stop me from living my life the way I see fit. You blew a damned good thing, baby.' She shoved her feet into her high heels and grabbed her carryall. 'I hereby resign my column for World News. From this moment on, I will free-lance for whom I want, when I want. Just like I will continue to fuck whom I want, when I want.'

Looking as if he were about to burst out laughing again, he flopped on this back, beating his hard meat with crazed energy. 'Let's fuck and make up.'

'Fuck yourself, Hum. Thanks for the good times. And for getting my career launched.' She snatched up the still 'on' tape recorder, switched it to 'off' and shoved it into her leather bag. '*Adieu, putz.*' Throwing the purse over her shoulder, she breezed out of the bedroom, head held high, her spine straight, the very image of a confident, secure, independent, and breathtakingly beautiful young woman. But inside, her heart had shattered into a million pieces.

At the bottom of the long drive leading up to the chalet, she had the driver of the rented limo stop and she got out to hold a hurried conference with the waiting man whose services she had so desperately hoped she would never need. He was a rising young video director, and behind him stood impatiently a motley assortment of the most bizarre freaks he had been able to line up on such short notice – from greasy bikers in black leather and chains to a trio of transexual nuns in short, gold lamé habits.

Honey gave the director the second half of the advance, ten grand in Swiss francs, and told him where he could find Hum. With mixed feelings and flowing tears, she climbed back into the limousine. As it pulled away, she looked back at the troop of grotesque weirdos and efficient-looking video crew heading up the hill to record the wild abandonment of Humboldt Harrison Hamilton. '*Adieu, mon cher.* Have a ball,' she murmured and broke down completely, weeping into her pale hands.

244

21
DIRK

At San Francisco International Airport, Honey stepped from the passengers' tunnel, looking like a million bucks – which, considering what Wildon Enterprises stock was going for at the close of the New York Stock Exchange that day, was about a-hundredth of what she was actually worth. She spotted Dirk in the crowd and waved, flashing a bedazzling smile. In a raw silk, bud green suit, she ran toward him looking vibrantly alive, radiantly composed and effusively happy. Groomed to the nines, her hair a mass of casually coiffed, tumbling Titian waves, she was so strikingly beautiful heads turned to follow her progress and he felt damned proud that it was he she was aiming for.

There was nothing short-changed in her full-armed embrace, nor in the sisterly-but-'thrilled' kiss of greeting that she bestowed upon his cheek. She fairly bubbled, she was so damned 'up', and he began to suspect that the sparkling façade was one giant cover-up. As they climbed into his 'west-coast wheels', metallic silver brand-new Lamborghini, he was about to tell her to come clean, but thought better of it.

For the short drive to Hillsborough, he raced the sleek silver bullet, forgetting until they were almost home that she never felt comfortable unless she was driving. He slowed deliberately, listening carefully to her chatty end of the conversation for clues as to the real state of her mind. She indicated that she was glad the whole horrid business was over with and how much she was looking forward to freelancing. Only when she dropped very casually that she had stopped in New York briefly to remove her things, both from her offices at *World News* and from Hum's Fifth Avenue triplex penthouse, did he catch a slight tremor in her tone.

Not until he was powering the sleek auto up the winding drive of the Hillsborough estate of their late parents did Honey's outward demeanor change. As the frothy yellow blossoms of the acacia trees lining the drive swept past and the rambling two-story brick mansion appeared on the crest of the hill, Honey's astonishingly convincing façade crumbled. At the sight of the house, she broke down completely, weeping silently. He knew then that his suspicions had been correct — she was in deep, deep pain. As soon as he braked to a stop in front of the portico above the main entrance, Honey bolted from the car and fled into the house in which they had been raised.

For an entire twenty-four-hour period, Dirk did not see her. Despite the many notes of humorous pleadings that he slipped under her door, she refused to come down for meals, even let him into her old bedroom to talk. There was so much he wanted to discuss with her, he was beside himself with concern. He gave all the servants, except the cook and the gardener, an indefinite paid vacation and batted around the comfortable but elegant house looking for things to occupy his time within range of her call. He knew it was useless trying any tactics with her except to wait and let her work it out of her system by herself. There were certain matters even the closest of relationships could not ameliorate. Especially those dealing with affairs of the heart.

On the bright, sunny morning of the second day, she suddenly appeared as he was having a solitary breakfast in the sun-room overlooking the bay clear up to the Oakland bridge and way down to San Jose. She swept in wearing a floor-length dressing gown of lucent blue velvet and despite her wan, dewy-eyed appearance, she looked like she was ready to tackle life again.

He took note of the antiquated gown and drawled teasingly, 'Why, Miss Scarlet, what makes you rise so soon?'

'Morning, babe,' she greeted, smacked a wet kiss on his brow, and plopped into the opposite ice-cream-parlour chair. She smiled at him, it was genuine and warm, and his spirits began to lift. 'I'm ravenous,' she growled and started heaping her plate with scrambled eggs, lean ham and loads of toast.

'Hey,' he said, trying to get her attention. 'Why is life like a cock?'

She groaned good-naturedly. 'When it's hard, it's fucked . . .'

He joined in with her for the last of the old chestnut, 'And when it's soft, you can't beat it.' They both laughed.

'You know, Dirk, what I was thinking about up there? A line I read once from George Santayana: "There is no cure for birth and death save to enjoy the interval." That's fairly relevant isn't it?'

He shrugged, other things on his mind. He kept his tone light. 'Guess what came in the mail this morning?'

For a fleeting moment, her deep blue eyes flickered with alarm before firming with renewed resilience.

'Whatever it is, it can't be worse than what we've already been through . . . so shoot. What came?'

'The tape of Hum's debauch. Want to see it?'

'No,' she said firmly and fell to eat her food with great gusto. 'By the way, do you still have my tape with Koka and Kola?'

'Yes.'

'Good. Because I want you to send *both* tapes to Hum at Hillsprings,' she said mischievously. 'He paid for them in more ways than one.'

'Is that a good idea?' he voiced cautiously. 'There's no telling what that asshole will do with them.'

'If we're lucky – which we are, you and I – Hum will look at them the *rest* of his life and see what a complete fool he was . . . and is.'

They laughed together and Dirk offered as a topper, 'Too bad we destroyed those films Snead took of us. Now *those* would *really* get Hum's goat.'

When their mutual hilarity had faded a bit, she scowled charmingly. 'Speaking of the old goat . . . we never found out what Sweet Dew did with that gold waist-chain.'

'Miss it?'

'*Au contraire.* I've sent back to Hum every piece of jewellery he ever gave me. And every gift that I could remember.'

Dirk whistled. 'That's a sizable fortune right there.'

'A tainted fortune, Dirk,' she said and grew pensive. 'You know, as I woke up in my old room this morning, I realized that I have never really had a place of my very own. Ever. A few apartments and flats scattered hither and yon, but not a real home.'

'Wouldn't you say it was about time? Baby bro, here, has had his Soho pad for a couple years already.'

'A new life,' she murmured as if dreaming aloud. 'A new freelance career . . . new lovers, new house. What else should I change?'

'You're the one who keeps telling me, there are no "shoulds". I don't want you to change one damn thing . . . except . . . ' He held her gaze pointedly, with a suggestion of genteel lasviciousness.

She put down her coffee cup with great deliberation, not breaking the visual bond. 'If you are speaking of you and me, babe, *that* aspect of our lives will never change.'

'Never and always are two words we banned long ago, Honey.'

She giggled and the colour of her high-boned cheeks looked healthy and rosy once more. 'I just had the most delicious idea.'

'I'm all ears.'

'Let's throw a reunion party,' she said excitedly. 'For all those terrific folk we met on this adventure. Starting with Sweet Dew.'

'I'd sure as hell love to meet that Koka.'

'And Kola is a real champ, Dirk. If his big cock isn't too intimidating for you,' she teased.

'Hey, I can handle my own.'

'Did I say you couldn't?' she rejoined breezily. 'Now who else . . . ahh, yes, Lokka the Laplander. He was very generous with his *shitka*.'

'Among other native items,' Dirk quipped. 'Maybe I could get Won Fat to tape the whole party?'

'I'm serious, Dirk. Let's fly them *all* over here for a big, big blowout. We haven't really used this lovely home that much. It's time we did. Mom and Dad, I know, would approve wholeheartedly. And Disa! Darling, Disa, how could I forget her?'

'And Carla Kopit . . . she's a gem.'

'But of course. Did I tell you she's gone back to school? Oh Dirk, we have so many terrific, wonderful new friends. And old, too. Why should either one of us ever feel down because one or two didn't work out?'

'I'll drink to that,' he said and reached for the silver

ice container on the nearby buffet. He extracted a chilled bottle of 1914 Château d'Yquem. 'I found this gem in Dad's wine cellar the other day. Been keeping it on ice for this very moment.'

'Divine,' she sang out, and giggled as fresh and youthful as a schoolgirl when he pulled the cork, making a big show of sniffing and tasting it. He poured two glasses of the priceless vintage Sauterne and they raised their glasses.

'What should we drink to first?' he asked.

'How about Catherine the Great's favourite toast? "God grant us our desires and grant them quickly." '

'Here, here,' he approved and they clinked glasses across the table. Eyeing each other over the rims, they sipped and savoured the grand premiere rarity, marvelling in its light brown colour and its sweet, almost creamy breed, enthusiastically making plans for their big reunion of all the 'positive' people they had encountered so very recently.

Shortly, he refilled their glasses, watching her exquisite face laughing delightedly over something he'd said and relishing her swift reemergence back into the 'Honey' he so dearly loved.

She read the gaze of her most precious friend and companion and linking her arm through his, thanked him silently for being there when she needed him. They stood at the window looking out on the view that seemed to stretch forever. 'Dirk, this toast is yours . . .' she said softly, raising her glass, waiting expectantly.

He thought for a moment and then, holding her gaze tenderly, said, 'Here's to us. Side by side. Whatever may come.'

DIRK & HONEY: SIN-DICATED

Roland De Forrest

Of course, there has always been a relationship between love and death. But Dirk Wildon, famed photographer and connoisseur of beautiful women, never expected that his highly acclaimed expertise in the former would get him so close to the latter. Making love to the wives of humourless gangsters can, however, lead to some surprising climaxes. Still, Dirk could not have known that his much-loved sister, the delicious Honey Wilde, would be held carnal captive as a result of his indiscretions. Or that New York's most notorious mobster would fall in love with her. Thank goodness that New York's finest, in the sultry shape of Sergeant Donna Devine, is finally living up to its name. Thank something that both Dirk and Honey know how to make the best of any situation.

DIRK & HONEY: SIN-DICATED

When Dirk and Honey mix with the mob everybody carries a piece.

FUTURA PUBLICATIONS
FICTION
0 7088 4257 7

DIANA'S DEBUT

Lytton Sinclair

She came, she saw, she conquered . . .

Travel is meant to be a broadening experience. And even the delicious Diana, who though a simple girl from a little town in Pennsylvania had seen and done a thing or two, found that travel can always teach you something. For it was in Rome that, despite an international incident of unforgettable violence and bad taste, she met so many warm-hearted people with fantastic bodies eager to communicate with a voluptuous down-home American girl; in Rome that she learned to let go of her small-town hangups about sex and *really* enjoy herself; in Rome that she discovered just what her mother's beloved minister (who was, in fact, her own first great love) meant when he told her, 'Diana, you have so much to give.'

DIANA'S DEBUT

They call Rome the city of Love – but it took Diana to prove it.

FUTURA PUBLICATIONS
FICTION
0 7088 4028 0

WHITE MOON, BLACK SEA

Roberta Latow

There is no limit to ecstasy and desire, no end to the wildest dream . . .

From the sophistication of Paris to Long Island's sublime confection of luxury and wealth and Istanbul, market of fabulous antiquities and sweet young flesh . . . the wide world was their temple of delight, uncharted territory of sensual excitement and fevered gratification . . .

At the top of her profession, at the height of her sexual powers, Mirella is the complete woman. Rashid, her Turkish playboy lover, laid the world at her feet and became himself her thrall, craving the piquant strand of treachery underlying their complex relationship. A tantalising threat of betrayal enhances their abandon, drawing them towards ecstasy and to the very brink of destruction. While Adam, Mirella's husband, dallies with tall ebony-skinned Aida, the epitome of royal insouciance, an Ethiopian princess with an untamed animal pride in her sexual skills. Her primitive hunger becomes his challenge, her insatiable passion his snare . . .

The dancing kaleidoscope of interrelationships sparkles, changes, combines again, glowing in light and life and lust –

WHITE MOON, BLACK SEA

FUTURA PUBLICATIONS
FICTION
0 7088 3783 2

EROTIC TALES

Alberto Moravia

Moravia, master story-teller, is at his most excitingly
explicit in this extraordinary collection of provocative
short stories. More than merely erotic, they are acute and
chilling portraits of human desire in its most obsessive
and elusive forms. There – at the point where fantasy and
reality meet – Moravia weaves his tales of passion and
sensuality, innocence and frenzy with a precision and
honesty you won't easily forget.

FUTURA PUBLICATIONS
FICTION
0 7088 3383 7

All Futura Books are available at your bookshop or
newsagent, or can be ordered from the following address:
Futura Books, Cash Sales Department,
P.O. Box 11, Falmouth, Cornwall TR10 9EN.

Please send cheque or postal order (no currency), and
allow 60p for postage and packing for the first book
plus 25p for the second book and 15p for each additional
book ordered up to a maximum charge of £1.90 in U.K.

B.F.P.O. customers please allow 60p for
the first book, 25p for the second book plus 15p per
copy for the next 7 books, thereafter 9p per book

Overseas customers, including Eire, please allow £1.25
for postage and packing for the first book, 75p for the
second book and 28p for each subsequent title ordered.